STEPPING TO A NEW DAY

Also by Beverly Jenkins

STEPPING TO A NEW DAY

A BLESSINGS NOVEL

Beverly Jenkins

WILLIAM MORROW
An Imprint of HarperCollinsPublishers

STEPPING TO A NEW DAY. Copyright © 2016 by Beverly Jenkins. All rights reserved. Printed in the United States of America. No part of this book may be used or reproduced in any manner whatsoever without written permission except in the case of brief quotations embodied in critical articles and reviews. For information address HarperCollins Publishers, 195 Broadway, New York, NY 10007.

HarperCollins books may be purchased for educational, business, or sales promotional use. For information please e-mail the Special Markets Department at SPsales@harpercollins.com.

FIRST EDITION

Map of Henry Adams by Valerie Miller

Library of Congress Cataloging-in-Publication Data has been applied for.

ISBN 978-0-06-241263-8

16 17 18 19 20   OV/RRD   10 9 8 7 6 5 4 3 2 1

To everyone searching for a new beginning

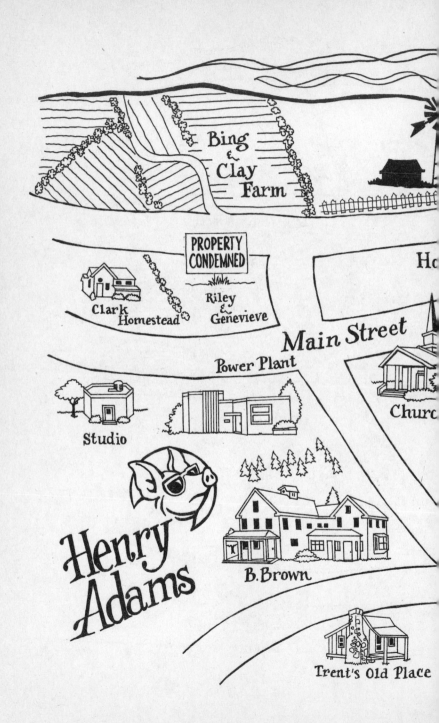

CHAPTER
1

Riley Curry, the former mayor of Henry Adams, Kansas, stood on the balcony of the seedy LA motel he now called home, and wondered how he was going to sneak out of town. He owed money to everyone from his landlord to the utility company to the trainer boarding his six-hundred-pound hog, Cletus, and he didn't have a dime to his name.

When he first came to LA a year and a half ago, he just knew Cletus would be the next big thing and make Riley so much money he'd be swimming in it. Hadn't turned out that way, though. The only thing he was swimming in was debt. None of the big-time movie producers or television execs would see him so he hadn't been able to pitch the scripts he'd written, or show them just how smart his hog was. He was told he needed an agent to get a foot in the door and after weeks of poring over the Internet, he finally found one. However, when the only acting job she could find Cletus was a walk-on in a no-budget horror flick, Riley fired her. Cletus was talented enough to star in his own project and Riley wasn't about to let all that charisma go to waste in a slasher flick headed straight to DVD.

"Hey, Mr. Big Time! You got my rent?" It was his landlady, Vera, a mean-eyed, foul-mouthed, purple-haired, ex-professional wrestler as seedy as the motel she owned. She was on the walk below standing next to an industrial-sized laundry hamper filled with the dirty sheets and towels she'd collected from the rooms.

"I'll have it for you on Monday."

"Friday!" she shot back, "or you're out on your ass!" She and the hamper moved on. Riley hated her as much as he hated LA.

He had to find a way back to Henry Adams. It was the only place he knew to go. He'd called his former wife, Eustacia Pennymaker, hoping to get a loan, but the maid said she was in Spain and wouldn't be back in the States for a month. His calls last winter to Bernadine Brown and his other ex-wife, Genevieve, weren't even answered. In Riley's mind, his life being in the toilet was still Genevieve's fault. If she hadn't walked out on him, he and Cletus would still be living in the house her father gave her as a wedding gift, the old loan shark Morton Prell wouldn't be dead, and Riley would still be secretly tapping into Genevieve's bank account. Having access to her money would also solve another looming problem. Wheels. Or lack thereof. His old truck died last week and the jackleg mechanic he'd found quoted him a repair price that almost gave him a heart attack. The little bit of cash he had left was enough to pay for the gas needed to get him and Cletus back to Kansas, but not if he had to repair the truck, too. What he needed was Bernadine Brown's junior felon, Amari, to steal him a car, but that wasn't an option, so he'd have to come up with another way to escape LA before Vera tossed him out on his rear

A couple of time zones away, TC Barbour drove his brand-new silver Dodge Ram the short distance from the home of his nephew, Gary Clark, to the building the Henry Adams locals called the Power Plant, site of the town's administrative offices. He'd arrived a week ago on a cross-country drive from his hometown of Oakland, California. Being retired, he had no real destination in mind, but he hadn't seen Gary in decades, so when they talked on the phone TC decided to accept his nephew's offer to stop in and stay awhile with him and his teen daughters, Leah and Tiffany. TC's business at the Power Plant had to do with a part-time job Gary mentioned in passing, one that entailed being the driver for the town's owner, Ms. Bernadine Brown. He'd driven a big rig at one point in his life and having never gotten a ticket driving it or anything else, he figured he was qualified. TC didn't like taking handouts, even from family, so if he was going to be bunking at Gary's and eating his food, he thought it only right that he contribute.

The town wasn't large by any means and the last time he'd visited, a good thirty years ago, it was so isolated and undeveloped it could've passed for the setting of the *Little House on the Prairie* television show. The surrounding area was still nothing more than wide open spaces with a house here and there, but the town center had changed dramatically. Paved streets replaced the dirt roads. There were streetlights and sidewalks. He drove past a diner with the head-scratching name of the Dog and Cow, a large school, a church with beautiful stained glass windows, and a long building with a sign out front that read: "Henry Adams Recreation—Senior Center." None of this existed on his last visit, and even more surprising was how cutting-edge they all appeared—as if they rightly belonged in a big metropolitan location like his hometown or LA. TC was impressed. After pulling into the parking lot of the equally impressive, low-slung red building that was the Power Plant, he got out and walked to the entrance.

This was his second interview. He and Ms. Brown met briefly a few mornings ago when he turned in the required resume. Gary's teenaged daughter, Leah, had helped him with the computer typing and formatting—a blessing, otherwise he would've never gotten the thing done.

Now, inside the office, TC sat patiently while the woman he hoped would hire him went over his resume.

"As I stated during your initial interview, you'll be the town driver," she explained, looking at him from where she sat fine and brown behind the desk. "Mostly taking folks back and forth to the airport down in Hays. Nathan Nelson, the young man you're replacing, left to attend college in Lawrence."

TC knew from Gary that Bernadine Brown's hand turned the world in the small town of Henry Adams. It was founded in the 1880s by freed slaves and she'd bought the place a few years ago, hook, line, and sinker. He'd never met a woman who'd owned a town before, and true to Gary's description, she was both classy and professional. She also had a man, which was fine with TC because he hadn't come to town to get tangled up with a woman—especially somebody else's.

"This is a pretty extensive resume," she continued, sounding impressed. "You've done everything from working as a longshoreman, to short-order cook and driving a big rig."

He'd also lost his wife, Carla, to lupus back in the '90s, but resumes didn't cover heartache or the challenges of raising three kids alone.

Ms. Brown went on to explain his benefits package, one he found surprisingly generous considering the job was only temporary. "We ran a background check and there are no red flags, so if you want the job it's yours. Just need you to sign the agreement."

She passed the document his way and the words on the paper swam before his eyes like letters in a bowl of alphabet soup. He patted his empty shirt pocket and sighed audibly. "I forgot my reading glasses. Can you show me where to sign?"

She smiled and pointed a perfectly manicured indigo-polished nail at the line needing his signature. He quickly scrawled *Terence C. Barbour* and handed it back.

"Welcome to Henry Adams, Mr. Barbour."

"Glad to be on board. When do I start?"

"Tomorrow afternoon. One of our residents, Ms. Genevieve Gibbs, is flying in from Washington, DC, at four p.m." She opened a desk drawer and withdrew a set of keys that she passed his way. "The town car is in the lot outside. If you want to park it at Gary's place, that's fine."

"Okay. What does Ms. Gibbs look like?"

"Caramel skin. Gray bob. Elegant."

"Gotcha." He stood. "Thanks so much, Ms. Brown."

"You're welcome, and please, call me Bernadine. We're pretty informal around here."

"Then call me TC."

She nodded and TC made his exit. Being born and raised

in Oakland, he knew next to nothing about living in a small town, but he was looking forward to the new experience.

Over at the church, Reverend Paula Grant glanced at her schedule for the afternoon. Having earned degrees in both theology and child psychology, she was actually Reverend Doctor Paula Grant. She served as priest at the Henry Adams African Episcopal church and as counselor to the town's lively children. The day's docket included a session with twelve-year-old Devon July, the adopted son of mayor Trent July and his wife, Lily. Devon started life in Henry Adams wanting to preach the Word but had given that up, and now Paula, his parents, and everyone else in town was trying to help the boy find himself. His acting out and rigid opinions had earned him two serious beatdowns from his BFF, Zoey Raymond Garland. As a result, he'd sort of gotten his act together, but his counseling sessions remained ongoing. She was also scheduled to meet with high school senior Eli James, whose dad, Jack, taught at the local school. Eli had never been one of her regulars. His dad had suggested the visit in order to try and determine what was going on with his son. Apparently Eli had become withdrawn and moody. It was a common stance for kids his age but Paula wanted to talk to him to make sure there wasn't something serious happening beneath the surface.

Devon arrived after school.

"Have a seat, Dev. How was school?"

He shrugged off his backpack and sat on her orange office couch. "It's school," he replied unenthusiastically. "Mr. James gave us a lot of homework. As always." Devon was thin, the color of a chocolate drop, and had a round head. He'd grown a few inches over the winter and was significantly taller than he'd been when Paula first came to town three years ago.

"Mr. James gives you lots of homework because he wants you to be as smart as you can be. Helps out when you become an old adult like me."

He flashed the smile that had won him the hearts and screams of the groupies he'd collected during last winter's performance of the band he was in before his parents, Lily and Trent, made him cut his online and off-line ties to the girls. "When's the band's next performance?"

"Not sure, but we're still practicing on the weekends."

"You guys are really good."

"Thanks."

"So you and Zoey still BFFs?"

"Yep. No more fighting."

"Good." Although everyone understood why Zoey reacted the way she had when Devon pushed her buttons, she too was one of Paula's clients because of her sometimes over-the-top temper. "Anything you want to talk about today?" She watched him think that over.

"Not really."

She waited.

"I think I want a girlfriend."

Knowing what she did about him, Paula wasn't surprised by the response. "May I ask why?"

"Amari has one—at least he used to until she moved—but Preston does, and Zoey likes Wyatt, so I need somebody to like, too."

Amari was Devon's older teenaged brother and Preston was Amari's BFF. Wyatt and his grandmother were recent arrivals in town and he was Devon's age. "Do you have someone in mind?"

He shook his head.

"Then I wouldn't worry about it. The right person will show up at the appointed time."

"You think so?"

She nodded. "And whoever it is should like you for being Devon—not because you can sing and are in the band."

"Oh."

He was one of the most talented kids in the state and his parents, who'd turned away more than a few unscrupulous would-be agents, were determined he not be sucked into the hype tied to that. He'd been raised by his now-deceased grandmother and she'd spoiled him rotten. His adoptive parents were doing a great job of undoing that as well. "So how are you and Amari getting along?"

"He's an awesome big brother. Makes me think about stuff."

"Like what?"

"Like what kind of person I should be. I told him I want to be him but he said he's already taken so I have to be myself."

"And what do you think about that?"

"I want to be a boss like him but I'm boring."

"I don't think you're boring."

"Girls think I am, at least when I'm not on the stage."

"Your time will come. Just keep doing the right thing and believing in yourself."

"Okay." But he didn't look convinced.

Because Devon's early life had been steeped in the Bible, Paula counseled him differently than she did the other kids. "God knows what your future holds so just wait and let Divine Order do its thing. Everything in its own time, right?"

"I guess." He still didn't seem convinced.

"You're still real young, too. Amari didn't get a girlfriend until recently. You have plenty of time."

He nodded and said, "Okay."

"Anything else for today?"

"No, ma'am."

"Then I'll see you next week. Give me a hug."

As she held him, her heart filled with the love she had for this special young man and she whispered, "You're going to be such a boss one day."

He smiled. "Thanks, Reverend Paula." He picked up his backpack and put it on. "I'll see you later." He exited and closed the door behind him.

In the silence that followed she'd be the first to admit that in the past few months Devon had come a long way. He still had miles to go, but that was okay.

A few minutes later Eli walked in. Tall, with dark hair and eyes, he was looking more like his handsome George-Clooney-resembling dad, Jack, every day. "Hey, Eli."

"Hey." He didn't take a seat. Instead he stood, as if not planning to stay.

She gestured. "You're welcome to sit."

He did, but she noted his reluctant body language. When he and Jack first moved to town Eli had been surly and hard to like due to the pain he'd been carrying inside over the recent loss of his mother, but Henry Adams filled him with the tough love it was so famous for, and over time the poison drained away, leaving behind a kid who was no less hurt but seemingly focused on looking forward. In the fall he'd be enrolling in community college, as would Bernadine's adopted daughter, Teen Queen Crystal. "So, how are you, kiddo?"

He shrugged his thin shoulders. "I'm good, I guess. Not sure why Dad wanted me to come see you. Nothing's going on."

She noted the way he wouldn't meet her eyes. "All set for school in the fall?"

He nodded. "Yeah."

"Excited?"

"Yeah." And he gave her his first smile.

"What are you looking forward to the most?"

He shrugged again. "Living in an apartment and being sorta on my own."

"Ready for Eli unplugged, huh?"

Another smile.

"You've earned it. You pulled your grades up. Got your head together. We're all really proud of you. Losing your mom when you did is not an easy thing to handle. When I lost mine, all the light in my world seemed to disappear."

Surprise brought him up straight. "You lost your mom? How old were you?"

"Fourteen."

He sat back, seemed to think on that for a moment, and said finally, "So you know how it is."

"I do," she answered softly. Only she hadn't received an iota of the support, love, and understanding Henry Adams showed Eli. The embers of that old pain quickened and she turned her mind back to the present before it flared to life. "I'm over fifty now and I still miss her."

"I still miss mine, too."

"I don't think it's anything we ever get over, but we get through it. Does that make sense to you?"

"It does. I dream about her a lot." He glanced her way as if needing the reassurance that it was okay to share his feelings. "For a while I thought I might forget what she looked like, but Dad has a bunch of pictures, so every now and then

I take them out and look at her. God, I miss her so much," he whispered. Tears shone in his eyes and he hastily dashed them away. "Sorry."

She handed him a tissue from the box sitting nearby. "No shame here. It's a measure of how much you loved her. Has losing her been hitting you pretty hard lately?"

"Yeah. Like out of nowhere almost. I thought I had the grief thing under control. Guess not, huh?"

"Nothing wrong with admitting that, nor do you have to apologize to anyone. Okay?"

He gave her a tight nod. They spent a few minutes sharing stories about their mothers. Paula told him about the birthday cake her mother would bake for her every year, and Eli told her that his mom always took him to the zoo on his birthday—even if it was a school day. "She made sure I got my homework the day before, though."

"You have an advantage I didn't have when my mama died."

"What do you mean?"

"You have your dad. My mom was a single parent." And she'd never shared the name of Paula's father.

"He probably didn't think it was an advantage. I treated him like crap." His eyes were earnest. "I want to apologize to him but I don't know how."

"Admitting that you do means the right moment will show up."

"You think so?"

"I know so. You'll feel it. Just promise yourself you won't let it slip by, okay?"

He nodded. "I won't." He was silent for a long moment before saying, "I'm glad I came to see you today."

"So am I."

"I know it's been a long time, but my condolences on losing your mom."

"Thank you, and the same to you. Anytime the grief starts rising and you need to talk, you know where to come."

"I do. Thanks, Reverend Paula."

"You're welcome. We'll always have this bond, Eli."

He picked up his backpack and like Devon closed the door softly behind hm.

Paula took a tissue out for herself and wiped her eyes. She hoped he would talk to his dad when the moment presented itself. It might not only bring them closer but would let Jack know his son was doing okay.

With nothing else on her schedule, Reverend Paula decided to have dinner at home for a change. Like most of the people in town she ate at the Dog more often than not but that day she felt like cooking for herself.

As she prepared to gather her things and lock up, there was a knock on the door and she looked up to see Rochelle "Rocky" Dancer on the threshold. "Hey, Rock."

"Hey, Rev. I know I don't have an appointment but are you busy?"

"No. Come on in. Have a seat." Although Paula wasn't licensed to counsel adults she was always willing to lend a shoulder or an ear.

Rocky took a seat on the couch. She was one of Paula's favorite people. Their trailers were near each other out on the July family's ancestral land, and when the weather was warm, she often awakened in the mornings to the lilting beauty of Rocky's flute. "So what's up?"

"Jack asked me to marry him."

"And?" Paula asked, hoping to keep her excitement under wraps.

"I'm not sure if I want to."

"Have you told him that?"

"I have, and he's willing to wait because he never pushes, but I'm wondering if I'm being selfish, or keeping him at arm's length because I'm scared."

"Of?" she asked easily.

"Honestly? That he'll wake up one day wondering what in the world he's doing with somebody as screwed-up as I am and leave."

Paula smiled. "You know he loves you, right?"

"I do, or at least I think I do, but I still can't figure out why."

"Have you asked him?"

She gave a tiny shrug. "I have, and he's so kind and considerate, and puts up with my crazy moods. I suppose I'm still waiting for the gotcha."

"Like your other relationships?"

"Yeah. Hard to be trusting when you find the man you married prancing in front of the window wearing your underwear."

"But what does that issue with your first husband have to do with Jack?"

She sighed audibly. "I don't know, Rev. Nothing, really. Guess I'm still trying to wrap my mind around Jack being so good to me."

"Feel you don't deserve it?"

"Maybe."

"But you do, you know. We all deserve love and peace and safety in our lives."

"I guess."

"No guess, Rock. We do."

Rocky stared off for a minute. "I know this is a decision I have to make for myself, but I needed to bounce it off of you, too."

"Always available."

"I know. You're the best. You can have your couch back. I have to get to work. Thanks."

"You're welcome."

Paula shook her head after the town's resident bombshell left her office. In spite of all the toughness on the outside, a scared and scarred woman lived inside. Paula was convinced Rocky being the beneficiary of Jack's unconditional love would go a long way in helping her heal, but convincing Rocky of that might take some time. Paula puttered around for another few minutes just in case someone else showed up at her door. When no one did, she picked up her coat, keys, and purse and went outside to her truck to head for home.

Eli came home to the smell of burgers frying and his eighteen-and-a-half-year-old stomach sat up and took notice. His dad was in the kitchen, and the skillets on the stove were sizzling. "Hey, Dad. Smells awesome."

"Good to know. How are you?"

Eli sat at the barlike counter and shrugged. "Okay, I guess." He wasn't ready to talk about his visit with Reverend Paula yet and was glad his dad seemed to know that. "You teaching GED class tonight?"

"No. New term starts in two weeks. Do you have to work next weekend?"

Eli had a part-time job as a member of the wait crew at the

Dog, the town diner managed by his dad's girlfriend, Rocky Dancer. "Yeah. Saturday morning. Why?"

"Apparently your grandparents are flying in that Friday."

"Your set or Mom's?"

"Mine."

"When did this happen?"

"My mother called about an hour ago. She never bothers to check if other people have plans. Her plans are always your plans whether you want them to be or not."

Eli loved his grandparents but sometimes his grandmother Stella acted like she was the Queen of England the way she ordered people around. His grandfather Jack Sr. was really the only person who could make her take a seat. "So I assume they'll be staying with us?"

"Yep." He took the now-done burgers from the skillet and put them on a plate. Eli could tell he wasn't happy.

"How long are they staying?"

"Just for the weekend supposedly, but who really knows." He sighed and looked over at Eli. "Go wash your hands. These sweet potato fries will be done by the time you get back."

"Aye, aye."

When he returned everything was ready. He sat at the table and after adding his preferred condiments to the burger and dousing his fries with ketchup began eating. "Not as good as the Dog's but it'll do."

"Hater."

Eli grinned and took a draw on the straw in his cola. "Why do you think Gram's coming?"

"Truthfully? To try and convince me that Rocky's not the one."

"Didn't you tell me she did the same thing with Mom?"

"She did, and you know how that turned out."

"She's batting zero."

"And that losing streak will continue."

Eli noted the fire in his dad's eyes. Personally, Eli liked Rocky a lot. She was tough both on and off the job, but underneath all that steel she seemed to love his dad. "You don't think she'll stoop to using the race card, do you?"

"I hope not, but she did use the *class* card with your mother. 'Blue bloods don't mix with no bloods,' she had the nerve to tell me."

Eli was appalled. "Because Mom was Italian?"

He nodded as he dipped the end of a fry in the small pool of ketchup on his plate. "I was furious, to say the least."

Eli was furious for him. Since moving to Henry Adams, the two of them had gone a long way toward being father and son. After his mom died, Eli had been so full of grief, he'd turned on him like a mad dog, accusing him of everything from not loving him to trying to ruin his life by taking him away from California and his friends. Now that he was older and been set straight by the likes of the town elders and Crystal, he knew his dad loved him a lot. "I went to see Reverend Paula today."

His dad paused and studied him for a long moment before asking, "How'd it go?"

"It went okay. She lost her mom when she was a teenager, too."

"I didn't know that."

"Yeah. We talked about that and Mom dying, and how I felt. She said I had an advantage she didn't have."

"Which was what."

"You," Eli said softly. He saw his dad's eyes glisten. "Dad, I'm so sorry I was so mean to you."

"You were hurting, son."

"But still. I've been wanting to apologize and could never find the right time. Reverend Paula said because I wanted to do it, the time would show up and that I should promise myself not to let it slip by, so the time is now." He took a breath. "Thanks for putting up with me and not leaving me on the side of the road. And thanks for telling me to go see her. She helped a lot."

"You're welcome."

"I've been thinking about Mom a lot lately—about how proud she'd be of me getting ready to go to college even though I'm a year behind and it's just community college."

"That you're continuing your education is the most important thing."

"I know. I have Tamar to thank, too." The town matriarch hadn't taken any crap from him, and that made him grow up a lot.

"I agree."

"And Crystal."

"How are you two getting along?"

Eli shrugged. "Okay, I guess. Even though I'm dating Samantha I still got a thing for Crystal if that's what you're asking. Not sure where she really stands though. Probably still waiting on that loser Diego to ride in on his bike and save the day." Diego July was a cousin of the town's mayor. Crystal fancied herself in love with him and she'd been crushed learning Diego didn't feel the same way about her.

"Women tend to be complicated."

"Yeah. Finding that out."

"It'll all work out in the end. Maybe the way you want and maybe not, but it will work out."

Eli noted that his dad didn't judge. He rarely did. Even when Eli and the other kids were busted surfing the Net in places they all knew were off-limits, his dad had screamed and yelled and dropped down on him hard, but hadn't judged. "So are you going to be able to handle Gram?"

"Yes. I figure it's only a weekend. How crazy can she make me in two days?"

"I got your back."

"Good. I'll let you know if we need to hide the body."

Eli chuckled and went back to his burger. He had something else weighing on his mind that he hadn't talked to Reverend Paula about, and until he figured out how to approach his dad about it, he planned to keep it to himself.

TC sat with Leah and Tiffany at the dining room table. He could smell something burning in the kitchen but being a guest he was too polite to go and see what the problem was. "Does your dad do all the cooking?" he asked the girls.

Leah sighed. "Yes. He's not very good at it, though."

"You two cook?"

Tiffany shook her head. "Before they got divorced, Mom used to do all the cooking so we never learned. Dad says he doesn't have the time to teach us and that he can do it faster."

"I see." TC's daughter Bethany began helping him in the kitchen as soon as she was tall enough to see over the table. Both his boys, Keith and Aaron, learned to cook from their mom before she got too sick, and after her passing TC helped them refine their skills. TC was an excellent cook and his great-nieces were correct in saying Gary was not, if the meals put on the table since his arrival were any indication.

Dinner consisted of burnt pork chops, overcooked broccoli,

undercooked mashed potatoes, and packaged biscuits. While Gary took his seat, Leah looked at her plate, glanced TC's way, and chuckled softly while shaking her head at her father's lack of skills.

"Tiff, your turn to say grace," their dad said.

She offered up a short, quietly spoken prayer, and once she was done, they began eating.

"So, you got the job?" Gary said, attempting to cut into the dried, burnt chop.

"I did," TC replied. "I start tomorrow. Have to pick up a Ms. Gibbs at the airport."

"Yes, Genevieve," Gary said, smiling. "She's coming back from Washington, DC. Very nice lady."

"She really is," Leah added. "We kids like her a lot."

TC saw Tiffany moving her food around on her plate as if doing so might make it disappear. TC wished the same thing. Not only was it badly cooked, it was so tasteless due to the lack of seasoning they may as well be eating cardboard, but he ate it all.

Later, while the girls were upstairs in their rooms doing their homework, he and Gary sat outside on the old-fashioned back porch watching the end of the day. "I think I'm going to like it here," he said.

"Good. Town's real slow and real quiet but everybody gets along for the most part."

"Are you enjoying running the store?"

"I am. Didn't think I would at first. I spent most of my life selling cars, not food, but I'm doing pretty good. Having a good staff helps, not to mention Bernadine's full support."

"How long have you been the manager?"

"We opened just before Thanksgiving. Still trying to learn

how to juggle my time, though. Rushing home to make sure the girls have dinner, checking their homework, and doing all the other stuff tied to parenting leaves me just enough time to breathe, go to bed, and get up the next morning to start it all over again."

"The girls seem happy."

"I think they are. The divorce was hard on Tiff, though. She's just starting to make peace with the idea that Colleen isn't coming back. Our priest, Reverend Paula, is also a child psychologist and she's been helping Tiff sort stuff out."

"And Leah?"

"My rock. Handled the divorce pretty well. Colleen always favored Tiff over her so . . . But as long as Leah has her telescope and her physics, she's good."

"Physics?"

"Yes. Wants to be an astrophysicist. My daughter has a brain big as the Milky Way."

TC chuckled. "Wow."

"She and her boyfriend, Preston, are two of the best young physicists in the state—so good they're taking college courses online. You'll meet Preston. He's a good kid."

TC couldn't get over that. *Physics*. He couldn't even spell the word. He'd have to make a point to talk to Leah about the subject and her goals. He was always interested in learning new things. "Are you old enough to remember the show *My Three Sons*?"

Gary looked confused. "Yeah, sort of. Why?"

"In addition to the dad, Steve, and his boys, there was a character named Uncle Bub—older guy, lived with them, cooked all the meals, did the housework, which freed Steve to go to work and not stress over the daily stuff that needed doing at home."

Gary gazed out at the fields leading to the horizon. "Be nice to have an Uncle Bub."

"Or an Uncle TC."

Gary paused. "What do you mean?"

"After your aunt Carla died your cousins were all still living at home, so I did the cooking and cleaning and all the other Uncle Bub stuff. Have to say I was pretty good at it, too. So, how about I be Uncle TC for you? I'll do the meals, keep the house up, do the laundry, and teach the girls to do the same along the way."

"I can't ask you to stick around and do all that, and I can't pay you."

"Not asking for pay but you could use the help, Gary. True?"

"Lord knows I do."

"Then I'm your guy. You get to do the homework, though. I don't know physics from a hole in the ground."

Gary chuckled.

TC added, "Tell you what. Let me cook breakfast in the morning, and after I run down and get Ms. Gibbs, I'll come back and make dinner. If at the end of the day you don't think I've helped, I'll turn in my apron. Deal?" He extended his hand.

The emotion in his nephew's eyes let TC know that making the offer was a good thing.

"Deal," Gary said softly.

They shook.

CHAPTER
2

The following morning, the Clark family awakened to the smells of bacon and they weren't sure what else, but the house smelled like heaven. When they entered the dining room, on the table sat a bowl of steaming scrambled eggs, a plate piled high with strips of bacon and a pan of biscuits made from scratch. Leah, Tiffany, and Gary stared, amazed.

"Eat before it gets cold," the smiling TC invited. "Who wants juice?"

They all did, and while he went to grab a bottle from the fridge they sat and began eating.

"Oh," Leah cried around a mouthful of eggs. "This is so good."

Tiff laughed. "No burned bacon!"

That earned her a critical look from her dad, but he finally smiled. "It's okay, Tiff. Cooking is not my strong suit, and I agree, this is really good."

There was orange marmalade and honey to go with the biscuits and because the biscuits were so awesome they all treated themselves to some of both.

They were eating and smiling when TC took his own seat.

Leah said, "You know you can't leave town until I go away to college, right?"

Tiff replied, "Until *I* go to college, you mean. Thank you for breakfast, Uncle TC."

"You're welcome, Little Bit."

Shyness seemed to come over her. "I never had a nickname before."

"Little Bit okay?" TC asked.

Her answer was a soft "Yes."

He shared a look with Gary who gave him a nearly imperceptible nod of approval. TC sensed the Clarks needed him to not only run the household but to help them navigate back to being a family, and he felt up for the task.

An hour later, the girls and Gary left to go about their day and TC had the quiet house to himself. He poured himself a second cup of coffee, then stepped out onto the wide back porch. The weather was a bit chilly for a man born and raised in California but he knew it was something he'd get acclimated to. Having been a big-rig driver he knew how beautiful the sky could be on a spring day in the plains, but to be able to sit down and enjoy it without having to push on to the new stop was something new. If all the smiles at the table were any indication his first morning as Uncle TC had been a hit. Later he'd drive down and fetch Ms. Gibbs, and he hoped that part of the day would be a hit, too.

On her flight home from Washington, DC, Genevieve Gibbs was exhausted, but it was a happy exhaustion. She'd had such a good time. In addition to taking the White House tour and a nighttime tour of the monuments atop a double-decker bus, she'd visited the Smithsonian, the African American Civil War museum and the Native American museum, and had some of the best salmon she'd ever eaten at a quirky little restaurant called Busboys and Poets. This was the first time she'd ever traveled alone and as a woman in her sixties, she was pretty proud of herself. Not that she'd wanted to go solo. She'd asked her friend and roommate Marie Jefferson to come along, but Marie was still acting like a teenager in middle school in response to last Christmas's surprise visit from long-lost classmate Rita Lynn Bailey. How Marie could hold onto a forty-year-old grudge about nothing was something Genevieve still didn't get. She and Marie had been best friends since they were eight years old. Now? Gen had hoped that having Marie with her on the trip to Washington would be a way for them to have some fun and rescue their friendship. Since she didn't want to come along Gen used the time to do some well needed soul-searching. For as long as she could remember someone else had held the reins to her life: first her parents, then her no-good ex-husband Riley, and after Gen walked out on him, Marie had been the one she'd looked to for guidance. After sharing Marie's home for the past few years and being influenced by how women like Bernadine Brown and Lily Fontaine July fearlessly approached life, Gen felt as if she'd finally come into her own. She now possessed the confidence she'd always lacked. The old Genevieve would've never given her embezzling ex-husband a right cross that knocked him into next week the way she'd done when he had the nerve to return to town a few years back with his so-called new wife, Eustacia Pennymaker. The punch broke a bone in her hand but the pain was secondary to the satisfaction that came from watching him slide to the floor out cold. Just thinking about him and his murderous hog

Cletus enraged her all over again, but she drew in a deep breath and willed herself calm. She was a new Genevieve—*large and in charge* in the words of her young friend Amari July, and she loved who she was becoming.

The plane finally landed at the Hays Airport and she made the short walk to baggage claim to get her suitcase. She didn't know the man holding the sign with her name written on it but Bernadine had texted her last night about having hired a new driver. She'd described him as Gary Clark's uncle and being near Gen's age, but she'd left out how nice he was to look at. Dressed in a well-tailored black suit and a crisp white shirt that showed off his large trim frame, he could've been a CEO. The small silver hoop in his ear added a bit of intrigue to his dashing appearance. The old Gen would never dare think such a thing, but the new and improved version of herself definitely appreciated his tall dark handsomeness. In spite of the changes she'd made to herself, she was still a lady and so she approached him and extended her hand. "Hello. I'm Genevieve Gibbs."

"Nice to meet you. I'm Terence Barbour. Most people call me TC."

"What's the C stand for?"

"Christopher."

For a second she looked at him and he looked at her, until he finally said, "Um, let me take that bag."

As she handed it off, she wondered why she felt so warm. Before she could analyze it his voice brought her back. "When we get outside, will you be okay waiting by the curb while I bring the car around? It's in the lot."

"That will be fine."

Once they cleared the doors and stepped out into the chilly early April sunshine, he said, "Be right back."

Yes, Genevieve decided, he was very handsome. Maybe even more so than Mal, or Clay for that matter. Thinking about Clay made her realize she needed to make a decision about whether their slow-moving relationship was still viable. Clay was a sweet, lovely man but he seemed to prefer the meek doormat Genevieve that she used to be, and since she didn't, they were having issues.

The black town car slid smoothly to a stop beside her. TC got out, opened the door, and held it for her. "Thank you," she offered quietly.

Once she was settled, he closed her in, took his seat behind the wheel, and off they went.

After clearing the airport property, he caught her eye in the mirror. "Some people like to talk while riding, others like silence. Which would you prefer?"

"A bit of both, I suppose."

He nodded. "Sounds good. You want music? I found some jazz on one of the streaming channels."

"That would be nice."

As they turned onto the interstate, Gen listened to the music and mused upon being back in Henry Adams. She had to admit that little Dorothy from Kansas was right: there was no place like home. That also got her to thinking. When a woman her age decides to reinvent herself, living with someone like Marie who used every day to throw a pity party for herself was not her idea of fun—nor was it healthy. Marie needed to deal with her issues, make her apologies to everyone she'd offended and move on, but since she wouldn't, Gen would be the one moving on instead. The idea broke her heart, but rooming with the cold and silent Marie was like living in a freezer and Gen wanted warmth in her life.

The station played an instrumental that was so memorable

and familiar both she and TC said at the same time, "Haven't heard this in years."

They both laughed. It was Wes Montgomery's "Bumping on Sunset"—a classic.

"Still sounds good," TC said.

"Yes, it does."

They listened with quiet appreciation to the groundbreaking guitar virtuoso who'd paved the way for greats like George Benson, Lee Ritenour, and others.

When the tune faded away, TC said, "Can you imagine how big he would've been in the music world had he lived?"

"If I remember correctly, he died rather young."

"Yes. A heart attack at age forty-five," he informed her solemnly. "Tomorrow isn't promised."

"No, it isn't." She sensed a sadness in his tone that made her wonder about its roots but she'd never be so rude as to ask.

A few more classic tunes played: "The Sidewinder" by Lee Morgan and "The Sermon" by organist Jimmy Smith. Her father Nelson had loved jazz. Growing up, she had her Motown and Stax, and he'd had his Blue Note and Verve labels.

TC's voice interrupted her musings. "Ms. Brown said you were visiting Washington, DC?"

"Yes. My first trip and I had a great time. Have you ever been there?"

"No. Haven't had the pleasure."

"You should go. I toured the White House. Although going through the security checks was longer than the tour."

He smiled at her in the mirror.

"I saw the African American Civil War museum and their beautiful monument across the street. It has the names of every man of color who served in the Civil War."

"Wow. I'd really like to see that. I served in the Army during 'Nam. What else did you do—if you don't mind me being nosy?"

She didn't. "I took a fabulous nighttime tour of the monuments on a double-decker bus. And I saw the Native American museum."

"I didn't know there was such a museum."

"There is, and the National Museum of African American History and Culture will be opening in the fall and I'm definitely going back to see it."

"I've heard a lot about it. Saw specials on *60 Minutes* and on C-SPAN."

"C-SPAN? I don't know too many people who watch C-SPAN, TC."

"Impressed you, have I?"

She laughed. "Definitely."

"Good." He caught her eye in the mirror again, and Gen's heart began a dance it hadn't done in years. Surprised because she didn't know Gary's uncle from a can of paint, she forced herself to turn to the window and gaze out at the passing landscape lining the highway.

When they arrived at the Jefferson place, he parked, came around, and opened her door. She stepped out, thanked him and waited for him to remove her suitcase from the trunk.

"I'll take this up to the porch for you."

Once that was accomplished, she handed him his tip.

He declined it. "Not necessary. Ms. Brown pays me well."

"But—"

He was already on his way back to the car. "Pleasure meeting you, Ms. Gibbs."

Before she could respond, he drove away. Having enjoyed his company, she said wistfully, "Pleasure meeting you, too."

Putting him out of her mind, she stuck her key in the lock and went inside.

Marie, wearing her signature cat-eye glasses, was seated in the front room watching *All My Children*.

"I'm back," Gen said cheerily. "How are you? What have I missed?" Because there was always something going on in Henry Adams.

Marie shrugged. "Nothing. Same old same old."

"I had a really good time. You should have come."

No response. Gen sighed silently. Lately, trying to have a conversation with Marie was like pulling staples out of concrete. "I'm going up to my room and unpack. Do you want to do something later? Dinner at the Dog?" The Dog, formally named the Dog and Cow, was owned by their lifelong friend, Malachi July.

"No. I'm good. You can go if you like."

Swallowing her disappointment, Gen and her suitcase climbed the stairs. It was official. She was definitely moving out, and the sooner she did the better.

That evening Genevieve checked herself out in her vanity mirror and nodded approvingly at her reflection. The new black velveteen jacket she'd purchased in Washington looked very classy with her red turtleneck, charcoal-gray wool pants, and black short-heeled boots. The simple gold chain around her neck matched the bangle on her wrist and the small hoops in her ears. She'd gone back to wearing her gray hair natural and she thought the elegant cut she'd also gotten in Washington set the tone for the image she wanted to convey: trim and fashionable yet classic. She and Clay had talked earlier on the phone and were going to have dinner at the Dog.

In spite of their issues, she'd missed him and looked forward to the evening. They agreed on a time and that he'd pick her up—since Gen didn't drive—something else she needed to remedy. She'd relied on other people to get her around all her life and it was time to step up. She wondered if Clay would be willing to teach her.

When she got downstairs, Marie was still in front of the TV watching *Wheel of Fortune*. "Clay and I are going to the Dog for dinner."

Marie replied with a distant nod. Gen wished she could help her friend find peace but that seemed impossible at the moment, so she left her and stepped outside to await Clay's arrival.

He pulled up in his truck and she hurried down the walk to meet him.

"Hey, good-looking," he said as he got out and came around to open the passenger-side door. He gave her a quick peck on the cheek. "Good to have you home. Worried about you being in DC alone."

She waved him off. "I was fine, just like I told you I would be." She climbed in and he closed her door. Before her trip to Washington they'd had a small argument about her traveling alone. She'd appreciated his concern but her mind had been made up and that was that.

After getting into the truck on his side, he started the ignition, looked her way, and said, "I know you think you're all that and a bag of chips, too, but no more trips by yourself. Okay?"

"Not okay." His lips tightened but she didn't care. Keeping her voice soft she asked, "Can we fuss after we eat?"

The smile that he showed cut the tension. "Yes, ma'am."

As he drove toward town she sighed inwardly. His treating her like he always knew what was best was driving her nuts, but she reminded herself that she'd loved him since high school. Marrying Riley Curry instead had been the worst decision of her life. Now they were trying to rekindle what they'd lost decades ago and she was doing her best to ignore the tiny voice in her head that kept whispering it was too late.

The Dog and Cow was the only diner in town and, as always during the dinner hour, the place was jumping. The booths lining the walls and tables positioned in the middle of the large room were filled with people, and myriad conversations competed to be heard over the sound of the flashy red jukebox playing "Cowboys to Girls" by the Intruders. The family of the Dog's owner, Malachi July, had lived in Henry Adams for over a century. Mal was also Clay's BFF.

Upon seeing them enter, Mal came over and gave her a hug. "Welcome home. Did you have a good time?"

"I did."

"Good. Hold on a minute and I'll get you two a booth."

While they waited Gen shared smiles and waves with a host of people she knew: from members of the young waitstaff like Bernadine's daughter, Crystal, to Sheila Payne, the town's director of special events, and Sheila's husband, Marine Colonel Barrett. When Gen was young her main goal in life had been to leave town and see the world, and she thought by marrying Riley with his boastful plans it would happen, but as the years passed she found herself stuck in a loveless marriage with a man who cared more for a hog than he did for his wife. Now that she was finally in charge of her own life, she was content with this small town and the wonderful friendships she'd made because she was no longer stuck. In spite of Riley's embezzlement, she was still financially secure—thanks to Bernadine's advisors—and if she wanted to spend a week in Washington, DC, or even Paris, she could.

Mal waved them over to a booth on the far side of the room. When the smiling Crystal came over to take their order, Gen ordered the trout and veggies. Clay opted for steak, salad, and a baked potato. "I'll get this right out," Crystal promised.

She headed off to the kitchen to put in their order and Gen asked Clay, "So, what have you been doing while I was gone?"

"Besides worrying?"

Lord save me from this man! "Besides worrying."

"Not much. Bing and I drove over to Topeka for the Black Farmers' meeting. We're still dealing with the fallout of the lawsuit. Some people with legitimate claim numbers are being told their cases were filed too late for them to be compensated."

He was a member of the class action suit filed by Black farmers nationwide against the Agriculture Department for its decades of unethical loan disbursements and illegal land forfeitures. "Do the people who were denied have any options?" she asked.

"It doesn't look like it, but we'll see. We were also told that the ombudsman hired to look after our interests is raking in millions that should be going toward the settlement."

She knew that Clay, his elderly housemate Bing Shepard, and some of the other farmers in the area had already received their portions of the landmark settlement, but others, particularly many of the women, had yet to receive a dime, and she found that shameful. "Did you see Marie at all while I was gone?"

"No. She's been keeping to the house just like she did before you left. I'm worried about her."

"So am I, and I wish I knew how to help. Living with her is like living in a tomb. I think I'm going to look into getting a mobile home."

He paused. "Really?"

She nodded. "Time for me to move out and be on my own. I'll talk to Lily and see what I need to do."

"Are you going to put it on your land?"

"Yes. And sometime in the near future I'm going to have another house built." And once it was ready she'd replace the roses and the sunflowers Riley's damn hog had rooted up at her old place. She wouldn't be able to replace the heirlooms and knickknacks given to her by her mother or grandmother, though. They'd been lost when Cletus trashed the house so thoroughly the county condemned it and then bulldozed the place. Her heart still ached over the loss. She glanced up to find Clay staring at her. "What's the matter?"

"Why are you building a house?"

"So I'll have a permanent place to stay, Clayton."

"But what about us?"

"What do you mean?"

"I mean, I thought you and I would be together."

"We are, but I'm not ready to jump back into a marriage right this minute, and I'm too old-fashioned to live with a man who hasn't put a ring on it." Gen was a huge Beyoncé fan.

Once again his lips tightened. She wanted to ask him if he was planning to propose to her, but afraid he might say yes, she left the question alone.

He took a sip of water, and after putting the glass down leaned in and revealed quietly, "I'm not comfortable with who you're trying to turn yourself into, Genevieve. You're acting like you're twenty-five."

Her lips tightened this time. "I'm turning myself into the woman I should have been when I was twenty-five, Clay. Why is that making you uncomfortable? Don't you want me to be happy with myself?"

Crystal's return with their food stayed his response. After setting their plates in front of them, Crys asked, "Anything else I can get you two?"

"No, honey," Gen answered. "I think we're good."

"Okay. Enjoy."

Once Crystal moved away, Clay cut into his steak.

Gen asked gently, "Aren't you going to tell me why you're so uncomfortable?"

"Let's just eat before our food gets cold."

Shaking her head with exasperation, she began to eat.

The ride back to Marie's place was as silent as their meal had been. When he stopped in front of the house, he confessed, "Honestly, I'm uncomfortable because I like the old Gen better. I enjoy looking after you, doing things for you, and you needing me. This new version doesn't seem to need any of that."

"I'm sorry I'm no longer helpless, Clay. For the first time in my life, I'm in control of me. Not my parents. Not Riley. Me. And I'm enjoying that. Can't you be happy for me?"

"I'm an old-fashioned guy, Gen. I want to take care of my woman."

She chose her words carefully. "And I appreciate that, but I don't want to be taken care of, Clay. I'm finally figuring out who Genevieve Gibbs really is. Her strengths, her likes, her dislikes, and I would love it if you'd come along with me on this journey and cheer me on."

He didn't reply.

"You won't even try, Clay. For us?"

He stared stonily out of his window and when he didn't relent, she reached down and opened her door. "Okay," she said, trying not to be overwhelmed by the sadness in her heart. "I'll see you." She got out, closed the door again, and started to the porch. He drove away and she didn't look back.

Hearing Gen moving around upstairs, Marie couldn't decide if she was glad to have her back or not. On the one hand, she'd been lonely knocking around in the big old house alone, but on the other hand, being by herself fed the funk she'd descended into since Rita Lynn's visit last Christmas. Her cringe-worthy behavior and the bridges she'd burned on that awful afternoon made her want to climb into a hole and never come out. Apologies to friends like Genevieve were warranted, yet she couldn't bring herself to offer them due to her inner shame and humiliation. As a result, she hadn't been to the Dog, attended the town meetings, or checked on how things were going at the beautiful school that bore her name. She knew she had to reenter the world at some point, but it was much easier not to. *How do I face people again?* She didn't want to see the pity in Mal's eyes now that he knew she'd been pining for him since middle school. They'd been friends over sixty years and he'd always viewed her as a sister. Marie had always prided herself on her inner discipline but when Rita Lynn, who'd given birth to Mal's son while they were in high school, coolly revealed the truth about those feelings all that discipline flew out the window and she lost her mind. Age-old anger and resentment rose up like unleashed toxic lava, and next she knew she was spewing it all over the place—at Genevieve, Mal, and yes, Rita Lynn. If Rita Lynn hadn't ended the encounter by dashing a glass of ice water in Marie's face, there's no telling how much more damage might've been done. Marie dragged her hands wearily down her face. And now, here she sat almost four months later, wallowing in self-pity and mad at a world that seemed to offer nothing but heartache. From her cold and distant mother, Agnes, to the son she'd been forced to put up for adoption and who wanted no contact, to her failed relationships with men. Marie was tired of being strong, optimistic, and hopeful. Her life had been one beatdown after another and she was tired of fighting back.

When Riley entered the crowded car dealership that Friday morning, he didn't have much of a plan but hoped and prayed something would work out. Since he hadn't had Vera's rent money she'd kicked him out as promised, so with no place to live going back to Kansas was his only option. The showroom floor was packed with people checking out the shiny new cars and SUVs. Balloons were everywhere and huge, large-lettered signs announced a sale in progress which he supposed accounted for all the lookie lous. Wearing his signature black suit with its fake red carnation pinned to the lapel, he just knew he looked the part of a man prosperous enough to draw attention, and sure enough a tall blond salesman wearing khakis and a blue, short-sleeved polo walked right over. "May I help you, sir?"

Liking the "sir" part, Riley puffed up and said, "Yes. I'm visiting from my hometown in Nebraska. I'm the mayor, and we're in the market for a fleet of SUVs. I've test driven your competition but thought I'd swing by and see what you have before making my final decision."

"Excellent. I'm sure we have something that will meet your needs. I'm Adam Reed. Come this way, please." He led Riley through the crowd and over to a nice-looking red SUV that Riley thought would fit his needs perfectly. "What's your name, sir?" the tall blond salesman asked.

Riley panicked. "Uh. July. Trent July."

"Nice to meet you, Mr. July. Where 'bouts in Nebraska are you from?"

"Hays. It's right outside of Omaha."

"Ah." Reed opened the door and stepped aside so Riley could slide in under the steering wheel.

Riley's short stature positioned him eye level with the bottom of the windshield and he was stung by red-hot embarrassment. If the salesman had any cracks or short jokes he kept them to himself and simply demonstrated the workings of the seat, and soon Riley was elevated enough to see over the hood. "I like this," he offered, taking in the fine leather interior and all the bells and whistles on the dash.

"How many vehicles is your town thinking of buying?" Reed asked.

"Maybe three, possibly four."

"Would you care for a test drive?"

"Sure would."

"There are a couple gassed up on the lot. Let me grab a plate and the keys."

Outside, while the salesman attached the plate Riley got in and adjusted the seat. There were a large number of people outside, too. He spotted a man and woman checking out a stylish black minivan parked just a few feet away. After peering in the windows the couple began looking around as if needing assistance from the sales staff. Reed was watching the two people as well, and Riley sensed he was torn between staying where he was and heading over to see if they were serious buyers. Riley seized his opportunity. "How about I just take a quick ride around the block so you don't lose those customers?"

The couple seemed to have given up and were walking back to their car. Reed's eyes widened in panic. "Yes, but do me a favor. I need a copy of your license. Can you go back in and have one of the girls at the cashier station copy it for me and leave it with her?"

"Sure can."

"Good. I'll see you when you get back."

True to his word, Riley went inside, but that was all he did. Keeping an eye on Reed through the glass, he walked around for a quick few minutes then went back out to the SUV. He waved at Reed and gave a thumbs-up. Reed returned the sign and as Riley left the lot and merged into the LA traffic, it was the last that salesman Adam Reed saw of Mayor Trent July.

Feeling like a million bucks, Riley steered the sweet red SUV through the open gates of the farm owned by the man boarding Cletus. His hog was in the large pen with a few others. Cletus got along with them pretty well for the most part, especially the white sow, Cleo, who'd done a few commercials and was slowly climbing the ladder to success. The farm's owner, a likable elderly man named Ben Scarsdale, was also an animal trainer. Scarsdale said he'd rarely seen a hog as smart as Cletus and enjoyed working with him. Riley owed him a ton of money but the man seemed to take Riley's promises to pay in stride and never seemed upset when payment didn't materialize.

Riley parked and got out. Cletus lumbered over to the fence. "How you doing, big boy? Came to break you out. You ready to go home?"

Cletus raised his head and let loose a few loud snorts which Riley took to be, yes.

"Hey, Riley. Didn't see you drive up."

Riley jumped, startled. "Uh, hey, Ben," he replied, hoping he didn't sound or look guilty. He also wondered how much the man had overheard. "Thought I'd take Cletus out for a picnic. He and I haven't had any family time in a few weeks and I miss him."

"That's nice. Where you going?"

"Not really sure, but there's going to be ice cream. Clete loves vanilla."

"Is that a new car?"

"Yeah," he said, clearing his voice due to the guilt clogging his throat. "Cousin died last week and left me a little bit of money. If Cletus doesn't break me eating ice cream, I'll pay you just as soon as I get back."

"That's good news, because your bill's pretty high. Don't keep him out too long. He and Cleo have a thing going and she gets upset when he's not around."

Riley saw the sow eyeing Cletus and Cletus eyeing the sow. He hoped this wouldn't be a repeat of Cletus and Chocolate, the sow his hog married a few years back. When Eustacia walked out on Riley and took her sow with her, Cletus was depressed for months. "Then let me get going. Don't want Cleo to get upset."

"I'll get the trailer."

Riley wasn't sure if the new SUV would be strong enough to pull Cletus's trailer but found he had nothing to worry about. He waved at Scarsdale and the man waved back, but Riley was so busy congratulating himself on his cleverness, he missed the angry set of Ben's jaw and the fire flashing in his blue eyes as Riley and his hog drove out of sight.

TC had never attended a town meeting before, so when he entered the diner Monday evening with Gary and the girls he checked out all the smiling people milling about and visiting, heard the Temptations singing "Don't Look Back" from the red chrome jukebox, and smiled. He liked the homey feel of the gathering right off the bat.

"Let's grab a seat," Gary shouted over the din. "And I'll introduce you around."

Following his nephew to a booth, TC estimated there were about fifty people inside, some Black, some White and all carrying plates piled high with appetizer-type food like wings, pot stickers, and cut-up raw veggies. That pleased him, too.

Since there were more people than booths, Gary stopped at one already occupied by the mayor, Trent July, and his wife, Lily. "Can we join you?"

TC had met both briefly over at the Power Plant while seeing about the job.

"Sure." Trent and Lily moved over so he and Gary could

join them. Leah and Tiffany were already squeezing into another booth filled with a group of teens.

"Welcome to the town meeting," Trent said.

"How often do you do this?" TC asked, still glancing around.

"Once a month. Gives us the opportunity to stay connected and keep up with what's going on around town."

"This is amazing," the impressed TC offered. "You won't find anything like this in Oakland."

Lily said, "One of the advantages of small-town living."

"I see," he replied.

Gary asked, "I know we just had dinner but do you want something to munch on?"

"Sure. How long do the meetings usually last?"

Trent answered. "No more than an hour or so. Not much on the agenda this evening."

"How much is the food?"

Gary smiled. "Free. Courtesy of the Boss Lady Ms. Brown."

TC saw her over on the side of the room speaking with a tall guy about his age. She looked elegant even when wearing jeans and a soft blue sweater. The tasteful gold bangles and the hoops in her ears seemed to emphasize the fact.

Gary said, "Let's grab a plate. We'll be starting soon."

The buffet table offered lots of finger food. TC helped himself to a few wings, and some little filo squares filled with spinach. The woman standing behind the line was knock-your-socks-off gorgeous. Gary said to her, "Rock. Want you to meet my uncle, Terence Barbour."

Extending her hand, she offered up a smile that made TC melt. "Hi, Mr. Barbour. Pleased to meet you. I'm Rocky Dancer. Welcome. You're the one taking over from Nathan?"

TC nodded. "I am. Call me TC, please."

"Will do. Help yourself to the fixings. My assistant Siz does most of the cooking. Best chef this side of the Mississippi."

TC eyed the bounty. "Looking forward to trying it out. Nice meeting you, Ms. Dancer."

"Same here. Call me Rocky."

He nodded.

He and Gary moved down the line, and as they did he got a wave from Ms. Brown. He asked Gary about the man she was talking with.

"Malachi July. Owns the place. He's also Trent's dad. Their family has lived here over a hundred years. Mal's mother, Tamar, is the town matriarch. I'll introduce you to them later. You got enough?"

TC eyed his plate. "I think I do."

On the way back to the booth, Gary stopped so TC could meet Clay Dobbs and his buddy Bing Shepard, whose beautifully carved ebony cane was as stately as the man holding it.

"Welcome," both men said to him.

"Thanks."

As they moved on, Gary said, "Clay and Genevieve Gibbs are lovebirds."

"Ah" was TC's reaction. He hadn't seen her yet and wondered if he would. He'd had a nice time driving her back from the airport and had to admit to being disappointed that she and Clay were an item, even though he wasn't looking to hook up with anyone while in town.

Gary stopped and introduced him to Reverend Paula. She invited him to the church and he told her how much he liked her navy blue cowboy boots. He then met the Paynes—Sheila and Barrett. The retired Marine was fit and still appeared capable of scaring the pants off a green recruit. His wife was a beauty and TC wondered if all the women in town were fine. Ms. Gibbs certainly had been. After leaving the Paynes, Gary said, "Their son, Preston, is Leah's boo, as the kids say."

TC wondered if the boy ever got out of line with a dad like Barrett. TC's dad had worked on the docks and had arms the size of redwoods. Anytime TC got out of line he made sure his daddy never found out.

Back at their booth, they found that Trent and Lily had been replaced by a new couple TC had yet to meet. Gary did the introductions. "TC, this is Reggie and Roni Garland."

Reggie said, "Nice meeting you. Trent and Lily are up front getting ready to call the meeting to order. They asked us to hold down the booth while you were gone."

TC swore Roni looked just like singer Roni Moore but he knew he had to be wrong. What would the Grammy-winning songstress be doing in Henry Adams? "Nice meeting you, too. Ms. Garland, you probably get this a lot, but you look just like the singer Roni Moore."

She smiled serenely. "I do get it a lot and I'm always flattered."

Beside him, his nephew was grinning and her husband wore a secretive smile. TC studied her features closely again and finally said to himself, Naw.

Trent rose to his feet. "Okay, let's get this show started." All eyes including TC's turned to the front of the room. At that moment, Genevieve Gibbs hurried into the diner accompanied by a young man and woman, each carrying a toddler in car seats. TC viewed her arrival approvingly.

Feeling harried, Gen hastily apologized to the folks at the head table for being late and she, Kelly, Bobby Douglas, and their twin little ones, Kiara and Bobby Jr., squeezed into the booth with Mal and Bernadine. Marie hadn't attended a town meeting in months so Gen rode over with Kelly and Bobby.

As Trent began to speak Gen hazarded a glance around the room and saw Clay. He met her eyes briefly before turning away. His refusal to accept her for who she wanted to be still pained her, but no way was she going to veer from her path. His loss. Just like Riley. She discreetly swept the rest of the room and found her gaze caught by the new driver, TC Barbour. He nodded politely and she offered a small nod in reply. Wondering why in response her heart was beating like a sixteen-year-old's, she focused her attention on Trent.

Trent opened the meeting by introducing Mr. Barbour to the gathering. "He's Gary Clark's uncle. Wants to be called TC, and will be filling in for Nathan as town driver until Bernadine can find a permanent replacement. Can you stand up, Mr. Barbour?"

A round of applause greeted him and he raised a hand in acknowledgment. He had on jeans and a charcoal-gray turtleneck and Gen found him as attractive in casual clothing as he'd been in the crisp black suit he'd worn at the airport.

Bernadine leaned over. "Not bad on the eyes."

"Hey!" Mal groused with a laugh. "I'm sitting here, too, you know."

"I'm just saying."

Gen silently agreed but in spite of his good looks and her reactions, she had no room in her new life for a man. If Riley hadn't taught her that, Clay certainly had. Going forward, it was going to be all Genevieve all the time.

So for the rest of the meeting, she sat and listened as Trent gave the latest on the new swimming pool he and his team would be breaking ground for in a few weeks and the plan to turn the old dilapidated Henry Adams Hotel into a loft space. He also brought them up to speed on the small strip mall that would be built and opened by the fall. Kelly's new beauty shop would be one of the businesses going in, along with a pharmacy and real clinic space for Doc Reg so he could move out of the school. Speaking of the school, teacher Jack James stood and announced the opening of the new term for GED classes for those who didn't want to take the classes online. Over the winter Gen had gotten her literacy certification to teach reading to adults who couldn't read or wanted to improve and Jack announced that as well. "See Ms. Gen about setting up a schedule," he said before retaking his seat.

She saw TC give her a quick glance before returning his attention to the front of the room. She wondered if he knew of someone who needed her help or was checking her out just because.

New resident and town fire chief Luis Acosta took the floor next to give an update on how his department was progressing. "So far we have twelve volunteers. Some have experience but most don't. Training and classes are ongoing. Lily has two state-of-the-art engines on order and as soon as the construction on the new firehouse is complete and passes inspection they'll be delivered and we'll be up and running."

Tremendous applause greeted the news. No one wanted a repeat of last year's deadly fire set by the now imprisoned Odessa Stillwell.

After the meeting, the mingling and visiting resumed. Kelly and Bobby were heading home to put the twins to bed. Gen thanked them for letting her ride with them. "I'll find a way back so go on and don't worry about me."

"Are you sure?" Kelly asked. The young family had moved

to town that past winter and Gen had come to love them very much. She was also godmother to the twins

"I'll be fine." She kissed the babies. "Be good for your mama and daddy, you two."

Both toddlers gave her sleepy smiles.

"We'll see you tomorrow, Ms. Gen," Bobby said in parting.

Gen nodded and watched them make their way to the door. Having them in her life made up for not having been blessed with children of her own. She also watched Clay leave with Bing. Something telling must have shown on her face because Mal walked to her side and asked, "You and my buddy fighting?"

"Honestly, Mal. I don't know what we're doing. No, I take that back. I do know. We've called things off."

"Really? What happened?"

"*I* happened, I suppose. Clay doesn't like the new and improved Genevieve. Said he prefers the old me."

"That's asinine."

"I know, but it is what it is. He said I'm acting like I'm twenty-five." Once again she refused to let the sadness take hold. "I'm not going back to who I used to be, Mal."

"And no one with any sense wants you to. Nothing wrong with what you're doing. Sometimes you have to shed the old to be the new. Take it from someone who's been there done that."

She gave the former alcoholic and Casanova a kiss on the cheek. "Thanks."

"No problem. Do you want me to talk to Clay?"

"If you want to, but I don't think it will make a difference. He's got his mind made up and we both know how rigid he can be sometimes."

He nodded knowingly. "Well, hang in there. For what it's worth, I like the new you."

That earned him a smile. "I like the new me, too."

"How's Marie?"

"Still the same. I want to smack her and shout, 'Snap out of it!'"

"Same here. While you were in DC I went to the house to check on her, hoping we could talk, but she wouldn't even answer the door."

"This is so stupid."

"Tell me about it."

"I want her to talk to Reverend Paula, but I don't see her agreeing to that."

"Me either. We'll just keep hoping and praying that she comes to her senses."

He left her to help with the cleanup and she was grateful to have him as a friend. Putting Marie out of her mind for the moment, Gen looked around for someone to hit up for a ride home. She saw TC Barbour talking with Gary and the Garlands. He glanced up casually and their gazes locked. He nodded and smiled. She nodded back, and while their gazes held, time seemed to suspend itself to the point that it took her a moment to realize Lily was standing beside her.

"Does Clay know you're ogling another man?" Lily asked.

Embarrassment heated her cheeks. "I'm doing no such thing." Even as she wondered why he kept drawing her attention.

"You could've fooled me. Although for a man of a certain age, Gary's uncle is kind of hot."

Laughing, Gen asked with mock severity, "What do you want, Lily July?"

"I wanted to know if you enjoyed your trip to DC."

"I did." And Gen filled her in on some of the highlights before asking, "Can I stop by your office tomorrow? I need your help and advice on some things."

"Sure. I have something to work on in the morning but I'm free in the afternoon."

"I volunteer for the seniors' lunch tomorrow at the rec. How about one-ish or so?"

"Works for me. We can talk business and then about what's going on with you and Clay."

Gen responded with a soft chuckle. *Nothing like living in a small town.* "Okay. I'll see you tomorrow."

Lily moved on. Gen spied Mal's mother, Tamar, putting on her coat. The July matriarch didn't live far from Marie's.

When Gen asked for a ride, Tamar replied, "Sure. Grab your things and meet me outside."

Gen picked up her coat and purse, and although the urge to glance TC's way one last time whispered, she didn't succumb on her walk to the door.

Outside, she got into Tamar's truck. The ninety-year-old Tamar drove her ancient truck, Olivia, as if they were qualifying for the Indy 500, so the drive home seemed to take only seconds. Tamar was one of the wisest women Genevieve had ever known, so before getting out she asked, "Do you think I'm being silly for trying to remake myself and my life?"

"Do *you* think you're being silly?"

"No, but apparently Clay does."

"Giving you grief?"

Genevieve nodded.

"Would you be happier being who he wants you to be?"

"No."

"Then step into your new life without him," Tamar advised easily. "You wouldn't be the first woman to do so. Or man for that matter. Some people spend their entire lives trying to live up to someone else's expectations and go to their graves wondering why they were never happy."

Gen felt the rightness in that.

Tamar continued. "In the scheme of things you're still relatively young. The Spirit willing, you have a good twenty, maybe thirty years left and you want to greet the sunrise with the smile you put on your own face, not the frown worn by someone else."

"Wise advice."

"Haven't lived this long for nothing."

Gen smiled. "Thanks, Tamar."

"I've been watching you these last few months, Genevieve Gibbs, and I like what I'm seeing. Keep being you and damn the torpedoes."

"Yes, ma'am. In fact, I'll be talking to Lily tomorrow about ordering a double-wide because I want to move out."

"Makes sense. You want to ride into town with me in the morning?"

"That would be great. I need to learn to drive, too."

"Another good idea. Who're you going to have teach you?"

"Are you volunteering?"

"I love you a lot, but not enough for that. I'm elderly, remember?"

Gen scoffed and laughed. Tamar was the youngest elderly woman in the county. "Then I'll ask Lily or Trent or maybe Bobby."

"All good choices."

Gen thought about the main reason for wanting to move out. "What are we going to do about Marie?"

"As much as it hurts me to say this, nothing. The only person who can do anything about Marie is Marie. She's in my prayers, though."

"Mine, too. Thanks for the ride and the advice."

"Anytime. I'll see you in the morning."

Gen got out, and beneath the beam of the porch light stuck her key in the door. Once she stepped inside, Tamar and Olivia roared off into the night.

CHAPTER
4

Eli dropped his backpack on his desk and removed his books. This would be his last year at the Marie Jefferson Academy. He was pretty sure he'd miss interacting with the other kids on a daily basis, but he wouldn't miss being taught by his dad. When your teacher was your father he knew when you had homework or a big test coming up. He also knew when you had a major paper to do and what day it was supposed to be turned in. The other kids could scam their parents on that kind of stuff, but not Eli. Case in point, last night after the town meeting instead of going up to his room to chill and maybe fire up his Xbox, he'd been asked about his readiness for today's test on the solar system, particularly Jupiter and its moons. Eli knew he was ready, well, sort of, but when his dad asked him to name the Galilean moons and what they were composed of he'd stumbled a little. His dad raised an eyebrow and said, "You might want to look over the material again."

So he did, and now knew Io from Calisto but like most teens had no idea when he'd use the knowledge IRL—in real life. It wasn't as if he planned to be an astrophysicist. He'd be leaving that to Leah and Brain. Eli was a sculptor and was pretty sure when Rodin created *The Thinker*, not knowing Jupiter's Galilean moons hadn't kept him awake at night.

Speaking of sculpting, news from the artist competition he'd entered a few months back was due in the mail anytime now. He'd submitted a bust of his mom. Working on it had been one of the toughest experiences of his life. Memories kept rising and some nights he'd cried so much over losing her he couldn't see the clay for his tears, but he'd been proud of the finished likeness and so had his dad. Crystal had also sent in an entry. She was a painter though, and submitted a triptych based on her life. First prize was scholarship money and the opportunity for the winner's work to be displayed in a big-time California art gallery. He and Crystal really wanted to win, but seeing as how only one of them could come in first, they'd agreed to be happy for each other no matter the outcome.

While the other students like Amari, Preston, and the Clark sisters filed into the classroom and took their seats, he glanced Crystal's way. The grin she shot him made his heart speed up. He continued to have deep feelings for her even though she'd made it clear she'd rather be friends, which was why he was dating Samantha instead. He and Sam had a good relationship and he thought she was pretty special, but she wasn't Crystal. Seeing Sam enter the room, he shot her a wink and settled in for the start of the day.

As always, class began with the pledge and the Negro National Anthem. It was Zoey's day to accompany the singing on the piano. Eli had been in Henry Adams going on three years now and knew the words by heart. When he and his dad first arrived it had been weird being one of only two White kids in town and he'd been pretty sure he wasn't going to like it, but nobody made a big deal about it and he'd done a lot of growing up since then. He'd also learned a ton of Black history and realized people were people. As Amari once pointed out, Eli was now bicultural and personally he thought there was a lot of cred in that.

After their math lesson and the test, it was time for lunch. Having been born and raised in California, Eli still had no love for the Kansas winter but the day's weather was filled with sunshine and temps that confirmed spring's warmth would show up for real sometime soon, so they all put on their coats and headed outside.

Once they were seated at the picnic table, Amari said, "I think we should go big for our dads on Father's Day."

They all knew that the former Detroit car thief seemed to wake up each morning with a plan tied to something big, so Eli said, "Okay I'll bite. Big as in how?"

Amari shrugged. "Not sure. Thought we'd brainstorm. We have some awesome fathers so why not celebrate."

Crystal cracked, "Some of you might have awesome dads but mine kidnapped me and held me for ransom, remember?"

Eli did. Ray Chambers wound up being a tornado snack and impaled on the points of a picket fence for his efforts. As far as Eli knew no one mourned his demise.

Amari's little brother, Devon, asked, "Is this going to be a secret?"

"Maybe," Amari replied.

Brain, always the voice of truth and reason, offered, "Good luck with that."

He was right, of course—there were no secrets in Henry Adams.

Zoey took a sip from her juice box and added, "Even if we did try and keep it secret, we'd still have to get permission from somebody for whatever it is we're doing. Probably Tamar."

She was right, too. Eli believed the sun didn't rise without the town matriarch's okay.

"How about we have an all-day picnic?" Leah asked.

Amari's face brightened at the idea.

Eli's did, too. "Maybe Tamar would let us use her field."

After that the brainstorming session began to flow hot and heavy. They discussed decorations, maybe having a short program and what kind of food they might want to serve. Tamar's homemade ice cream topped the list. In the middle of the planning, Wyatt got up and walked away from them without a word.

Eli asked, "What's up with him?"

Zoey speculated softly, "Maybe he's feeling kind of left out because he doesn't have a dad."

Wyatt's soldier mom died in Afghanistan and he was being raised by his grandmother, Gemma, one of the clerks at the town's grocery store. Eli didn't remember the boy ever mentioning his father.

"Damn," Amari said. "I forgot. Be nice if we could find him one."

"True," Brain said as they all watched Wyatt walk stiffly toward the school's doors. "But it's not like we can hook him up with one on eBay."

Eli felt bad. He couldn't imagine not having his mom *and* his dad.

"So do we call off the idea because of Wyatt?" Leah asked.

Amari shook his head. "I say we go ahead. We'll figure out

a way to help Wyatt somehow. And Eli, since you suggested we use Tamar's field, you get to ask her. Let us know what she says."

Eli sat there dumbfounded while everyone else gathered up their trash. Lunch was over.

Crystal smiled. "I saw that coming the minute you opened your mouth. You are such a sucker."

Smiling, he lowered his head, then joined the trek back.

The Henry Adams Ladies Auxiliary provided lunch to area seniors three days a week, and once the cleanup was done, Genevieve put on her coat, waved goodbye to her friends, and walked the short distance down to the Power Plant for her appointment with Lily. Inside, lush green plants filled the red-brick atrium and basked in the sun streaming down through the skylights overhead. A few small fountains had been recently added and the soft sounds of the water added to the space's calming Zen-like feel.

The administrative offices lay beyond the double glass doors and a short walk down the carpeted, art-lined hallway led Gen to the space occupied by the lady whose hand turned the world. She poked her head in the open door. "Afternoon, Bernadine."

As always the Boss Lady was at her desk. "Hey there, Gen. How are you?"

"I'm well. Have an appointment with Lily. I'll tell you about it later."

"Okay. I'm all yours if you need my input."

"Thanks."

Lily was working on a laptop when Gen arrived and she looked up with a smile. "Come on in, Gen. Have a seat. Be with you in just a sec. I need to send these blueprints for the Henry Adams Hotel to Mayor Hottie. He and Bobby are in Franklin talking to a supplier."

Gen took a seat. It was no secret how much Lily loved her husband Trent. Gen envied their relationship. That she'd never experienced such a special connection was one of her life's biggest regrets.

Once Lily hit *send*, she asked, "Can I get you some coffee? Juice?"

"Coffee would be wonderful."

After they both had their cups, Gen revealed what she'd come to discuss. When she finished, Lily asked, "How soon do you want to move?"

"As soon as I can find a suitable mobile home. And after, when Trent has time, I'd like to get with him and have some blueprints drawn up for a new house."

"You're going big."

"Go big or go home, as they say. And I want to do both."

"Has the county said it's okay to rebuild on your land?"

"Yes. I talked to them before I went to Washington." The last testing showed no toxins, but the soil was rich with pig poop. Perfect for the roses she wanted to plant.

"So, what's Marie saying about you moving out?" Lily asked.

Marie was Lily's godmother. "I haven't told her yet. Wanted to speak with you first so I'd know what kind of time line I'd be working with. Honestly, in her present frame of mind, she'll probably see it as just one more betrayal, but I can't stay there any longer. Even the air feels oppressive."

"I understand. I've tried talking to her too, but decided until she has her own come-to-Jesus moment, there's nothing any of us can do."

"Tamar said the same thing."

"And that's sad."

"It is because I've loved her like a sister all my life."

"I know, but in the meantime, let's get going on this move. Depending on what you want and what's in stock I might be able to have a home on your land sooner than later. How big do you want it to be?"

They spent the next few minutes discussing square footage and amenities. Lily pulled up the website she'd used for the double-wides Bernadine had on Tamar's property for new residents. Genevieve saw a two-bedroom that she thought might suit her needs, and loved that it had a small front and back porch. "I like that one, Lily."

Lily checked availability and to their delight there was one in stock on the lot. Gen handed over her credit card. Lily made the deposit online, and once all the paperwork was printed out, reviewed, signed, and scanned back, Gen had a new leased double-wide.

Lily added a small warning. "Trent has a ton of projects on his plate. I'm telling you up front he probably won't get around to building your home until next year."

"That's fine." And it was. That she'd have a new home to live in as early as the middle of next week was godsend enough for the present. "Thank you, Lily."

"No problem. If you need help moving you know everyone in town will volunteer."

"Everyone except Clay."

"So what's up with him?"

Genevieve filled her in.

"That is so sad. This isn't the fifties. Why is he expecting you to act like it is?"

"I don't know." And truly she didn't, but she did know that he'd been changed by his service in Vietnam. He'd left Henry Adams a carefree, laugh-filled jokester and returned joyless and rigid. Mal had been changed by the experience, too. She couldn't imagine the horrors they'd lived through. As far as she knew, unlike Mal, Clay hadn't sought help from the VA or anyone else, but then again, the country hadn't been kind to the returning vets of that era, and as a result many men and women continued to suffer in silence to this day. Clay never talked about his time overseas but it was the only possibility she could point to as the reason for him changing. That and the fact that she'd thrown him over for Riley just a few months before he was drafted.

"Gen?"

She startled at the sound of Lily's soft voice. "Sorry. I was drifting in the past. Forgive me."

"No problem. How about asking the Ladies Auxiliary to help you pack. We're always looking for a way to get together. Maybe us being there will help Marie out of her funk."

"I'd love that, and if it helps Marie, so much the better."

"Do you have a lot of stuff to move?"

"Not really. I left Riley in a huff and most of my belongings were still in the house when Cletus trashed the place." She remembered how devastated she'd been upon viewing the aftermath of the hog's rampage on the news. Curtains hanging listlessly on torn-away rods. Floors littered with pieces of broken furniture, lamps, and her precious curios. "I'm looking forward to buying new things." Things that gave her comfort, fed her soul, and reflected her and her new life.

When the girls came in from school, TC had snacks of fruit, cheese, and juice waiting just as he'd done for his own kids years ago. The smiles on the girls' faces made his heart swell with memories. "I wasn't sure what you liked, so I had to guess. If you have a preference for something else just let me know and we'll pick it up when we go to the store tomorrow."

Leah, in the process of biting into a crisp red apple, paused. "We?"

"Yes, ma'am. You and Lil Bit will do the shopping with me tomorrow. Preparing you for independence, and so you'll know exactly how much food costs."

"Oh."

"Problem?"

"Uh, no. It's just we never did anything like that before."

"Think of it as an adventure. Do you have anything scheduled after school?"

The girls shared a brief look and Tiff said, "No."

"Good. Also want to have a pizza party for you girls and your friends, say Saturday?"

Leah's eyes narrowed suspiciously. "Why?"

"So I can get to know them and for them to know me too, since I'll be here for a while." He asked again, "Problem?"

Leah appeared ready to say something but apparently changed her mind. "No. No problem, but the only pizza place is in Franklin and they're always cold when they get here."

"We aren't getting them from Franklin."

Tiff asked, "Where then?"

"We're making our own."

Both girls stared with round eyes.

TC enjoyed the reactions. "It'll be fun. Promise. I just need to know how many people are coming to make sure we have enough dough."

They were viewing him as if he were an alien who'd just

walked through the front door. "Take a minute to chill and then get started on your homework. I'll let you know when dinner's ready."

Eyeing each other with what appeared to be amazement, the girls left him in the kitchen alone.

Eli backed his car out of the driveway on his way to the neighboring town of Franklin to have dinner with his girlfriend, Samantha, and her parents, but his mind kept replaying how rigid Wyatt appeared walking away during lunch. The kid had been real silent for the rest of the day and something made Eli want to make sure his friend was okay. Following the death of his mom, Eli hadn't cared about anybody's feelings other than his own. Living in Henry Adams had changed that. So he pulled up in front of the boy's house and got out.

Wyatt answered the door and eyed Eli suspiciously before saying, "Hey, Eli."

"Hey. Just stopped by to check you out. We didn't mean to hurt your feelings at lunch."

"I'm good. Thanks." And he promptly shut the door.

Stunned, Eli stood there. *I know this kid didn't just close the door in my face.* But he had and Eli could either pound on the door or leave. Holding onto his temper, he chose the latter. *So much for trying to help.*

By the time Eli got to Sam's house he'd let it go, but would be talking to the other kids about the incident because Wyatt hadn't acted *good*.

Sam answered the door and unlike Wyatt met his arrival with a smile. "Come on in."

She lived in a nice house. Her parents seemed to like him and he thought they were okay as parents went. They didn't hassle him or make him feel uncomfortable and that's all a kid could ask. Her mom, Natalie, wasn't a very good cook though, and as they sat down at the table he politely ate the spaghetti and meatballs because he was supposed to.

"You looking forward to community college, Eli?" her dad, Phillip, asked. He was a plumber.

"Yes, sir."

Her mom glanced Sam's way. "Sammy's pretty excited about going to Columbia in New York City. Aren't you, honey?"

"I am," she said with a happiness that showed.

Her mom sighed. "I just wish you'd gotten the scholarship to KU, so you'd be closer."

"I know, but Columbia came through first."

Sam was incredibly smart. Her big brain ranked right up there with Leah's and Preston's. She'd set her sights on leaving small-town Kansas the moment she became eligible to apply for colleges. She'd also been smart enough not to apply to KU, even though she told her parents she had. Neither of them had gone farther than high school. Sam was their only child and because they weren't familiar with the application process they'd relied on her to handle the paperwork and keep them informed.

"What are you going to major in, Eli?" her father asked.

"Art with a minor in business."

He nodded approvingly. "Smart. Having business as a backup is a good thing. Art won't pay your mortgage."

Eli didn't like hearing that, but nodded as if he agreed. He glanced at Sam. She showed a tiny eye roll. Hiding his amusement, he went back to his plate.

At the end of the meal, Eli stood. "I'll help clean off the

table, Mrs. Dickens?" It was what polite guests offered, but as always, she waved him off.

"Thanks, Eli, but you two go ahead and get your studying started. Can't have you flunking out right before graduation." Her dad didn't offer to do anything and left the table to head for the flat screen in the den.

Eli and Sam moved into the living room.

As they took out their history assignments, he gave a quick look around to make sure they were not overheard and asked quietly, "Are you ever going to tell them you didn't apply to KU?"

She chuckled. "Maybe after I graduate from Columbia. Have you talked to your dad about letting you move back to California?"

"No, because he'll probably tell me no. I'm waiting on my friend Geoff to call me back. He's going to ask his mom if I can live with them until I finish school." Eli's mom and Geoff's mom had been good friends. If she said yes, he'd have a better chance of getting his dad to agree. Eli enjoyed living in Henry Adams. He liked the people, the friends he'd made and the maturity he'd found, but he wasn't a small-town kid and he was feeling stifled by the slow pace and having nothing to do but go to school and hang out at work. He missed the energy of California, the people, his friends, surfing, the music. And like Sam, he wanted out, but unlike her, he didn't have the grades to get him into a big college—his own fault—so he had no golden ticket. "Maybe I'll have some leverage if I win the art competition."

"Maybe."

"No matter what happens though I'll do my best to come and see you at Columbia." She went so still in response, he paused. "What's the matter?"

She shook her head. "Nothing. Let's get started."

He reached out and gently turned her chin so he could look into her eyes. "Talk to me, please. Is something wrong?"

For a moment their gazes held. She backed out of his hold and stared off for a moment. "Do you really want the truth?"

"Yeah."

"Okay. It's like this. I don't want a boyfriend back home when I leave in August."

That confused him. "What do you mean?"

"You and I have had a good time together but you don't love me, Eli. You never have. And please don't lie to me and say that you do."

He blinked.

"I knew going in that you still had a thing for Crystal and it was okay, but when I leave I'll be stepping into a new life with new friends and maybe eventually somebody who'll be all mine and I'll be all theirs."

"Wow," he said softly. He hadn't seen that coming. At all.

She reached out and cupped his cheek. "You're a pretty amazing guy and you've been really sweet to me, but we don't have a future so there's no sense in pretending that we do."

"So is this goodbye?"

"I still want to go to the graduation dance together, if you do. I still want to go to the Friday night movies and do all the other fun stuff we've been doing, but as friends."

He studied her and realized he'd really screwed this up. All this time he'd been basically playing her but she'd played him, too. He felt like such a fool he wanted to rewind time and start over with this incredible girl because she'd deserved better. "I'm sorry, Sam."

"Me, too."

Damn!

"Do you still want to work on this assignment?" she asked quietly.

In truth, he wanted to slink home with his tail between his legs. "Yeah. What's the first question?"

Later, lying in bed in the dark, Eli thought back on Sam's startling confession. He felt an inch high. What might have happened had he dealt with her like a real girlfriend and not as a placeholder for Crystal? Would she have been so quick to dis their relationship? Would she have been sad about their being separated by so many miles? As it stood she'd been pretty matter-of-fact about the whole thing and his ego felt stomped on. No more than he deserved. Treating her the way he had he'd earned having his feelings bruised like the loser in an MMA bout. Like most boys, he'd grown up believing girls were emotional and fragile little things. Since moving to Kansas it was obvious the women he'd interacted with didn't know that.

CHAPTER
5

The following morning, as Paula prepared to leave for her office, she received a text from her uncle Calvin in Oklahoma. *Tyree gone. Della making funeral arrangements.* Sadness flooded her and she whispered a prayer for her grandfather's soul. That he was no longer in pain from the cancer was a blessing. She was then beset by a different set of emotions. His death meant she'd have to go back to Oklahoma and she sent up a prayer for herself.

Once in town, Paula stopped by Bernadine's office. As always she was at her desk.

"Good morning, Reverend. Come on in and have a seat. What can I do for you?"

Paula sat and said, "My grandfather's passed, so I'll be going to Oklahoma as soon as the funeral arrangements are finalized."

"My condolences on your loss."

"Thank you."

"Is this the same grandfather you went to see over the Christmas holidays?"

"Yes, he had cancer, but he hung on longer than the doctors said he would."

"So sorry," Bernadine said again. "Do you want Katie to fly you there?" Katie piloted Bernadine's personal jet.

"No. I'll fly commercial. Less drama that way."

Seeing Bernadine's puzzlement, Paula explained, "My aunt Della already thinks I'm a stuck-up so-and-so. If she finds out I flew in on a private plane she'll really go to town on me."

"You're kidding."

"Wish I were. I am persona non grata in her eyes. So was my mom."

"May I ask why?"

"My mother left there as soon as she finished high school. After her death when I was fourteen my grandfather took me in. I left too, as soon as I was able. Most folks born there die there."

"You are one of the kindest and most loving people I know. How dare she hate on you."

"Thanks for that, but it is what it is. I pray for her and for me."

"Is this more of your being kind as opposed to being right scenarios?"

That made her smile. "I suppose so." Bernadine was referencing a sermon Paula had given a few months back. The theme had been: Choosing to be kind over being right.

Bernadine cracked, "That's why you're the pastor here and I'm not. So when are you leaving?"

"Not sure, or how long I'll have to stay after the funeral, either." She had no idea if he'd made a will.

"Okay. Let me know if I can help in any way."

"I will." Paula stood. "Thanks, Bernadine."

"You're welcome. God bless you."

She gave the Boss Lady a nod and slipped out.

On the short drive to the church, Paula thanked God again for bringing Bernadine and Henry Adams into her life. Three years ago when the diocese in Miami informed her it would be closing her aging inner-city parish, she'd also been encouraged to retire. Knowing her call was still strong and viable she'd eschewed the advice and prayed for direction instead. A short while later the remarkable Ms. Bernadine Brown entered her life. Like everyone else in town, it took Paula some time to wrap her head around the depths of Bernadine's generous spirit, but through it Paula gained a community, a brand-new church, and the opportunity to combine the two things she loved most: serving God and helping kids.

Inside her office, she hung her parka in the office closet and checked her planner. She had a session with Zoey Garland after school. As far as Paula knew, Zoey, aka Miss Miami, as she was affectionately called, hadn't gone Muhammad Ali on anyone in quite some time. She assumed the anger management talks they'd been having were helping—either that or no one had made Zoey mad enough recently to set her off. Smiling, she closed her planner. Until Zoey arrived the day was her own, so she sat down at her desk to fine-tune her sermon. One of the upcoming Sunday readings was from Ecclesiasticus. Chapter 44, verses 1-15. It paid tribute to the ancestors, particularly those unsung. When she began working on the sermon earlier in the week, she'd thought the verses apropos in light of her grandfather's cancer fight. Now that the disease had won, the words resonated louder still, even though living with him represented a dark, painful period in her life, and Tyree Parks hadn't feared God or anyone else. *Their descendants stand by the covenants; their children also* . . . Paula wasn't looking forward to returning to Oklahoma. When she visited her grandfather in the hospital over the Christmas holiday she'd hoped things in the small town of Blackbird had changed for the better—they hadn't. The people had gotten older of course, but the petty jealousies, backbiting, and the abject poverty remained firmly entrenched. Her mother's sister, Della, was still bitter, resentful, and venomous. Every word she'd spoken to Paula had been laced with barbs, even going so far as to deride Paula for being a priest. The hate-filled words hurt—always had, and probably always would because she didn't see her aunt changing. When it came time to return there for the funeral she'd need God's help because Blackbird, Oklahoma, was a snake pit and anyone who ventured in without fangs was prey.

Needing to find out about the funeral arrangements, Paula picked up her phone and mentally prepared herself to speak with her aunt because she knew it wouldn't go well. When Della answered, Paula said, "Hey, Aunt Della, this is Paula. My condolences."

"How'd you find out?"

"Uncle Calvin sent me a text."

"What do you want?"

"To see if the arrangements have been made. I'll be coming for the funeral."

"Why? He didn't leave you anything, if that's what you think."

Paula prayed for patience. "I don't want anything from him. I'm coming to pay my respects. I owe him that."

"You owed him so much you left, just like your mama did."

"Can we not go there? He was my grandfather."

"And my father and your mother's father. Didn't stop her from breaking his heart when she left. And you turned around and did the same thing. Apples don't fall far from the tree."

As difficult as it was, Paula refused to be baited.

Della continued, "And don't think you're going to have a say in the service."

"I wasn't planning to."

"Good. Because nobody wants any of that mumbo-jumbo you and those Catholics use."

Paula gave up long ago trying to explain to her aunt that she wasn't Catholic. To Della if you weren't Baptist or Methodist, you were Catholic. "How's Robyn?"

"Got her head in those damn books so much, have to remind her to do her chores. She's going to turn out to be as useless as Lisa." Della's daughter, Lisa, disappeared fifteen years ago, leaving behind her then two-year-old daughter, Robyn, for Della to raise. No one knew where she'd gone or if she were alive or dead, and Della didn't seem to care. Paula worried that Della's constant berating would kill her granddaughter's love for learning just as she'd tried to do with Paula.

"I'm looking forward to seeing her again." The seventeen-year-old was quiet and withdrawn but smart as the proverbial whip. Paula wished there was a way to help her but trusted God to make a way out of Blackbird for her just as a way had been made for Paula.

"Just stay away from her. The last thing she needs is you filling her head with more of your college nonsense." On Paula's visit last winter she'd offered to help Robyn pay for college if she chose to attend. Della had been furious but Paula planned to keep the promise no matter what because the girl deserved to have as bright a future as possible.

"Let me know when the arrangements are set."

When no response followed, Paula waited. A glance at the phone's face showed: **Call Ended.** Della had hung up. Tight-lipped, Paula tossed the phone aside and wiped at the hot tears in her eyes. Her aunt was going to make her lose her religion but she was determined to stay forthright.

Gen had a literacy session that same morning with a student in Franklin. Usually Nathan chauffeured her there and back, but with him gone the driver would be TC. Lily's assessment of Henry Adams's newest resident played back in Gen's mind. *For a man of a certain age, Gary's uncle is kind of hot.* Gen agreed. Granted, she knew nothing about him, which meant he could be a serial player like Mal before Bernadine entered his life, or have some other major fault, but he hadn't given off that vibe. In fact, he'd been nothing but polite and respectful on the ride from the airport. They even shared a similar taste in music, not to mention the man watched C-SPAN, of all things. That alone was enough to add the words *and intriguing* to the end of Lily's description. If he panned out, TC Barbour might be quite the catch for a woman of a certain age, even though that woman wouldn't be her.

As the time to leave approached, Gen went to the closet for her blue leather jacket and the tote holding her books and supplies. Nathan was sometimes late picking her up. What with a wife needing to be dropped off at her job and a baby to drive to day care it was a wonder he showed up at all some mornings, but a glance out of the curtained windows showed TC right on time. Seeing the black town car made the gloomy April day seem brighter somehow. Marie was still upstairs doing whatever behind her bedroom's closed door, so Gen called out a goodbye and left.

He was standing beside the opened car door when she stepped out onto the porch. "Good morning, Ms. Glbbs," he said as she approached.

"Good morning, Mr. Barbour. How are you?"

"Doing well." As she walked by him and took her seat she caught the faint scent of his nice-smelling cologne.

After closing her in, he took his seat up front. He swiveled around to face her. "You'll have to direct me, if you don't mind. Couldn't get the GPS to wake up and do its job. Ms. Brown said you're headed to Franklin?"

"Yes, it's the next town over. Go out to the road and turn left. Franklin's not that far."

"Okay." He followed her instructions and soon they were underway.

"Do you want some music?" he asked.

"I do. Thanks."

Soft jazz played lightly against the quiet interior.

After a few moments, he asked, "Is the weather ever going to get warmer? As in really warm? I'm not liking these forties one day, sixties the next."

That amused her. "It'll settle down soon. Where are you from?"

"Oakland."

"Ah. California weather."

"Yes. It can get cold there too, but it doesn't hang around like this. Are you from here?"

"Yes. Lived here all my life."

"Then you must like small towns."

"I didn't when I was younger, but now, I'm content. Finally realized there's a lot to love."

"Such as?"

"Lifelong friendships. Goodhearted people. No crime."

"Gotcha. Enjoyed the town meeting. Never been to anything like that before."

"Not many communities gather the way we do. We get together on Friday nights too, to watch movies at the recreation center."

"Really?"

"Yes. We show an early one for the kids and a late one for the adults—usually classics. *Carmen Jones. Casablanca.* I think we're showing *Pinocchio* and *Dream Girls* this Friday."

"And everybody turns out?"

"Yes. Kids, babies, teenagers, grown folks."

"That sounds really cool."

"It is. I missed them when I was married. My ex-husband didn't really care to go, but I'm there most Fridays now."

"How long were you married?"

Gen sighed. "Truthfully, forty years too long. It took me a while to admit that he loved his hog more than me, but once I did, I left."

He caught her eye in the mirror. "He loved a hog."

"Yes. One of the downsides of being in a small town is that there are no secrets, so you may as well hear the story straight from the horse's mouth."

And when she was done with the telling, he asked, amazed, "The hog killed a man?"

"Sat on him until he went splat. And when the authorities carted the hog off, my idiot of an ex-husband broke the animal out of the county pen and the two went on the lam, like maybe they were the Dillinger Gang. It was unbelievable."

"I'm sorry but this is funny."

"It's okay. In some ways it was, but it was also off the wall, stupid, and when the health department bulldozed my home, infuriating." Just thinking about it made her temper spike so she calmed herself.

"Does your ex and his hog still live here?"

"No. Riley took him to Hollywood last year to make him a star."

"What!"

"Truly crazy, right?"

"Yes. You've been through a lot."

"I have, but I'm still standing and that's what counts."

"Amen."

His approving tone made her add one more star to his name. "So what about you. Married? Divorced?"

"Widower. Lost my wife Carla to lupus almost thirty years ago now."

"Oh, I'm so sorry."

"Thanks. Loved her madly."

Gen wondered what it felt like to be loved so deeply. "Children?"

"Three. Two boys and a baby girl. All grown now of course. How about you? Any kids?"

"No."

She saw him watching her from the mirror and she gave him a tiny shrug in response as if the gesture summed it up. She never knew whether she was the one with the fertility issue or Riley. Her doctor said she was fine. Riley never went.

They were now driving down Franklin's main street. She directed him where to turn and to the address. He stopped the car out front. "Do you have my number so you can call when it's time for me to take you back?" he asked.

She didn't. After adding him to her contacts, she placed her phone back in her purse. "I'll call you in about an hour."

He came around to open the door for her. She wanted to tell him it was unnecessary but she knew it was his job so she kept it to herself and got out. "Thank you."

"You're welcome. See you in an hour."

She nodded her agreement and climbed the steps to the porch. When Mrs. Rivard opened the door and ushered Gen inside, the black car eased away.

TC didn't think it made much sense to drive back to Henry Adams and then immediately turn around and come back. He decided to check out Franklin instead. He had a good eye for landmarks so he was sure he wouldn't have a problem finding his way back to the house to pick up Ms. Gibbs. Franklin was larger than Henry Adams. He passed a couple of national chain hotels and the many businesses lining the main street. Some had plywood over the windows though, as if they were closed, and houses in the neighborhoods sported plywood as well. He wondered what the story was on that. He made a point to ask Ms. Gibbs. Thinking of her made him replay the conversation they'd had on the drive. Her ex-husband sounded like an idiot. What kind of a man chose the company of a hog over a woman, especially one so fine? When she first came out of the house dressed in her blue leather jacket, black jeans, and flat black suede boots, she looked pretty fly. Were he in the market for a lady friend it would be someone like her. She was witty, had a sense of humor, but as he'd noted, had been through a lot. It took a strong woman to walk away from a marriage of over forty years and strike out on her own. Knowing what he did of Henry Adams though, he was sure she'd received plenty of support because it impressed him as the kind of place that looked after its own. She said she'd been in the area her entire life. He'd bet she'd been a showstopper when she was young. Even now she was a stunner.

He glanced up at the mirror and froze seeing a cop car behind him with its overhead light flashing. Sighing, he pulled over, rolled down the window, and assumed the position—hands on the steering wheel so they'd be in plain sight.

A big burly White cop in a brown uniform came to the window. "Morning, Mr. Barbour. I'm Will Dalton. County sheriff."

TC's voice mirrored his astonishment. "How do you know who I am?"

"You're driving Ms. Brown's town car and since you don't look anything like Nathan, I called her."

Amazed by that, TC shook his head with amusement.

"Small town," the sheriff offered by way of explanation. "Welcome to Graham County."

"Thanks."

"Just wanted to introduce myself and let you know you have a taillight out. Have Trent get you a new one when you get back. You waiting on Ms. Gen?"

TC was further surprised. "Yes."

"She's doing a good thing helping folks out with her literacy teaching." He handed TC a card. "My card. I'll let my people know you're Ms. Brown's new driver. Got a few knuckleheads who think hassling new people is part of the job. It isn't. If you have any trouble, show them that and have them call me. They'll back down pretty quick."

TC wondered if there was another word for amazement. "Thanks, Sheriff."

"No problem. Have a nice day. Tell Ms. Gen I said hello, and don't forget that taillight."

"I won't."

When Dalton drove away, TC fell back against the black leather seat. "Wow." In all his years he'd never had an encounter with law enforcement that even came close to this one. "Definitely not in Oakland anymore, Toto."

TC was waiting outside the residence when Ms. Gibbs appeared in the doorway. He watched her give a parting hug to the elderly woman and as she waved goodbye TC got out and opened the door.

She approached him with a cheery "Hello there, Mr. Barbour."

"Hey there. Ready?"

"I am." Getting in, she offered the same soft-spoken thanks he'd grown accustomed to hearing. After closing the door, he took his seat and they headed back to Henry Adams. "Sheriff Dalton says hello. Stopped me to introduce himself and to let me know my taillight is out. Gave me his card."

"Will's a good guy. He was in our town talent contest last summer. Plays a mean lead guitar."

"Really?"

"Brought the house down. Plays with a group called Five-Oh. They almost won."

He would have loved to have seen that. "Sounds like you small-town folks have a good time."

"We do. Hopefully you'll stick around long enough to see some of it."

"I hope so, too." And he meant it. "Do you want to be dropped off at your house?"

"No. I think I'll stop at the Dog and get some lunch."

"Okay."

"Do you have another run today?" she asked

"No. You're it."

"If you don't have plans for lunch would you like to share a table?"

He paused and looked at her in the mirror. "That would be nice."

"Then let's go eat."

As they entered the Dog it was the beginning of the lunch hour and the place wasn't as crowded as it would be in the next hour or so. Bobby Womack's cover of "California Dreamin'" was on the box. Gen didn't know what possessed her to propose they have lunch, and she hoped he didn't think she was trying to hit on him, but she enjoyed his company.

Mal came over and, seeing them standing side by side, paused a moment. "You two together?"

"Yes, Mal. I'm treating him to lunch for being such an excellent driver." She didn't care for the way Mal was eyeing him. "But it's not a date so please don't trip, okay?" Beside her TC chuckled softly, at what she didn't know.

Apparently reassured, Mal stuck out his hand. "We haven't been formally introduced, but I'm Malachi July."

"TC Barbour."

"Nice meeting you."

"Same here."

"Let me get you a table."

"Booth, Mal, please," she said.

"Okay."

A few seconds later they were seated in a booth along the wall of windows that looked out onto Main Street.

"How long have you known July?" he asked her.

"Since fourth grade."

"One of those lifelong friendships you mentioned earlier."

"Yes. He can be a bit mother hen-ish sometimes but his heart's in the right place. And I'm going to apologize in advance. This is a small town and being in other folks' business is in the water, so please excuse the looks you'll probably get because we're together."

"I think I can handle it. It's just lunch, right?"

The way he said it made her eye him for a moment. "Right." He gave her the impression that he knew something she didn't and was amused by it.

But before she could muse further, Rocky walked up with glasses of water and menus. "Hey, you two."

Gen said, "Hey, Rock."

"Hi, Ms. Rocky."

"Hey, TC. Do you know what you want or do you need a minute?"

They viewed the menus. TC pointed to the color picture of the burger and fries.

Gen opted for the salmon salad.

"Gotcha. They'll be right out. Oh, and you two look real good together."

Gen's jaw dropped.

TC burst out laughing.

"I'm just saying," Rocky said in parting.

When they were alone again the horrified Gen said, "See why I apologized in advance?"

"No problem. Who knows, maybe next time we'll make it a real date and really give them something to talk about."

She stared.

"I'm kidding. I know you have a guy."

"I did, but not anymore," Gen admitted.

"No?"

"Irreconcilable differences."

"Ah, I see. I'm sorry."

"I am, too. But life moves on."

When their food came, Rocky had nothing else to say about them as a couple but she did give Gen a wink. Gen knew by dinnertime everybody in town would know she and TC had had lunch together. Clay too probably, and speculation would spread like wildfire. As it stood they were already the center of attention in the increasingly crowded diner if all the curious eyes turned their way was any indication. *This was so not a good idea.*

But over the course of the meal, they had a good time. He told her about growing up in Oakland and all the jobs he'd had. She told him about growing up as the pampered ladylike daughter of an undertaker and that she still wore gloves to church. They talked about their favorite music groups of the '60s and '70s and Gen revealed that she'd never been to a live concert.

He stopped. "Never?"

"Ever. Why in the world would Earth Wind and Fire or anybody else play Henry Adams?"

"So you never got to hear Phil Bailey in his prime sing 'Reasons'?"

She shook her head sadly.

"Well, the next time anyone of note comes within a hundred miles. Me. You. Going. Okay?"

She smiled. She knew he didn't mean that but it was the thought that counted. "Okay."

"And I'm not joking."

His firm tone made her pause, study him, and ask, "Really?"

"We're the first generation with its own sound track. Every baby boomer has to attend at least one concert before they die. That's the law, you know."

Gen was enjoying him so much. "Okay, Mr. That's the Law. I'll keep an eye on the newspapers."

"Good."

To their utter surprise "Reasons" sung by the aforementioned Philip Bailey filled the air and TC pointed a fry at her. "See, even the universe agrees."

Enjoying the song, Gen had to admit he was right.

When lunch was over, they went to the desk to take care of the bill.

"How was everything, TC?" Mal asked, running Gen's debit card.

"Best burger I've had in a while. I'll be back."

"Good." He handed Gen her card and receipt.

Outside, TC said, "Thanks for lunch. Next time it's on me."

"Sounds good." She put another star next to his name. Clay would never let her pay for their meals together. Ever. He took it as an affront to his male pride. TC, on the other hand, hadn't balked. She liked that.

When they reached the car, he opened the back door and she said, "You know, after having lunch together it feels kind of silly for me to be riding in the back. Is it okay if I sit up front?"

"Whatever the lady wants."

So she sat next to him and told herself she wasn't nervous. But it was a lie. She felt like a teenager on a first date.

He put the key in the ignition and looked over at her. "I had a good time."

"I did as well."

Silence filled the car for a long few seconds and as it lengthened her heart started doing that crazy dance thing again. He finally turned the key and drove her home.

As she was getting out, she glanced up at the house and saw the windows on the curtains move. Marie was spying but Gen gave it little thought. "Thanks again for the ride to Franklin and for the good time at lunch."

"You're welcome. I'm holding you to the concert."

"I will keep an eye out. I promise."

"Good. Enjoy the rest of your day."

"You, too."

Gen went inside and before she could close the door behind her, Marie, now seated on the couch, asked coolly, "Who was that?"

Gen didn't like her tone. "TC Barbour. Bernadine's new driver."

"Since when?"

"Since Nathan and Lou and the baby moved to Lawrence."

"If he's a driver, what were you doing riding in the front seat?"

Gen took off her coat and hung it in the closet. "Because we had lunch. And he's a nice guy."

"What's Clay going to say about you riding around with Mr. Nice Guy?"

Gen held onto her temper. "If you would leave the house or talk to me occasionally you'd know that Clay and I are done."

"Why?"

"Because he's Clay."

"So you're throwing yourself at this new guy? You don't know anything about men."

"And you do?"

Marie's lips tightened.

Gen didn't want to throw Marie's past relationships in her face but she wasn't putting up with this third degree any longer. She'd been putting off telling Marie she was moving out because of the uncertainty of how she'd react, but at this point, Gen was too upset to care. "So you'll know, I'm moving out."

"When?"

"Probably by the middle of next week. I'm leasing a double-wide and putting it where my house used to be."

Gen thought she saw pain cross Marie's face before it was immediately replaced by the familiar mask of disinterest.

Marie shrugged. "Fine with me."

Gen waited to see if she'd say anything more but when she didn't, Gen walked by her and climbed the stairs to go to her room.

Alone, Marie closed her eyes against the painful emotions and told herself it didn't matter. She was lying, of course, but it was easier to look upon Gen's plans to move as yet another low blow to her life rather than deal with reality. She was terrified of growing old and being alone and she resented Gen's newly found strength and independence. *How dare you do this to me!* she wanted to scream up the stairs. *How dare you!* Not that she'd given her old friend much choice. Having been distant and uncommunicative probably killed their friendship, but weren't friends supposed to stick together through thick and thin, no matter what? When Gen finally saw the light and walked out on Riley who'd taken her in? Who'd taken her to Las Vegas for the first time? Who'd stood by her when her home was razed, and had her back when Riley's embezzling came to light? She'd supported Genevieve when nobody else had and this is how Gen repaid her. *I'm moving out.* Marie knew laying all this at Gen's door wasn't right, nor was any of it her fault, but it was easier than looking in the mirror and facing the truth that this was the bed she'd made.

CHAPTER
6

As Eli drove home with Crystal riding shotgun, he asked her, "Do you think we're ever going to hear back about the art contest?"

She shrugged. "Wish they'd hurry up, though. This waiting is about to kill me."

"Tell me about it. I wonder how many entries they got total."

"Couple of hundred probably, but who knows."

"You going to this pizza party Leah's uncle is giving?"

"Yeah. She said he's going to show us how to make pizza from scratch so since I'm into the cooking shows, I'm interested. You coming?"

"I don't know. Sounds kind of lame."

She rolled her eyes. "Everything is lame to you."

"No, it's not."

"Yeah, it is. You had the easy life growing up—two parents, nice house, too, I'll bet. Grandparents. The whole American dream thing."

"So I'm supposed to deny that?"

"Nope, but you're content to not put too much effort into things because you've always had them—like delivered pizza. You're happy just opening a delivery box and not wondering how that pizza got made."

"You're not making sense. You know that, right?"

"I am making sense. It's just easier for you to say I'm not so you don't have to dig beneath that comfort zone of yours."

"No comfort in losing my mom."

"True, but kids like Amari, Preston, and myself had to deal with the loss of ours from day one. You don't know how blessed you are, dude."

"I do."

She didn't look convinced.

"Changing the subject. I went over to check on Wyatt the day he walked away from the table and he closed the door in my face."

"Really?"

"Yeah. I think there's a lot more going on with him than he's letting us see."

"Probably. Lost his mom. Grew up on the South Side. Probably one of the few White kids. I'd have a lot going on underneath, too. You going to try and be big brother?"

Eli hadn't given that any thought. It sounded like a good idea though, and would probably win him points with her. "Yeah. If he'll let me."

They were now in front of her house. She gathered her stuff from the floor of the car. "Sounds good. Let the rest of us know if we can help, and if you learn anything new about him we might need to know."

"I will."

"God, I hope the letter from the contest is in the mailbox," she said, looking at her house.

"Me, too."

"Now, remember you're supposed to be happy for me when I win."

He laughed. "Get out of my car, girl. I'll text you later."

Giving him a smile, she did just that.

Backing out of her driveway, he drove across the street to his own house.

Once inside, Eli made himself a sandwich. His dad wouldn't be home for at least another hour, so he needed something to tide him over until dinner. If he knew how to cook he could get their meal started but his dad had always done the cooking and he'd done the eating, so he didn't know how. He thought back on the conversation he'd had with Crystal in the car. Was this what she'd meant about him not looking past his comfort zone? Eli didn't expect to have the world handed to him, or did he? He certainly expected his dad to cook dinner, but he helped out, too. He cleaned his own bathroom, did his own laundry—well, sometimes. He also put the dishes in the dishwasher after dinner. Since his mom's death his dad had taken over the chores she used to handle and Eli never really thought about how his dad felt about carrying the load. He just expected his dad to do it. It never occurred to him until that moment that maybe his dad would like to come in after school and chill sometimes instead of heading straight to the kitchen to cook for his almost nineteen-year-old son every day. He winced at that truth. He supposed he was being selfish. *Damn you, Crystal.* Now he was going to have to learn to cook.

After school, TC and his nieces piled into his truck and drove the short distance to the grocery store. Once there, Tiffany grabbed a cart.

"You have our list, Leah?" he asked.

"Yes, sir."

"Okay. What's first?"

She looked at her phone. "Tomato paste."

When they reached the right aisle he stood back and watched Leah pick up a can, before asking her, "Is that paste or sauce?"

She read the label. "Oh, this is sauce." She put it back, studied the other red-labeled products nearby and grabbed another can. "This is paste."

Tiff asked, "What's the difference?"

"Paste is thick. Sauce is loose, almost like juice," he explained while Leah put a number of the correct cans into the cart.

"Never knew there was a difference," Leah admitted.

"That's why we're doing this," he said with a smile. "What's next?"

She consulted the list on her phone again. "Yeast."

In the baking aisle Tiff stopped the cart at the yeast.

TC said, "We need rapid-rise."

Both girls studied the offerings. Tiff found it first.

"You sure it's rapid-rise?" he asked her.

"Yep. Says so right here," and she pointed at the wording before tossing the packets into the cart.

"Cheese next," Leah told them. "Parmesan and mozzarella."

When they reached the dairy aisle he once again made the girls double-check the package labeling to ensure they'd picked up the correct product. They then moved on to the meat. After adding ham and pepperoni, sliced turkey, bacon, and a few other choices to their cart, Leah said they needed dried oregano, so they grabbed a bottle and because TC liked mushrooms on his pizza, a small package was added to the cart as well.

"Is that everything, Leah?" Tiff asked.

"I think so."

They were on their way to the checkout when Gary walked up.

"Hey, Daddy," Tiff said.

"Hey there. You guys find everything you needed for your pizza party?"

Leah nodded. "We did. This was fun."

That was music to TC's ears.

"Good. Just checking. I'll see you at the house. Thanks, TC."

"No problem. Like Leah said, we had fun."

Gary left them to go back to his duties. Their cashier was Wyatt's grandmother, Gemma, and after she checked them out, groceries were put in the truck and the happy trio drove home.

They were putting everything away when TC's phone sounded. Seeing his daughter Bethany's profile picture put a smile on his face. "Hey, baby girl."

"Hey, Daddy. How are you?"

Excusing himself from Tiffany and Leah, he walked into the living room and took a seat on the couch. "I'm doing good."

"How's Mayberry?"

That made him smile. "Stop hating on your cousin's town. It's a nice place. Slow but nice."

"Everywhere's slow compared to Oakland. So, are you still coming to see me this summer?"

Bethany managed a large resort on the Hawaiian island of Kauai. "That's the plan."

"Good. I may have found a class for you to take while you're here."

TC stilled.

As the silence lengthened, she asked, "Daddy? You still there?"

"I am."

"I know you don't want me up in your business—"

"You're right."

Her voice was contrite. "I'm sorry. Not trying to make you feel bad or anything but you can do this. The teacher promises it'll be a really small class, and I'll help."

"I have to go, Beth baby. I'll call you in a few days."

"Daddy—"

"Bye." Fighting off the troubling emotions triggered by the conversation, he went back into the kitchen to check on the girls.

Later that evening while alone in the spare bedroom that had been turned into his own, TC pointed the remote at the big flat screen and clicked it off. Lying there in bed, he thought back on Bethany's call. The father in him owed her an apology. She'd only been trying to help and he appreciated her concern even though it wasn't needed, or at least that's what he'd been telling himself all these years. He reached over and turned off the light. Sometimes a person could admit things in the dark that they couldn't at any other time and for him it was that he couldn't read. He was what the folks on a program he'd watched on PBS called *functionally illiterate*. He knew numbers and basic words but lacked the ability to read a book from cover to cover or pore over the sports section in a newspaper. His father, Elwood, hadn't been able to read, either. He'd grown up in Mississippi, the son of sharecroppers, and had chopped cotton instead of going to school because his help had been necessary to put food on the table. When he became a man and moved west, the dock supervisors hired him for his brawn, not his brain. He made a decent living for a man of color in the '40s so schooling hadn't been important, and with times being what they were he hadn't seen its importance for his son, either. Whether TC's mother was literate or not, TC would never know. She left him and his father when he was about six and he never saw her again. With his father working long hours and being dead on his feet when he finally did make it home, TC basically raised himself. No one cared if he went to school or not, nor was there anyone around to make sure he did his homework. When he grew old enough, he too went to work on the docks and a few years later, saw a pretty little brown beauty named Carla George at a dance one night and fell head over heels in love. He courted her for six months before admitting the truth and to his surprise she didn't walk away and eventually agreed to be his bride. Over the years, she kept his secret, covering for him when she could, but always gently encouraged him to bite the bullet and take a class. He never did and that was why he'd taken the girls to the store. He couldn't read the labels on the cans. He knew some things by sight like meat and eggs, and even though tomato paste and tomato sauce often came in different sized cans, he wasn't familiar with the brands Gary carried and he needed the girls to read the labels for him. He also needed them to get the yeast because rapid-rise was different than the regular kind. Yes, it had been a shopping exercise for them but it was also one of the tricks of the trade employed by a man with his deficiency. He thought back on Genevieve and her literacy classes. He sensed she might be the one to help him out, but like many people in his position there was an element of embarrassment and shame tied to his condition. They'd had such a nice time together at lunch. Would she think less of him if he confessed the truth and asked for her help? There was no way to know and he didn't want to mess things up with her. So he lay in the dark haunted by his future and his past. Right before Carla died he promised her that he'd learn in her memory but hadn't kept his word. "I'm so sorry, baby," he whispered. And he was.

He turned over hoping for sleep, but it was a long time coming.

Friday morning, Gen rode over to the rec with Tamar to help set up for movie night. There were hot dogs to take out of the freezer, packages of buns to count, cartons of soda syrup to mix and put into the fridge, and countless other duties that went into making the weekly gathering a success. Bobby Douglas had been tapped by Tamar to be their muscle for the morning. Under Gen's supervision he was moving the big popcorn machines into place when Clay walked in.

"Can I talk to you for a minute, Genevieve?"

Even at the age of sixty plus Clay Dobbs with his golden skin was still gorgeous as a sunrise, but when she unconsciously began to compare him to the tall dark handsome TC, she shook her thoughts back to the matter at hand. "Sure. Bobby, see what else Tamar needs help with. I'll be back in a minute."

"Let's go to the gym," Clay said.

Upon entering, she asked, "What do you want to talk to me about?"

"I hear you had lunch with Gary's uncle."

"And?"

"Are you trying to make me jealous?"

"It was lunch. It had nothing to do with you."

Obviously upset, he looked off for a moment. She hoped he didn't think he had the right to tell her what she could or couldn't do but he gave the impression that he did.

"I don't want you having lunch with him again."

"Don't be ridiculous. I'm not your child."

"Genevieve, I know we're having some issues, and you probably think—"

"Stop right there. You don't know what I'm thinking because if you did we wouldn't be having these so-called issues. You've stated your position. I stated mine. I'm not the woman you want. I can live with that."

"You're too old to be trying to turn yourself into somebody different," he gritted out.

That hurt. "Thank you, Clay. I really wanted to hear that. Excuse me, I have to get back to work." And she left so he wouldn't see her tears.

On her way down the hall, Sheila stepped out of one of the storage rooms. "Gen? Are you okay?"

"No, but I will be."

"What's wrong?"

An angry Clay passed them by without a word. As he barreled through the door leading to the parking lot, Gen said, "That's what's wrong." She told her about the hard time Clay had been giving her, and what he'd said.

Sheila shook her head disapprovingly. "You know I had the same sort of problem with Barrett."

"I do." Sheila left her husband for a brief time in response to his extramarital affair and returned revamped and stronger.

"He didn't like who I turned myself into but the more I

liked myself the more I didn't care what he thought. Stick to your guns, girl. There's nothing wrong with what you're doing. At all."

Gen wiped her eyes. It was good hearing Sheila affirm what she already knew. And she was not too old. "Thanks, Sheila."

Sheila draped an arm over her shoulders and gave her a squeeze. "Forget about Old Man Sourpuss Clay Dobbs. A man worth your heart will love who you are."

Gen raised her chin and smiled. "Thanks."

"You're welcome. Now let's get back to the kitchen before She Who Must Be Obeyed sends the bloodhounds to track us down."

Walking beside Sheila, Gen felt much better, but Clay calling her too old continued to resonate like a sore tooth for the rest of the day.

To TC, walking into the auditorium for the Friday night movies felt like walking into the town meeting or the Dog. The atmosphere screamed *community* and all the word encompassed. His plan had been to stay in Henry Adams through the summer and get back on the road before the snow fell, but the more he got to know the place and its residents the more it pulled at him to extend his stay. Granted, the slow pace was taking a bit of getting used to—after all, he was a city boy— but he was enjoying the small-town vibe.

Following his nieces and Gary down the aisle he marveled at how packed the place was and that the auditorium with its plum-colored seats and huge stage was grander than he'd imagined. To the left was the concession area with large hot-air popcorn machines, a hot dog station and others with people lined up buying nachos and ice cream. The facility would be a perfect venue for a big-time concert. Thinking about that made him discreetly scan the room for Genevieve Gibbs. She said she always attended the movies and he hadn't seen her since they'd had lunch together the other day. He spotted her serving up hot dogs. She wore a white apron over her blue sweatshirt and jeans, but even in the casual attire she looked elegant somehow.

"You ladies want food?" Gary asked his daughters.

Leah responded, "We'll get some after we get our seats."

Gary said to TC, "Which means: See you later, old guys."

Leah grinned, and she and Tiff headed for a group of young people farther down the aisle near the stage.

"Do we old guys have a designated area, too?" TC asked.

"Not really. We just can't sit with them."

TC felt eyes on his back and turned to see a light-skinned man about his age glaring his way. "Who's the guy in the red-check shirt?"

Gary turned. "Clay Dobbs. Gen's boyfriend. Like everybody else in town, he probably heard you two had lunch."

TC remembered him now from the town meeting. "She said they aren't together anymore. Irreconcilable differences was how she put it."

"Interesting," Gary said, eyeing him closely.

TC held up his hands. "I think she's fine, but I had nothing to do with whatever their issues are."

"I'm not one for spreading rumors but this is a small town and word is he's having a hard time with her new personality," Gary said.

Seeing TC's confusion, he explained. "I guess she used to be pretty timid but she isn't anymore."

TC found that surprising. She seemed so confident he couldn't imagine her timid or why her man would want her to remain that way.

They found seats and TC asked, "You think I can go over and get a hot dog without Clay shooting me in the back?"

Gary chuckled. "I guess we'll find out. I saw Reggie when we came in. I think he can handle a buckshot victim."

"He's the doctor, right?"

Gary nodded.

"Okay. You want anything?"

"Bring me a dog and a cola. I'll hold down our seats."

"Okay."

On his way to the hot dogs, Dobbs shot TC another glare. TC ignored him. He'd never been a fighting man but if push came to shove he could handle his business. He was a good four or five inches taller than Dobbs and outweighed him as well, so unless the man knew some kind of karate or had a gun, TC figured he'd come out on top. However, he also knew not to underestimate any man—especially one who thought you might be hitting on his woman.

The woman in question gave him a smile when it was his turn to order. "Hey, Mr. Barbour."

"How are you, Ms. Gibbs?"

"I'm doing good. You?"

"No complaints."

"What can I get you?"

He told her and she filled his order. After giving him his change, she handed him two cups. "The soda machine is over there to your right. Help yourself."

"Thanks." He moved aside and the next person in line took his place. Loaded down with the drinks and dogs, TC made his way back to his seat. If Dobbs was still glaring, he didn't know or care.

TC was unwrapping his hot dog when a commotion in the back of the auditorium caught everyone's attention. County Sheriff Will Dalton was there along with two uniformed officers. They were speaking with Trent July.

Gary said, "I wonder what's going on."

Next they knew Trent was being handcuffed and an angry buzz went up from the crowd who by then were on their feet. Mal ran up the aisle, along with a teen who shouted, "Oh hell, no!" Tamar and July's wife, Lily, charged to the scene as well. Gary handed TC his food. "Be right back." He hurried toward the back along with a number of other men.

TC saw Dalton talking with the Julys and the others gathered around him. At one point the sheriff held up his hands as if to say he wasn't at fault. A few seconds later, Dalton and the officers escorted the shackled Trent from the auditorium.

An angry Tamar July took to the stage. "My grandson has been arrested for stealing a car from a California dealership. Will thinks it's a case of mistaken identity and promises to get it straightened out. The family is going with them to make sure that happens so in the meantime, movie night is cancelled. Everybody go home."

CHAPTER
7

Riley, with Cletus in tow, had been driving for days and he was tired. All he wanted to do was pull over and sleep, but that was impossible. One, Cletus was already mad about having crossed the Nevada desert in the trailer and would undoubtedly pitch a fit if he was confined too much longer; and two, Riley was pretty sure the car salesman had figured out he wasn't coming back, which meant the police were probably looking for him and he didn't want to be found. Having been on the lam before when he broke Cletus out of the state's pen a few years ago, he knew to cover his tracks as best he could, so before leaving LA, he'd replaced the dealer's plate on the SUV with the one from his old truck still sitting dead behind Vera's motel. (She'd have it towed eventually but there was nothing he could do about that.) At a fast food place outside Las Vegas, he'd placed the dealer's plate along with the meal's leavings into the empty bag and stuffed it in a trash can at a rest stop along the highway. Confident law enforcement wouldn't know where he was, he'd patted himself on the back once again for his cleverness.

But cleverness didn't help him drive or offer a solution to his other problem—a place to sleep. It was getting dark, he was having trouble seeing, and he'd learned after the disaster on the first night that pulling into a motel was out. While trying to sneak Cletus into the room, he'd been busted by the desk clerk. She'd ordered Riley off the property and threatened him with the police. Cletus had balked so much about going back into the trailer, Riley had to bribe the big hog with the candy bar he'd been saving for his own treat and they'd spent the night in the parking lot of the local Wal-Mart. The next night he'd tried a highway rest stop but Cletus created such a racket screaming and throwing his immense weight against the sides of the pen wanting out, Riley was cussed at by a bunch of angry semi drivers who promised to feed Cletus to a meat grinder if he didn't shut up. Having little choice, Riley drove back to the highway. He caught a few hours of sleep after Cletus dozed off, but for all intents and purposes he'd been awake for too many days to count and now he worried he was one nod away from crashing his sweet, stolen SUV and maybe killing them both.

The exhausted Riley finally arrived in Henry Adams just as dawn broke. He still had a key to Eustacia's half-finished mansion on the edge of town and it was his plan to sleep there until he figured out his next move. He pulled up next to the house and the state of it rendered him instantly awake for a few moments. The doors were gone, replaced with large sheets of plywood, and all the once fancy windows were boarded up, too. He wondered what happened. Getting out, his tired legs had trouble supporting his weight as he swayed his way to the listing porch that was missing many of its planks. The two stately columns installed by Eustacia's builders were no longer upright but looked about to keel over at any moment. He'd expected the landscaping to be overgrown but had no explanation as to why the front yard had been dug up. There were large deep holes everywhere. Cletus was screaming to be let out of the trailer but Riley needed to sit down for a moment in order to shake off the need to sleep. He placed his head against the leaning column and next he knew he was out like a light.

When he awakened he was so groggy he thought he saw Trent July standing over him. Not sure if he was dreaming or not, he opened his mouth to say hello, only to have a fist explode in his face, and just like that he was out again.

The next time his eyes opened he had trouble seeing and his face hurt. He sensed he was in a moving vehicle. He was lying on his side and tried to struggle upright but for some reason his hands were behind his back and he couldn't bring them forward. When he saw Sheriff Will Dalton's face he froze.

"Welcome back, Curry. You're under arrest for identity theft and car theft. You have the right to remain silent . . ."

Riley fainted dead away.

Leah and Tiffany's friends began arriving at noon for the Uncle TC Pizza Party. The younger kids rode their bikes over. Crystal and Eli came in Eli's old Subaru. TC had each of them bring a pie plate to put their pizzas in. The kids put their music on the wireless speaker system and after everyone washed their hands the pie making began. Tiffany, Devon, Zoey, Wyatt and the Acosta kids, Alfonso and Maria, worked together on the sauce. Crystal helped TC roll out the dough he'd made earlier that morning. Eli, Preston, Leah, and Amari sliced up the meat. When everything was ready TC showed them the process. Sauce first, followed by mozzarella. Meat and veggies came next and grated Parmesan finished it off.

Amari spooned sauce over the bare dough. "This is fun, Mr. Barbour."

"Is it?"

"Yeah. If I knew how to make dough this could be a regular thing for me."

TC said, "I used to do this on Saturdays with my kids."

"How many kids do you have?" Devon asked as he carefully laid out slices of pepperoni on his mozzarella.

"Three."

They spent the next little while finding out about each other. He learned where they were all from originally and they quizzed him about Oakland. Because of the number of kids, the pizzas had to be cooked in shifts, but eventually all were done and they were amazed by how good they tasted.

Zoey said, "Mr. Barbour, you're going to be our official pizza maker. Nobody is going to want delivery anymore."

"Especially since they always come cold," Tiff pointed out.

Amari said, "You should open your own pizza place."

Wyatt munched on a triangle oozing with mozzarella. "That's a good idea. We'd have to have a name for it, though."

Crystal said, "Just eat, Amari. You're always trying to put somebody to work."

Ignoring her, Amari said, "Speaking of work. Eli, have you talked to Tamar about us using her property?"

He shook his head.

TC's curiosity must've shown because Devon said, "Amari, I thought you said this was supposed to be a secret?"

Amari eyed TC. "I don't think he'll snitch. Will you?"

"Depends. You planning on breaking the law?"

"Nah. Just trying to put together a Father's Day thing for our dads."

"Then I won't snitch."

Preston said, "You remind me a little of OG."

"Who's that?"

"Mr. Malachi," Wyatt said.

"Ah. I take it you guys like him?"

"A lot," Amari said.

Zoey said, "He's like our grandfather."

"He *is* my grandfather," Amari said proudly.

"Braggart," Leah said.

Amari tossed back, "Old Big Word Suzy over there."

Everyone laughed and TC noted how much they acted like siblings. "You all like each other, don't you?"

Eli said, "Sometimes, but we just put up with Amari, though."

More laughter.

TC asked, "Tell me about this secret Father's Day thing. If you want to, that is."

Every eye turned to Wyatt who said, "I'm good. No sense in me being mad because I'm the only one in town without one."

TC's heart tightened. In his view the boy didn't look good at all. His eyes were hard and his words sounded borderline sarcastic. From the way the kids reacted this discussion had come up before. He made a mental note to ask Leah about it later.

Amari said, "You're a good manager for the band, Wyatt. Do you want to be manager for this?"

"No."

Crystal said, "I don't have a dad either, Wyatt, but I'm going to help out."

"Good for you." He stood up. "Mr. Barbour, I've had a great time and thanks for the pizza lessons. I'm going home now."

A startled TC glanced at Leah, who shook her head as if to say, Don't interfere. And because he didn't know any of them well enough to intervene he followed her unspoken advice. But he did ask, "Do you want to wrap up the rest of your pizza to take home?"

"Yes, thanks."

While the other kids looked on silently, TC got some foil and wrapped up Wyatt's uneaten slices. Wyatt stuffed the pizza and pie plate into his backpack.

TC asked, "Do you want a ride home?"

He shook his head. With a wave he exited.

After his departure Zoey said, "We need to find him a daddy, y'all."

An awkward silence fell over the group. It was finally broken by Leah. "Since we're talking about dads, what's going on with yours, Amari?"

Amari's lip tightened. "Sheriff Will let him go a little bit after they took him in. The real perp was Ms. Gen's crazy ex-husband with the killer pig. He told a car dealership in California that he was my dad and then stole an SUV. They found Mr. Curry in town this morning and now he's locked up."

"Good," Leah said.

Preston said, "He's really nuts."

Amari said, "Yep. I'm glad Ms. Gen got rid of him."

Because Gary had gone in to work early, TC hadn't heard any of this until now, but he was glad she'd gotten rid of the man, too.

The kids then began to discuss the Father's Day event.

"I think we should have flags representing our families," Amari said.

Alfonso jumped in. "Yeah, like the flags for the houses in *Harry Potter*. Each flag would have something on it that shows what your family is about. Maybe the Acosta house flag would have a picture of Mexico and a fire engine or something."

All the kids stared.

Amari asked, "Who are you and what did you do with the Alfonso who never talks?"

He dropped his eyes shyly before unleashing a high-voltage grin. "I just think the flags are a great idea."

The rest of the kids apparently agreed and for the next few minutes brainstormed about the flags and what might go on them. In the middle of the conversation Leah asked, "What are the flags going to be made of?"

Crystal said, "Maybe we can silkscreen them like the ones I did for the August First Parade."

"And we pay for them how?" Preston asked.

Zoey said, "Everybody should have some gold coin money left, right?"

Once again, TC was in the dark.

"But Alfonso and Maria weren't living here when you gave out the gold," Tiff reminded her. Eli then took a moment to tell the Acostas and TC about the coins Zoey inherited last fall after the death of the town's hermit, Cephas Patterson. "She gave one to everybody in town."

TC was impressed. "That's pretty fabulous, Zoey."

"Thank you."

TC said, "If you all can come up with a way to get the flags made, I'll pay for Alfonso and Maria's. Is that okay with you two?"

The siblings spent a few seconds whispering to each other and finally Maria said, "Our dad and *abuela* would tell us to say no, but I think we want to say yes. Right, Alfie?"

He nodded. "Thank you, Mr. TC."

"No problem. Wanting to give your dads a special day is cool. I'll help if you need me to."

So TC was allowed to be in on their secret plan and he felt very special indeed.

Riding home after the pizza party, Eli said to Crystal, "I like their uncle."

"Yeah. He was nice. Felt bad about Wyatt, though."

"I know. I'm going to go by his house after I drop you off and see if I can't convince him to come hang out with me. If you think about it he's like the lone wolf. Devon has Amari and Zoey. Leah has Preston and her sister. Zoey has you."

"And you and I are pretty tight and you have Samantha."

"Yeah." Guilt rose in response to Sam's name but he squelched it. So far he hadn't said anything to Crystal about the breakup. "Maybe I can take him to the skate park in Franklin. I haven't been on my board in a while. One of the other not-so-hot things about Kansas—you can only board when it's warm."

His phone sounded. Keeping one eye on the road, he peered at his phone. It was his friend Geoff in LA. He was so anxious to talk to him, he didn't care if Crystal overheard them. He put him on speaker. "Hey, Geoff. What's up?"

"Nothing, man. My mom said no."

"Aw hell. Really? Damn."

"I know. She said you were a bad influence."

He sighed. "Okay, man. I'm in the car. I'll call you back later."

"Okay. Sorry."

"No problem."

And because Crystal was Crystal she asked without shame, "What was that about?"

He glanced over. "I want to move back to California. I was hoping Geoff's mom would let me live with them while I went to community college, and once I finished I could find a place of my own."

"What's your dad saying?"

"Haven't brought it up because I know he'll tell me no, but if Geoff's mom had said yes, he might've said yes, too. Tired of small-town living."

"I understand."

"You're not going to call me stupid for wanting out?"

"No. I get it. So what's Plan B?"

"I don't know."

"Your dad's pretty cool outside of the classroom. Maybe he'll surprise you if you talk to him."

"I doubt it."

"You won't know until you do. Why do you think he'll say no?"

"Because I don't know anything about living on my own. Sort of the same thing you and I talked about the other day. That comfort zone thing? And you're right. I thought about him having to come home every day and cook for me."

"You can't cook for yourself?"

"Never had to or thought about it."

"You are truly pitiful. I cook for my mom at least three nights a week."

"Yeah, give you the Awesome Crystal Award."

"Better than the Eli Booby Prize."

"Shut it," he said, chuckling. "I'm going to see if Siz will teach me to cook."

"Good choice. Rocky and OG can hit up their insurance company if you burn the place to the ground."

"Hater."

"Truthfully though, you wanting to help out your dad is a good thing. I'm proud of you, Eli."

His heart sang. "Thanks. Now if I can just figure out how to help Wyatt."

"It'll come."

He hoped so. He was glad Crys hadn't asked him about his being a bad influence. Geoff's mom was right. He'd lost his mind after his mom died and acted out in ways that made him view that version of himself with shame. Shoplifting, stealing cars, one of which had been hers. Drinking. All the dumb stupid stuff a suburban kid could do, he did. His dad had been furious, especially the night he'd had to get out of bed to come bail Eli out of jail. To be truthful were he his dad, after all the drama he caused back then he wouldn't let him live on his own, either.

He dropped Crystal off and after parking the Subaru walked over to Wyatt's. But Wyatt didn't want to go skateboarding. "I don't have a skateboard," he explained, talking to Eli through the screen door.

"Why not?" At Wyatt's age everyone Eli knew had one.

"I grew up on the South Side. Think about it, Eli."

And once he did, he understood and felt incredibly stupid. "Sorry. Look, I'm just trying to be a friend if you let me."

"Why, because I don't have a dad, or because I'm a White kid like you, or both?"

Eli stared. "What!"

"Did you hit up Amari or Preston when they moved here?"

"No, you little jerk. They were already here when my dad and I got here and they hit me up. It didn't have anything to do with race. You need to talk to Rev. Paula about whatever you're going through because I'm officially done." And he stepped off the porch. Behind him the door slammed. He didn't care. *Little dumb ass!*

Wyatt's grandmother pulled into the driveway. He waited for her to stop so he could cross it and go home. She waved. He grudgingly waved back.

When she got out of the car, she said, "What's wrong? You look ready to punch somebody."

"Your grandson is an idiot."

She paused. "And you say that because . . . ?"

Eli debated telling her but went ahead. "We were talking about our dads at lunch the other day, and Wyatt got up and left. We thought since he's never known his dad we may have hurt his feelings. Same thing happened today at the pizza party with Leah's uncle. I stopped by to see if maybe he wanted to go skateboarding or something but he blew me off, just like he did the other day."

"I'm sorry, and thanks for telling me about what happened at lunch. Last few days he's been more withdrawn than usual and I didn't know why. He's never mentioned his dad because he's never met him. Neither have I for that matter."

Eli's anger dissolved and he went back to feeling sorry for the boy again. "I know he's got Zoey and Devon for friends, but I thought maybe I could be a friend to him, too. We both lost our moms."

"You're a good kid, Eli. When we lived in Chicago I didn't allow him outside a lot because of all the shootings and violence, so he's more into his maps and books. Now that we're here, I'd like for him to play outside."

"Is it okay if I get him a skateboard and a helmet and stuff?"

The offer put tears in her eyes. "That's so sweet. Yes, you may. I've signed him up for the Big Brother program but so far he hasn't been matched with anyone. He needs a guy in his life, especially now that he's getting older so, thank you, Eli."

"You're welcome. I'll bring the board by when I get it."

"Okay." She smiled at him and went into the house.

Feeling pretty good about himself, Eli walked the short distance home.

Back at the Clark house, the girls were helping TC clean up, but when Tiff began to load the dishwasher, he said, "Hold up, Tiff. Dishwasher isn't working."

"Since when?" Leah asked, walking over to it and opening the door.

"Since now. Good time to learn how to do dishes by hand."

Both girls stared.

"But that's why we have a dishwasher," Tiff pointed out.

TC smiled. "And when you go to college and live in a cheap apartment that doesn't have one, what're you going to do?"

"Use paper," Leah tossed back as if it was the dumbest question she'd ever heard.

"Wrong."

She whined, "Aw, come on, Uncle TC. This is the twenty-first century. Nobody washes dishes by hand."

"How about girls in Afghanistan?"

She blew out a breath. "Way to bring the guilt, Unc."

"Thank you. Now, go grab your music and let's get started."

Tiff looked confused. "Music?"

"Yes. Washing dishes and music go together."

Looking doubtful they trudged off to grab their phones and Bluetooth speakers and when they returned, he motioned them to the sink. "Leah, since you're the oldest, you get to wash."

"Thanks," she said, rolling her eyes.

"Watch the sarcasm," he warned.

Instantly contrite, she whispered, "Sorry."

"Lil Bit, you dry."

She nodded enthusiastically.

So for the next hour, while Rihanna, Taylor Swift, and a bunch of other singers TC didn't recognize filled the kitchen, the Clark girls learned to wash dishes the old-school way. He showed them how much water to put in the sink and how much detergent to add. When it came time to start, he told Leah to put the silverware in the soapy water first.

"Why first?"

"Because silverware goes in your mouth and you want the water to be clean. Some folks wash the glasses first or the plates but I raised my kids to wash the forks and spoons first."

"I guess that makes sense. I learned something today."

"Is that a good thing?"

She nodded and smiled. "Yes."

So the silverware was washed first. As Tiff dried the forks and spoons and placed them back in the drawers, Leah asked, "Do I make fresh water now?"

"No. Glasses and plates next. You can put them in separately or in together. Just be careful. You don't want a glass to break and cut your hands in the water."

Her eyes widened.

TC smiled. "There's a lot more to this than you thought, huh?"

"Yes."

He watched her wash the outside of the first glass and when she paused and stared at it as if puzzled by something, he asked, "Problem?"

"Yes. How do I wash the inside?"

He showed her and she said, "Duh, Leah. Simple."

"Not if you've never done it before."

Their dad appeared in the kitchen. "Whoa! You ladies are washing dishes? Is the dishwasher on the fritz?"

Tiff shook her head as she dried a glass. "Uncle TC said we needed to learn because when we go to college we may live in a cheap place that doesn't have one."

An impressed-looking Gary met TC's smile. "Way to go, Uncle Bub. Any of the pizza left?"

TC said, "Saved you some dough and the sauce is still on the stove. Cheese and meat in the fridge. You ladies think you can handle the rest of the dishes and show your dad how to make his pizza?"

They nodded.

"Then my work here is done. Going up to my room to watch my Oakland As play some baseball."

"Bye, Unc," both girls called.

He climbed the stairs to the laughter and voices of Gary and his daughters having a good time and said quietly, "Way to go, Uncle Bub."

Later that evening, Genevieve decided only an idiot like Riley would think impersonating Trent and then stealing a car was a good idea. She hoped the authorities would keep him locked up and throw away the key. According to the

text she'd received earlier from Lily, Riley was being represented by one of Eustacia's lawyers and they were scouring
Europe trying to find her so she could post Riley's bail. Why
the woman continued to take Riley's calls was something
Gen didn't understand because if he called her, even if he
claimed to be on fire, she'd still hang up on him. Putting her
silly ex-husband out of her mind, she took her jacket out of
the downstairs closet to wait for Tamar to pick her up for
the Ladies Auxiliary meeting. They usually didn't meet on
Saturdays but something must be going on for Sheila to call
them together by text on such short notice. Marie was still
in her room, so Gen assumed she wasn't going. After Gen's
announcement that she was moving, Marie had even less
to say, so Gen had all but given up on trying to save their
friendship.

When she and Tamar got to Lily's house all the women in
town were there. From Rocky to Gemma Dahl to Anna Ruiz
to Bernadine and Kelly Douglas. Everyone except Marie.

Tamar said, "Genevieve, please take that seat over there,"
and she gestured to the beautiful purple rocker Trent purchased especially for Lily when he built the room for her.

By the smiles on all their faces, Gen sensed this was not
going to be a regular meeting. "What are you all up to?"

Lily said, "Just sit. You'll find out soon enough."

As she sat, Bernadine stood. "Genevieve Gibbs, you've impressed us all with your quest to remake yourself. You've been
focused, strong and determined. You even have a new home
on the way, so, to show how much we support and love you,
we have decided to give you a house-warming party."

An amazed Genevieve watched as the women brought in

gift after gift after gift and laid them at her feet. She started to cry.

Sheila said, "Anything you don't like you can exchange, so not to worry. Okay?"

Hands trembling with emotion, Gen began opening her presents. There were towels and sheets, pillowcases and candles. Two sets of china. Cookware, bakeware, silverware. One box held a dozen crystal champagne flutes, another a gorgeous bathrobe in her favorite shade of gold. For the next ten minutes she opened the mountain of boxes and gift bags. Anything and everything she might have purchased for her new home, her friends supplied, and when she was done, she was a hot crying mess. Tissue in hand, she looked around at the women she loved most of all, and a part of her wished Marie had been there, too. The always intuitive Tamar said, "Don't worry about Marie. She'll be back with us soon."

Gen dearly hoped so.

Lily said, "In the meantime, champagne from the Boss Lady's collection."

"Let's use my flutes."

So the flutes were washed and once they were all filled, everyone raised theirs and Bernadine declared, "To sassy women everywhere. Long may we reign!"

"Hear! Hear!"

The women spent the next hour mingling and talking to Gen about her new place. She looked at her bounty and asked, "Where in the world am I going to store this until the trailer arrives?"

Lily said, "You can leave it here. We'll bring everything to your place when you move in."

Gen liked the simple solution. Three years ago, she had been standing on her front porch nursing her latest bite from Riley's hog and wondering what she was going to do with her life. Now, she was stronger, better, and feeling brand-new. She'd come a long way and just as she had the day she left Riley, she had no intentions of looking back.

Although Sunday brought a cold, bone-chilling rain to Henry Adams, Reverend Paula was pleased with the turnout at church and the positive responses she'd received on her sermon. She'd stayed after the service to meet with the parents of the teens going on the mission trip to Jamaica and now, she was home. She still hadn't heard anything about her grandfather's funeral, so she sent a text to her uncle Calvin. His immediate reply: *Funeral on Saturday. Della said she told you.* Paula sighed. Della hadn't told her a thing. Rather than expose her aunt's lie, Paula typed back, *Be there Wed. Thx!*

Putting the phone down, she walked over to the windows and looked out at the gray day. Obviously Della didn't want her at the funeral. She'd hated Paula from the day they met and Paula still didn't understand why. Her grandfather certainly hadn't favored her over her aunt. In fact, he had no problem telling Paula to her face how much of a burden she was and how much he resented her presence in his life and home.

Leaving the window, she entered her bedroom and sat down at her small desk to boot up her laptop. She needed to determine how much of her bank account the airlines would demand for a round-trip ticket on such short notice. The fare was only slightly staggering, but the idea of having to return to Blackbird continued to haunt her, so after securing her ticket, she turned on the TV, hoping the baseball game might distract her enough to keep the demons at bay. When that failed, she took down a book she'd been anxious to dive into but the memories of growing up kept playing in her head so she closed it and looked at the clock. It was half past four. She didn't really want to cook dinner but knew she had to eat something, so she decided to brave the day's still ugly weather and seek the balm and good food found at the Dog and Cow.

When she entered, the after-church rush was over so it wasn't as crowded as it probably had been an hour ago. Mal walked up. "Nice sermon this morning, Reverend. Table or booth?"

"Whatever you have is fine."

He scanned the interior for an open spot. "Okay, this way," and led her to one of the tables.

"Thanks, Mal."

"No problem. Eli will be with you in a sec."

Paula used the time alone to applaud herself for having left her trailer and to look around to see who else was there. She spotted town construction boss Warren Kelly and his auburn-haired wife, Jayne. Behind them Gemma Dahl and her grandson Wyatt shared a table with Zoey and her parents, Reg and Roni. When they waved Paula's way, she waved back. In one of the booths by the windows Sheriff Will Dalton sat eating with his wife, Vicky, who'd been diagnosed with ovarian cancer back in January and was undergoing chemo.

She looked frail as a baby bird and the treatments had taken her hair but she was laughing at something her husband was saying and that made Paula smile. Behind the Daltons sat Clay Dobbs and Riley Curry wearing a pair of oversized dark glasses. Since there was no sun outside, she assumed the shades were covering the two black eyes he'd reportedly been given by Trent July. Trent's cast-encased hand had been signed by nearly everyone during coffee hour that morning. Because she didn't condone violence of any kind Paula hadn't added her signature, but she certainly understood Trent's response to Curry's scam.

"Hey, Reverend Paula." Eli walked up and placed a glass of water on her table. He was wearing the black shirt and pants that were standard attire for the waitstaff.

"Hey there, Eli."

"What can I get you?" he asked. "Special today is baked trout, brown rice, and asparagus almandine."

"Sounds good. I'll have that."

He wrote it down. "By the way. That special moment you told me to look out for? It came and I talked to my dad. Turned out okay. Thanks for the advice."

"You're welcome."

He continued in a softer voice. "Don't tell anyone but Siz is going to teach me to cook. I figure I can do dinner a few times a week and give my dad a break."

"How thoughtful, Eli."

He blushed a bit. "Thanks. I'll get your order in."

He left her alone and Paula beamed. Like Devon, Eli had come a long way.

She picked up her glass to take a sip of water but paused when Clay approached her table..

"Can I talk to you for a minute, Reverend?"

She set her glass down. "Sure. Have a seat."

He took a seat opposite her and said, "Hate to bother you, but I need some advice on how to convince Genevieve to stop making a fool of herself with all this change nonsense."

Paula assessed him for a moment. It saddened her that he didn't support Gen's new view of herself so she said gently, "All I can tell you is the only person we can control is ourselves."

His lips thinned and he gazed off for a few seconds. She knew it wasn't what he wanted to hear but it was the truth.

"So you don't think a man should be head of his household?"

Paula paused. "If he has a household to be the head of. You and Gen aren't married, are you?"

"No, but— Never mind. I knew I shouldn't be talking to a woman about this."

And to her surprise he got up and stalked off.

Her eye caught Mal's and as if he knew what had been discussed, he shook his head in what looked to be disappointment, and offered a shrug as if to say: *What're you going to do?*

She shrugged in reply. She hoped Clay and Gen worked out their issues because knowing the path Gen was on, Clay was going to wind up on the curb permanently if he wasn't there already.

In the middle of thinking about that, Rocky appeared at her side. "Got a minute?"

"Sure." Paula was beginning to wonder if maybe she should've stayed home and had a nice quiet dinner there instead.

"I've decided to tell Jack yes."

"Are you at peace with the decision?"

"I am."

"Then congratulations," she offered genuinely. "You'll be good for each other."

"He'll be good for me. Not sure about the other way around, but I'm going to try and make it work. Thanks for listening, Reverend Paula."

"No problem. Let me know if the church can help in any way."

"Will do."

Watching Rocky head back to the kitchen, Paula was happy for her and knew everyone in town would be, too. She and Jack were well loved. Paula looked around and considered hiding under the table until Eli returned with her meal in order to avoid having to counsel anyone else, but smiling at the silly thought, she took out her tablet and played a few rounds of *Candy Crush* instead.

Her meal finally arrived and as always, it didn't disappoint. The fish was flaky and well-seasoned. The rice and asparagus were superb. Rumor had it that Siz was being courted by a fancy restaurant down in Lawrence. Paula didn't want to deny him the opportunity to advance his career but on the other hand, he could cook for her for the rest of her natural-born days.

That night in Paula's dream she was walking in her grandfather's backyard. The surrounding trees were covered with thousands of black butterflies and the sound of their wings filled the air like voices moaning an old gospel hymn. Out in the middle of the yard two women were on their knees. At first, she thought they might be praying, but as she looked closer she saw that they were using their hands to dig a hole in the dirt, and that their movements matched the cadence of the butterflies' eerie song. Just as she wondered who they might be, one of the women turned her way. The face was old, ancient, and tears streamed down her cheeks. Although she appeared familiar, Paula couldn't place her. When the second woman turned, Paula froze. It was her mother, Patricia, and she too was weeping.

"Mama?"

No response. Instead the two began digging faster and deeper. The dirge of the butterflies grew stronger. The sky darkened. Thunder boomed, lightning answered, and rising winds tore at Paula's robe. The dirge was now so deafening she covered her ears with her hands. The butterflies suddenly peeled away from the trees and swarmed her like a malevolent cloud. Razor-sharp wings beat against her face, fouling her eyes, stealing her breath. She opened her mouth to scream. The black cloud parted just as her mother reached into the open earth and withdrew a human skull. She raised it high against the violent storm and Paula bolted awake.

Shaking, Paula turned on the lamp on her nightstand. She dragged her hands over her eyes and felt the damp sweat on her face. *Good lord! What was that?* She drew in a deep breath and tried to calm herself. Aspects of the nightmare were already beginning to fade, but the skull in her mother's hand remained. Had the nightmare been fueled by her grandfather's upcoming funeral? And who was the old woman with her mother? Paula was sure she knew her, but her name and identity remained just out of reach.

Having no answers, she got up, washed her face, and walked through the darkness to the kitchen for a drink of water. Returning to her bedroom, she turned off the light and scooted back beneath the covers, hoping to go back to sleep, but remnants of the disturbing dream lingered and a strong sense of foreboding kept her awake for quite some time.

* * *

Over at the Clark house, the girls and Gary were asleep but TC was in his bedroom awake. There was a late-night NBA game on ESPN but he wasn't paying it much attention because he had other things on his mind. Years ago, his wife Carla saw a card company's commercial on TV about a man who couldn't read, who'd saved all the cards he'd received from his family and friends in a box. The commercial went on to show the man getting help from a kindly tutor, and at the end, sitting down and reading the decades of cards he'd hoarded. Carla encouraged TC to start a box of his own and he had. It originally held a pair of work boots. Why he'd placed the box in the truck along with his other personal stuff when he left Oakland he had no idea, but he opened it now and looked inside. It was stuffed with cards dating back to the '90s. Envelopes in every color of the rainbow held greetings he'd received from his kids for his birthdays, Father's Days, and myriad holidays. When the kids were young, he'd been able to trick them into reading them by saying he wanted to hear them express the written sentiments, but once they grew up and moved away, their cards came by mail and he could only open them, look at them, and put them away. *You're pretty pitiful,* he thought to himself. And he supposed he was. Lord knew he wanted to be able to read, and now that he was on the downslope of life the urge to set aside the fear and take the plunge grew stronger, but the fear was just as strong. Reverend Paula's sermon that morning about paying homage to the ancestors struck a nerve. Carla hadn't been an ancestor but she had been his wife, and tackling his deficiency once and for all would not only honor her but also people like his father, grandfather, and the others in his line, all the way back to slavery, who hadn't been able to read, either. His kids were the first readers in his family.

Carla's family read of course, but not the people on his side, at least as far as he knew. He'd tried to get around his lack by embracing audio books, and over the years convinced himself that that was enough, but it wasn't and he knew it. The face of Genevieve Gibbs floated across his mind's eye just as it had the last time he'd had this debate with himself. Carla always strongly believed that God put people in your life when you needed them. Was that the reason he'd ended up in Henry Adams? Fate? He didn't know but sometime soon he needed to take a trip to the wizard for some courage and find out.

As dawn broke, Riley hadn't gotten much sleep due to the throbbing in his nose, so he got out of bed and padded into the connecting bathroom. The mirror told him what he already knew. Both eyes were still as black and blue as the huge bruise spanning the bridge of his nose. Were it Halloween he could pose as a raccoon. He wanted to sue Trent July for his pain and suffering but Eustacia's big-time lawyer told him to forget it because once a jury learned that Riley used Trent's name to commit a felony, he'd lose the case on the spot. Never one to accept blame, Riley proceeded to argue with the lawyer until the man hung up. Granted, Riley didn't feel so clever now that the car dealership wanted him thrown in jail but self-reflection was also something he disliked, so he turned his mind to another pressing matter—finding a place to stay. At present he was bunking with his old pal Clay Dobbs. Clay's housemate, Bing Shepard, was down south visiting relatives but once he returned Riley was certain the old man would have him kicked out. Eustacia's lawyer and Sheriff Dalton advised him not to leave town. Cletus was making himself at home in one of Clay's pens but if Riley was forced to leave where would they go? His only hope was that the interior of Eustacia's partly built mansion looked better than the outside and he could stay there.

"So what did the lawyer say last night?" Clay asked as they ate breakfast.

Riley told him everything including the part about being warned off suing Trent.

"The lawyer's probably right," Clay noted.

"No, he's not. I want July charged with assault and I want him to pay for my pain and suffering."

"You tell the lawyer that?"

"I did. Argued with him until he hung up on me."

"Using Trent's name was not a good idea."

Riley ignored that and concentrated on eating his eggs.

Clay took a sip of coffee. "So, what's your next move?"

"You still seeing Genevieve?"

Clay paused and said finally, "No."

"Why not?"

"She's turned herself into one of those feminists who doesn't need a man. Even bought herself a mobile home."

Riley looked up. "Really?"

"Says she's going to put it where the old house used to be. She's also keeping time with Gary Clark's uncle."

"Who?"

Clay explained and finished by saying, "She said it was only lunch but I think something more's going on."

By then Riley was only half listening. He was thinking about her trailer. If he could finally convince her to own up to the error of her ways, maybe her guilt would allow him and Cletus to move back in. "She still staying with Marie?"

Clay nodded.

"Maybe after we check out Eustacia's place I'll stop in and see her. For old times' sake."

Clay looked suspicious but Riley was too busy forming a plan to notice.

After breakfast, while Clay cleaned up the kitchen—Riley didn't offer to help—Riley took Cletus a large mixing bowl of his favorite rice cereal that he'd had Clay buy at the grocery store. "Here's your breakfast, big boy."

Cletus trotted over and Riley slid the bowl beneath the bottom rung of the pen and set it on the ground. While the hog ate, Riley said, "Going to see Genevieve later."

Cletus raised his head and squealed.

"I know," Riley said. "I don't want to see her either but we need somewhere to live. Clay's not going to let us stay here much longer and she's getting her own place. This whole mess is her fault, and once I explain it to her she'll let us come back."

Riley heard a horn blow. It was Clay in his truck. "Okay, I have to go. You be good."

The ride over to Eustacia's took only a few minutes. The last time he'd seen the place he'd been too tired to really take it in and now as he and Clay approached the porch, he swore the front door was different. "What happened to the other door?"

"Had to be replaced."

To Riley's surprise Clay had a key. "Where'd you get a key?"

"Trent."

Before Riley could ask about that, Clay had the door opened. Riley followed him inside and for a moment all he could do was gape. The walls looked like someone had gone at them with sledgehammers. The carpets were ripped up as were the floorboards underneath. Ceiling fans lay like dead insects amidst piles of broken plaster, splintered wood, and shattered glass. "What happened?"

"People tore the place up looking for gold."

"What!"

So Clay explained about Cephas Patterson finding outlaw Griffin Blake's hidden stash of gold coins. "Last fall, when word got out, every treasure hunter within five hundred miles came to town looking for more."

"And they came here?" Riley asked.

Clay nodded. "Probably because the place looked abandoned. They broke into Patterson's place and trashed it. The new recreation center was hit, too. By the time the police showed up and put a stop to it, the damage had been done."

A grim Riley said, "Let's see the rest." Stepping carefully because of all the broken glass, they continued the tour and he stared around in shock at the gutted kitchen. "Where are the appliances?" The fancy stainless steel double oven and its companion fridge were nowhere to be seen. All the high-end sink fixtures were missing, too.

"Looted. When the rioters didn't find any gold they took whatever they could, including Eustacia's appliances, air conditioner, furnace, and hot water heater."

Riley wanted to cry. "Why didn't somebody let me know?"

"You didn't leave a forwarding address, remember."

It was apparent that he and Cletus couldn't live there. Moving in with Genevieve was the only option. It was either that or pitch a tent and live outdoors, and he didn't own a tent or anything else for that matter. "Take me by Marie's so I can talk to Genevieve."

"She's not going to take you back, Riley."

"Who said anything about that? I just want to say hello."

"Uh-huh. Instead of trying to bamboozle your way back into her life, you might want to look for a job. There's a new beauty shop in town run by Kelly Douglas. She'd probably let you rent a chair if you want to go back to barbering. The men here could use you."

"I'll think about it," he said, but in truth he wasn't. He just wanted to get back into Genevieve's good graces and maybe get access to her bank account again. "You driving me over to Marie's or not?"

Clay assessed him stonily. Riley sensed he wasn't liking the idea of him seeing Genevieve again even if they had broken things off, but he didn't care. She was his ex-wife and he had every right to see her if he wanted.

"Okay," Clay said finally. "Let's go, and just so you'll know, Marie's got a bug up her butt. Don't expect a friendly greeting from her, either."

Riley and Marie had never gotten along, so he didn't care.

On the drive over Riley racked his brain for a Plan B just in case he couldn't count on Genevieve's guilt. He thought back on how and where they first met and how much of a big shot she'd thought him to be and he knew he had her. Upon arriving at the Jefferson homestead, he puffed himself up. He and Genevieve hadn't parted on the best of terms but their forty years of marriage had to count for something. She'd take him back, he just knew she would.

Clay asked, "You want me to wait?"

"No."

"If she knocks you out again, have somebody call me."

"Ha. Ha." Putting on his shades, Riley left the truck and Clay drove away.

On the porch, Riley pressed the doorbell. Seconds later, the white lace curtains in the front window moved then dropped back. Someone was home. He waited. Nothing. He pressed the bell again. Still no response. He leaned forcefully on the bell for a good ten seconds. The door was snatched open and there stood Marie.

"What do you want?"

"Came to see Genevieve."

"She's not here." The door slammed closed.

Hopping mad, he laid on the bell again, but when she didn't respond, he sighed in surrender. It occurred to him that maybe he should have had Clay wait. He now had no way to get back and no phone. Although it was a cloudy day, the temperature wasn't bad, so he took a seat on the top step to wait for Genevieve's return. He just hoped she wasn't out of town.

Genevieve was just leaving her tutoring session with Mrs. Rivard over in Franklin. TC stood waiting next to the car.

"Ready?" he asked as she approached.

"I am."

He bowed elaborately and gestured for her to enter. She laughed and took her seat up front. A few seconds later he got in. No matter how hard she tried to dismiss it, riding beside him still made her feel like a teenager on her first date.

He started the car and headed them back toward Henry Adams. "How'd the lesson go?"

"It went well," she told him. "She's almost at the point of not needing my help and that's the goal. I'm very proud of her."

"How long have you been working with her?"

"About six weeks."

"Is that average?"

"It depends on the person. When I took the training, I was told it could be as fast as a month or as long as six. Some students are very motivated and some are fearful."

"I see."

Something in his tone made her look his way. "Something wrong?"

"Nope. Just thinking about Mrs. Rivard. I imagine it took a lot of courage for her to ask for help."

"It did. She couldn't read at all when we first got together."

"Did she say what made her decide she wanted to learn?"

"Yes. She wanted to be able to read to her new grandchild. She hadn't been able to with her daughter."

"That's pretty powerful."

"It is."

As always he had the jazz station on and a nice guitar tune began to play. "I like that," she said. The display on the dash showed the name of the tune and the artist.

TC said, "Since I'm supposed to be keeping my eyes on the road, who's it by?"

"Lee Ritenour. Song is called 'Windmill.' Says it's from his *World of Brazil* CD."

"I'll have to get that."

Gen took out her phone.

"What are you doing?"

"Downloading it."

He chuckled. "You're something else."

"I'll take that as a compliment."

"That's how it was meant to be taken."

She glanced up from her phone. His praise made her feel good inside and she said quietly, "Thank you."

"For what?"

"For taking me seriously."

"How could I not?"

She shrugged. "Remember those irreconcilable differences I mentioned the day we had lunch?"

"I do."

"My doing things like downloading music was one of them."

"Huh?"

"I was told I was trying to act like I was twenty-five and it wasn't becoming."

"That doesn't make much sense."

"I agree," she said firmly.

"As we used to say back in the day, I think you're very cool, Ms. Genevieve Gibbs. Don't change yourself for anybody. Okay?"

"I don't plan to."

"Good. Let the haters hate."

"Amen."

They rode the rest of the way to Henry Adams listening to the music in a companionable silence. Gen found herself enjoying his company more and more.

He turned the car into the drive. Upon seeing Riley sitting on the top step, she groused, "Oh, good lord."

"What's wrong?"

"That's Riley on the porch."

"Who's Riley?"

"My ex-husband."

"The pig guy?"

"Yes."

He leaned forward to check him out. "Day's a little cloudy for shades."

"He's wearing them to hide the black eyes he got from Trent."

TC looked confused.

"I'll explain later, or better yet, have Gary tell you about it."

"Okay, but I take it you weren't expecting him?"

"No."

"I thought you said he was in LA. Why's he here?"

"Obviously wants something. Always does." She opened the door.

"You going to be okay talking to him?" he asked with concern. "Do I need to stick around?"

"I'll be fine, but thanks for the offer."

"Are you sure?"

"I am. You go on and do whatever you were planning to do."

"I was planning on asking you to have lunch with me."

Gen eyed him and wondered if she'd ever breathe again. "Really?"

Smiling softly, he offered a small shrug.

"I'd like that." She forced herself to stop staring. "Can you wait while I take my tote inside?"

"For as long as it takes."

Filled with wonder, she left the car.

"Who's that?" Riley had the nerve to demand. He peered past her, trying to see into the car.

"Why are you here?"

"I came to see you."

"Why?"

"Just wanted to see how you were."

"I'm fine." She walked by him to the door and took out her key.

"That the fella Clay says you're seeing?"

"That's none of your business or Clay's."

"I'm only asking because I don't want you to be taken advantage of."

"Something you know all about, right?" She wanted to sock him and send him flying off the porch.

"Look, Genevieve. I—"

"No, you look," she said, cutting him off. "You stole thousands of dollars from me, and the only reason I couldn't put you in jail was because your name was on the account and the bank said I had no concrete proof you took it without my permission."

"But Genevieve—"

"Don't say another word to me, Riley Curry. You stole from me. You chose that damn hog over me. You even married another woman while you were still married to me. Go 'way. I don't want you in my life." That said, she went inside.

Marie was waiting. "What's he want?"

Gen was seething. "Probably money or a place to stay. I didn't ask."

"Why's Morgan Freeman still out front?"

Gen was putting her tote in the closet and upon hearing that she stopped and turned back. "Morgan Freeman? Really, Marie? This is why I'm moving."

Without another word, she slammed the closet door and sailed back outside.

Riley was still there. He opened his mouth but the glare she shot him made him rethink whatever he was planning to say and she stormed past.

Inside the car she was sure steam was curling out of her ears. "Can we go, please, before I punch something?"

"That mad, huh?"

"Madder. Riley's an idiot and so is Marie."

"Who's Marie?"

"The woman I live with. We've been friends all our lives but she's lost her mind. She just called you Morgan Freeman."

He chuckled. "*Driving Miss Daisy*?"

"Yes!"

"It's okay. I've been called worse. I didn't know you could get this angry."

"The last time I did, I punched Riley so hard I knocked him out and broke a bone in my hand."

He barked a laugh. "Really? Whoa."

"At the Dog in front of everybody, including his so-called wife. Riley's a bigamist too, you know."

"Wait. What?"

She nodded.

"Lots of drama going on for such a little town," he said, studying her.

"You have no idea."

"You still down for lunch?"

"Please, but do you mind if we get a takeout and go someplace quiet. I need to calm down."

"Whatever you want."

"Thank you."

Gen called ahead so she didn't have to wait long for their order to arrive at the desk. Once it was paid for and the speculation on Mal's face ignored she returned to the car.

"So where to?" he asked.

"Let me make a call." Once she did, she gave him directions.

CHAPTER
9

When they reached their destination, he took in the large old house surrounded by open land and asked, "Where are we?"

"The July homestead. Park here and we can walk down to the creek. There's a picnic table there."

They left the car and covered the short distance across the open land to the creek. As they sat, he said, "Nice spot."

"It is. Peaceful, too."

"All this wide open space takes some getting used to for a city boy."

She removed his sandwich and her salad from the bag. "Are you enjoying being here, though?"

"I am. Definitely different. Never lived any place so quiet."

"It grows on you."

They ate in silence for a while and she again thought about how much she liked his company. She wondered how he felt about being with her but was too shy to ask. "How long do you plan to stay with Gary and the girls?"

He took a sip from his bottled water. "For sure until summer. After that, I don't know. I'm supposed to go to Hawaii in August for my daughter's birthday. She manages a resort on Kauai."

"Sounds nice. Hawaii is on my bucket list."

"Beautiful place. She was stationed in Hawaii during her time in the Air Force and decided to stay. Real proud of her."

The pride on his face was plain. "And your sons?"

"Proud of them, too. My oldest, Keith, and his wife live in Atlanta. They're both big-time stockbrokers. Other son, Aaron, is a petroleum engineer in Alaska."

She looked up from her salad. "Alaska?"

"Yes. He's lived there almost five years now."

"Have you visited?"

"I have. A couple of times. Like Hawaii it has its own kind of beauty."

"Never been there, either." She mused on what it might be like to see those places with him and caught herself. When she looked up his eyes were waiting.

He asked quietly, "Where have you traveled besides DC?"

"Just Vegas. It's one of Marie's and my favorite places. She hits the casinos and I hit the shows, the Grand Canyon, and Hoover Dam."

"I've never seen either of those."

"The Grand Canyon is truly God's work. It's breathtaking. I've been there four, maybe five times and I always see something new. Feel free to tag along next time I go."

"I may have to hold you to that."

His tone and easy gaze had her at such sixes and sevens, as her grandmother used to say, she changed the subject. "So, do you have grandchildren?"

He shook his head. "No. Still waiting on the kids to cooperate."

She nodded understandingly.

"Keith and his wife arc trying, but they're so busy chasing stocks and bonds. I keep telling them if they actually took a vacation they'd probably have babies by now."

"Careers mean a lot to the younger set these days."

"I know. Aaron and Bethany are content with the single life, but I worry about them never finding the love their mother and I shared."

"You're a romantic."

"Not ashamed to admit that I am. Spoiled Carla rotten."

"Sounds like you had a good marriage."

"We did. I've gone on with my life but still miss her."

"That's sweet."

"Are you a romantic?"

She shrugged. "I suppose, but hard to be that when you're in competition with a hog."

He chuckled. "I still find that unbelievable."

"Think how I felt. And Clay wanted what he thought was the ideal me. He doesn't appreciate the woman I'm trying to be."

"His loss."

"In a way mine, too. At my age I'll probably never get to experience what you and your Carla had."

The empathy in his eyes moved her so intensely she looked away and went back to her salad.

As if to change the subject he looked out over the creek and asked, "Do people come out here often?"

"Yes, and Tamar doesn't mind as long as you call first. It is private property, after all."

"I see. Being out here with all this peace and quiet makes a man want to buy some land of his own."

She nodded. "I have land, too, but it's a much smaller plot. The Julys have been on this homestead since the 1880s."

"Gary told me about the history here."

"It's an honor to live in a place where the race has walked free for over a hundred years. I can't wait for my new mobile home to arrive so I can have a place of my own again."

"When's it coming?"

"Hopefully in the next couple of days."

"Do you need help moving?"

"I don't think so but if I do I'll let you know."

"Please."

"Okay, I will." Gen had trouble holding his gaze because of the connection she sensed growing between them. She wasn't sure what to do about it and lord knew she didn't want to be staring all cow-eyed at the man.

"I like being in your company, Ms. Genevieve Gibbs."

She somehow managed to reply, "And I enjoy being in yours, Mr. Barbour."

"Be nice if we could do this again."

"I'd like that."

"Have you found us a concert yet?"

She lowered her head to hide her smile. "No. Not yet."

"You are looking, right?"

"I am."

"Good." The silence between them stretched until he finally glanced at his watch. "Are you ready for me to take you home?"

In truth, the answer was no, but she said instead, "Yes. Hopefully Riley's gone by now."

"Where's he staying?"

"With Clay."

"Ex-husband staying with ex-beau?"

"I know. We all grew up together. I was sweet on Clay in high school and he was sweet on me but I married Riley. It's complicated. Nothing worked out for any of us, though."

"Sorry to hear that."

"At least I came to my senses and cut bait. Otherwise I'd still be in a bad marriage with a hog as a third wheel."

They gathered up their trash and placed it in the large waste can by the table's edge. "Thanks for the company," she said.

"You're welcome."

For a moment they just gazed at each other. Gen felt the connection tightening but had no idea if it was her imagination.

"Shall we?" he asked quietly.

She nodded and they walked back to the car.

When he stopped in front of Marie's, Gen was pleased to find the porch empty. "Thanks again."

"No problem. You'll let me know if you need help moving."

"I will." Wishing she had a legitimate reason to spend more time with him, she got out. "Have a nice rest of the day."

"You, too."

Up on the porch she stuck her key in the lock and gave him a wave. As she stepped inside she watched him drive away and wondered where their relationship might lead.

The house was quiet. She'd expected to find Marie in front of the TV but she wasn't. When Gen called for her and got no response, she grew concerned. Knowing Marie usually parked around back, she walked into the kitchen in order to see if the car was there, but found a note attached to the back door. *Back later. M.* Since Marie rarely left the house these days, Gen was surprised. The note dampened her concern somewhat, but she still wondered where Marie might be. Figuring the question would be answered soon enough, she went upstairs to her room to begin packing for the move.

Sitting in her car in the church parking lot, Marie regretted making the Morgan Freeman crack, mostly because of Gen's withering response. It was the same tone Gen used with Riley and Marie realized she had slipped so low in Genevieve's opinion that she and Riley were seated at the same table. It got her attention. No way did she want to be thought of in those terms. Riley was both despised and pitied. Granted, his sins against Genevieve were far more serious, but in a way they weren't because Gen trusted Marie as a friend, and in exchange, received a snide jealousy-fed comment about someone Gen might genuinely be interested in. Everyone knew that Riley had no plans to change and was content to be himself for the rest of his life. However, Marie wasn't—not with her life, her acerbic attitude, or the hole she found herself in. So she got out and walked to the doors.

Inside, she found Reverend Paula seated at the desk in her office.

"Marie," she said, looking and sounding surprised. "Hello."

"Hi, Paula. Do you have some time? I'd like to talk to you."

"Yes, I do. Take off your coat and have a seat. Can I get you something? Coffee? Tea? Water?"

"Tea would be nice."

"Okay. I'll be right back."

While she went to get the tea, Marie drew in a calming

breath and wondered if this was the right choice. She'd never shared her problems before because she'd always convinced herself that there was nothing in life she couldn't handle on her own. With her life spiraling out of control, that confidence had fled, and if anyone could put things in perspective without judging it would be Paula. Marie also trusted her not to run to the Dog and tell everyone in town her business. She'd been bitter and alone long enough. She needed someone to light the way back.

Paula returned with a tray holding a steaming mug, a spoon, and a few packets of sweetener. She set it on the table nestled against the sofa where Marie was seated and while Marie doctored the brew to her liking Paula settled into a nearby chair and waited silently.

Marie began. "I'm sure you've heard about the mess at the Dog last winter."

"I have, but I wasn't there so for me it's all hearsay. Why don't you tell me what happened."

So Marie did, and didn't spare herself in the telling.

Paula asked gently, "So what made you so angry at Rita Lynn?"

"Mal wasn't supposed to know that I loved him. I'd planned on keeping that to myself for the rest of my life but when Rita told him how I felt, I just lost it. I was embarrassed, hurt. I felt betrayed."

"Understandable."

"I wanted to crawl into a hole."

"And so you did."

She hadn't expected Paula to view it that way, too. "Yes."

"And now?"

"Now I want out. Genevieve is so upset she's moving. A

few weeks ago Mal came by to see me and I wouldn't answer the door. I'm a mess, Paula."

"You're not a mess. You're just hurting and I get the sense that it goes deeper than Rita Lynn. I never met your mother, so tell me a little bit about her. Did you two get along?"

"I loved her. She barely tolerated me."

"Explain that, please."

Marie shared the painful story of getting pregnant in college by a man who refused to marry her. "I came back to Henry Adams pregnant and ashamed. My mother thought it best to put the child up for adoption. The nuns whisked him away as soon as I gave birth." Her voice trailed to a whisper. "I never even got to hold him." Her heart tightened painfully at the still raw memory.

"I'm so sorry."

"And from then on I couldn't do anything right in her eyes. She didn't like the car I drove, the men I dated, taking Gen to Vegas when she asked me to."

"And your father?"

Marie chuckled bitterly. "I grew up believing he'd died in the Korean War because that's what she told me, but on her deathbed, she confessed that I was born out of wedlock, too."

Paula looked shocked.

"My mother was no better than I was when it came right down to it. She berated me and put me down my whole life for committing the same mistake she'd made. I was furious at her when I learned the truth."

"Have you reconnected with your son?"

"Another funny story," Marie said sarcastically. "He called me a couple of years back. Said he was in town and wanted to meet me. Lily drove me over. I just knew he wanted to be in my life but no, all he wanted was medical information."

"That had to be heartbreaking."

"It was and I felt stupid and hurt and broken inside for being so hopeful. My life seems to be one low blow after another."

"But your teaching brought you joy, no?"

"It did. My students were all the children I never got to hold. I loved them all."

And she had. She never felt so alive as when in the classroom. That made her think of Trent. He'd been one of her best students and because of the altercation with his mother, Rita Lynn, their relationship was strained, a strain that also affected Marie's relationship with her goddaughter, Lily. No woman should have to choose between husband and godmother, so to keep from negatively impacting their marriage, Marie had distanced herself from Lily as well.

"Your friends miss you, Marie."

Marie's lip trembled. She told herself she'd pluck out her eyes before letting the tears fall but fall they did. "How do I fix this, Paula? How do I look at Mal and not feel like a fool. How do I apologize to Trent for being so screwed up that when he and his mother came to see me I slammed the door in his face? And poor Genevieve. We've been sisters of the heart since we were eight. She can't stand me right now. I have burned so many bridges." Marie wept brokenly. Terribly. Paula got up and held her close.

"It's okay," Paula whispered.

"No it isn't. How am I ever going to face them again?"

"I don't think it'll be as hard as you imagine. They all love you." Paula handed her some tissues and waited while she tried to pull herself together. "You're one of the heartbeats of this community. Everyone knows you're hurting and they all feel powerless to help. As for Mal, please don't beat yourself up over him knowing the truth. Loving someone even if it isn't returned isn't something to be ashamed of."

Marie wanted to believe her, especially the part about reconnecting, but how could Paula be so sure?

As if having read her mind, Paula said, "And you know why I know it won't be hard?"

"How?"

"Because as I said, they love you, Marie. Very much. Gather your courage and talk to them. Then make peace with yourself so your blessings can flow."

Marie blew her nose and thought about how she might do it, and realized she knew. "When Mal first started AA, I went with him to some of the meetings. At one, they talked about making amends being a big step in recovery. The members were encouraged to apologize to everyone they'd hurt." She looked to Paula for reassurance. "Maybe I'll do that."

"I think that's an excellent idea."

Marie wiped her eyes and nodded to herself. "That's what I'm going to do." Coming to see Paula was the light she'd needed. "Thank you."

"You're welcome. Can I ask you something though?"

"Sure."

"What made you decide to come and see me today?"

"Riley."

"Curry?"

Marie nodded. "He came by to see Gen earlier and he was so . . . Riley—you just want to smack him 24-7. I looked at him and then at myself and I felt like Gen wanted to do the same thing with me, especially after the way I taunted her this afternoon. I don't want people here dealing with me the way they deal with him. Might not make sense to you but it did to me."

"The trigger doesn't really matter. I was just curious."

"There were no visions or directives from the Lord involved."

Paula laughed, then turned serious. "Welcome back."

"You can welcome me back for real after I make amends." She stood. "You're pretty good at this, Reverend Paula."

"Just using my gifts the way I'm supposed to. And if you need to talk more I'm always here."

Marie nodded and left the office. On her walk to the car, she felt lighter, freer. She was no longer Sisyphus pushing the boulder up the mountain. A part of her was afraid to go through with the apologies she needed to make and wanted to run back to the house instead, but as Paula suggested, she gathered her courage and drove to the Dog.

When she walked in, Mal was behind the counter and surprise filled his eyes. "Marie?"

"Hey. Can we talk in your office for a minute?"

"Sure. Come on back."

They entered and he closed the door. "Good to see you."

"Thanks. Look, about Rita Lynn. I need to apologize."

"No, you don't."

"I do, Malachi, so for once can you just shut up, so I can say what I need to say."

Humor twinkled in his eyes. "Floor's all yours."

"I was loud, obnoxious, and wrong that day."

"True."

She exhaled an exaggerated sigh of frustration. "I'm trying to be serious here."

He said softly, "I know, but I'm trying to tell you there's no need to be. If anybody should be apologizing, it's me. Marie, I'm sorry my cluelessness caused you so much pain. I truly didn't know. I've loved you all my life—and I still do, but not in that way. Nobody can kick me in the butt like you do and I've missed that and you these past few months."

Marie swore softly as the tears broke free again.

He held out his arms. "Come here."

He held her tightly and placed a solemn kiss on her forehead. "The love we have is strong. Always has been, always will be. And no, it's not the love I have for Bernadine but it's just as special and precious. Please forgive an old drunk for being so blind."

Marie cried silently as that love filled her soul. And it was precious. They'd had each other's backs since they were old enough to walk and it was a bond they'd take to the grave.

He leaned back and looked her in the eye and she saw that his were wet, too. "I love you, girl, in a way I'll never love anyone else. Square business."

She wiped her tears away and smiled. "Do you think kids these days say square business and mean it the way we did in the seventies?"

"Probably not, everybody's too busy lying."

She laughed and for the next few moments thought back on all they'd done together, the shared fun, the arguments that never lasted long enough to be memorable, and she knew how blessed she was to call him friend. "Thanks, Mal."

"You helped save my life, Marie. It doesn't get much better

than that. Now, before we both start bawling again, how about some lunch? My treat."

"You're on."

After lunch, Marie was still feeling good about herself and her friendship with Mal. When she pulled into the driveway at her home, she assumed Genevieve was home and she was hit by a bit of apprehension. Suppose Gen threw her apology back in her face because of the hell she'd put her through these past few months. She decided the only way to find out was to go in and see. And pray.

Marie heard her moving around in her bedroom, so she stuck her head in the partially opened door and knocked softly. "Gen?"

Gen turned and seeing Marie, frowned. "Yes?"

"I went to see Reverend Paula today to talk about my issues."

Her face softened. "That's so great, Marie. Did she help?"

"A lot. I'm so sorry for being such a witch. You of all people didn't deserve the treatment I've been dishing out. I'm apologizing to everybody I hurt, hoping they'll forgive me."

That earned her a soft smile.

"I've missed you."

"I've missed myself. Can you forgive me?"

"You know I can. What brought this on?"

"Riley."

"Huh?"

Marie laughed. "As the kids say: What had happened was . . ."

For the next hour they talked, shed a few tears over the pain that had divided them, and began slowly resurrecting their lifelong friendship. "I'm doing my own 12-step program by apologizing to everyone I've hurt. I already talked to Mal."

"How'd it go?"

Marie thought back. "It went well. I still need to talk to Trent and Lily and Rita Lynn."

Gen paused. "You sure you want to talk to her?"

"No, but I need to. She's Trent's mother and she'll be visiting again sooner or later, so I need to clear the air. We'll probably never be BFFs but I don't want drama between us spilling onto Trent and Lily's marriage."

"You're right," she said, and added, "Look at you being all mature and rational."

"And you don't have to move now."

But Genevieve's response was not what Marie thought it would be. "I do," she said gently. "It's time for me to fly on my own. We'll still be best friends and do what best friends do, but I need my own place. You taking me in after I left Riley has meant so much. You helped me grow up. A lot. Clay doesn't like this new me, but I hope you do."

"I do," Marie replied. "And thanks for not throwing my apology back in my face."

"I'd never do that."

"I know, but I worried I'd treated you so badly that you wanted to punch me out like you did Riley that day at the Dog."

"Which he deserved. I admit, there were a few times I wanted to punch you too but I was more hurt than angry."

"I'm so sorry."

"It's okay," Gen said reassuringly. "We're good now, right?"

"Yes, we are." Joy filled Marie's heart. "And let me apologize for the Morgan Freeman remark this morning."

"I appreciate that."

"So, tell me about him. Do you like him?"

"I do, but we're just friends."

"Uh-huh."

"We are, Marie."

Marie smiled. "You're blushing, Genevieve."

"Am not."

"Are, too."

"Go away unless you want to help me pack."

"Hand me a box."

CHAPTER
10

When Eli came home from school, he checked the mailbox first thing, hoping to get news from the art competition. He rifled through the small stack of envelopes at warp speed and stopped at the one addressed to him. The return address showed the name of the museum running the contest. He ripped it open as if it held gold and read:

> Dear Eli,
>
> Thank you for your submission. The judges found your sculpture to be outstanding. However it was not picked as the best in its category. Much success with your artistic endeavors in the future. Your bust will be returned via mail. Sincerely . . .

He dropped his head and went inside. Disappointed, he sailed the letter across the room and plopped down onto the sofa. "Damn!" He'd been so confident the bust of his mom would win first place and he'd planned to use the scholarship money as part of the leverage he needed to convince his dad to let him attend community college in California. Now, he was no closer to that goal than he'd been a week ago. He sighed dejectedly. Feeling sorry for himself, he sat there for a good twenty minutes before deciding to hell with it. He'd planned to surprise his dad with dinner so he got up, walked into the kitchen, and washed his hands.

The meal would be a simple one: broiled whitefish, a salad, and mashed red potatoes. His dad always left for school earlier than Eli so that morning, after his departure, Eli took the whitefish fillets out of the freezer to let them thaw in the fridge. Now, following Siz's written instructions, he put the potatoes in a pot of water to boil, put the lid on it, turned on the burner, and began working on the fish and the marinade. Once the seasoned fillets were ready, he placed them on the foil-lined broiler pan, set it aside, and checked the potatoes. His eyes widened seeing white foamy water boiling out from beneath the lid and sizzling down the side of the pot. He quickly grabbed the lid, singed his fingers, and immediately dropped the thing onto the floor. Cursing, he danced around a minute before turning on the faucet in the sink and sticking his hand into the stream of cold water. With the lid removed the over-boiling water subsided. His hand felt better too, so he dried it gingerly, said a small prayer of thanks, and made a note for the future not to use a lid when boiling potatoes. He put the lid in the sink.

He let the potatoes boil for another twenty minutes and placed the fish under the broiler. Siz said it would only take a few minutes, so Eli very carefully poured the water and softened potatoes into the colander waiting in the sink. Siz suggested rinsing the pot and quickly putting the potatoes back inside, adding some milk and butter and putting the lid back on so they'd stay hot while Eli searched for the potato masher. He found the masher and began mashing, and other than burning the heck out of his fingers he thought he'd done a pretty good job. There was a knock at the door. He put the lid back on the potatoes and went to answer it. Crystal.

"I came in first place!" Crystal exclaimed.

He wanted to slam the door on her. Instead he grumbled, "Cool."

"Not really," she confessed. "I got a Dear Crystal letter saying thanks for submitting."

"So did I."

"Well, we tried. You okay?" she asked gently.

"No. I wanted to win so bad."

"Me, too."

So they talked for a few minutes more and then Crystal asked, "Are you cooking something?"

And he turned to see smoke filling the air. "Oh, no! My fish!"

He ran to the kitchen to find black acrid smoke rolling out of the oven like dry ice in a horror flick. The smoke detectors screamed shrilly.

Crystal shouted, "Look through the glass in the door first! Make sure it isn't on fire. Where's your extinguisher?"

Ignoring her advice, Eli yanked down the oven door and billowing smoke rushed out like a fast-moving cloud. Coughing, he grabbed pot holders and quickly pulled the pan out. The fillets looked like charred black hot dogs. "Aw, man!" He was walking the pan to the sink counter when he noticed his dad standing beside Crystal.

"Hey, Eli," his dad said, eyes twinkling with muted amusement.

An angry Eli tossed the pan in the sink. "No jokes, Dad. Okay?"

"No jokes here. What was that supposed to be?"

A chuckling Crystal said, "I'll see myself out. *Bon appetit.*"

Eli glared at her retreating back. When he heard the front door close, he answered, "Whitefish fillets. I was going to surprise you with dinner. Thought I needed to step up so you could come home and chill and not have to cook for me all the time."

"I appreciate the gesture."

"Too bad it turned out to be crap."

"The thought counts, though."

"Can't eat thoughts."

"No."

"Didn't win the art competition, either. The letter came today."

"I'm sorry. I know how hard you worked on the bust."

Eli shrugged. "Thanks. Today sucks."

"Mine didn't. My son tried to make my life easier, and that's a good thing in my book. Do you want to eat at the Dog?"

"No, because Siz will ask me how my cooking went and I don't want to have to tell him I screwed up after he spent all last week giving me lessons."

"Then how about we make a quick run to the store, pick up some fish, and start over?"

"You'd trust me to try again?"

"Of course."

His fingers tingled. "Burned my fingers learning not to put a lid on the pot when you boil potatoes."

"We all learn that the hard way," his dad assured him. "Do we need to swing by and have Doc Reg check you out?"

"No. I think I'll live, but I may have trouble typing that paper due next week."

"Don't even try it," his dad tossed back.

Eli grinned. He felt better. "Then let's go to the store."

"I'll drive."

Eli's second attempt at dinner turned out to be better than the first. There was no smoke, no singed fingers, and although the mashed potatoes had lots of lumps, not even he could screw up a salad.

When they were done eating, his dad said, "Good job, Eli. When you live in your apartment you'll need to know how to cook."

Eli thought this might be the perfect time to bring up California, but he let the moment pass. His dad was just going to say no and he'd had enough disappointment for the day. "I'll try not to burn the place down."

"Good plan."

And they shared a smile.

"You haven't been going to Sam's in the evening lately. You two call it quits?" his dad asked.

Eli squirmed.

"Sorry. Didn't meant to get in your business."

"It's okay. She called it quits. Said she didn't want to have a boyfriend when she goes away to school in the fall."

His dad studied him. "And how do you feel about it?"

Eli shrugged. "It's not like I can tie her up and keep her in the basement like the mayor of Franklin did that kid last fall. I told her fine. We agreed to stay friends." He wanted to change the subject. "Gram and Jack Sr. still coming this weekend?"

"Far as I know. And I want to tell you something before I tell anyone else. I asked Rock to marry me. She said yes."

His mouth dropped. "Awesome, Dad." He was genuinely pleased. Finally something to make the day better. "Can I be the ring bearer?"

His father laughed. "No, but I do want you to be my best man."

Eli stared and the sudden lump in his throat made it hard to breathe. "Really?" he croaked.

"Really."

"Then, yes."

"Thank you, Eli."

"Have you set a date?"

"Not yet, but I'll let you know."

"I'm real glad for you two. Rock is a boss."

"Yes, she is. I didn't think I'd love anyone else after your mother died, but . . ."

Eli wanted him to be happy and with Rocky he was pretty sure he would be. Which meant she'd be his stepmother and that was pretty awesome, too. When he and his dad first moved to town, she, like everyone else, had had no time for Eli's whining and complaining, even nicknamed him Oscar the Grouch, but since then he'd grown to care about her and she for him. "Do you think she'll let me ride the Shadow now that we're going to be family?" She'd restored a classic Vincent Black Shadow and it was the most badazz motorcycle Eli had ever seen.

"No."

"Aww, come on. I can probably handle it."

His father gave him the side-eye. "Probably?"

"Maybe."

His father chuckled like dads do when their kids are talking crazy. "Take it up with Rock."

Which also meant no, so he let it go.

"Have you been looking for apartments over by the community college?"

"Uh, not yet. I've been waiting to have a weekend free of work. Planning on taking Crystal with me when I do go."

"Okay, I'll want to see the places you look at before you decide."

"No problem."

His dad stood. "And now, since you cooked, I'll clean up so you can start your homework. Thanks for dinner."

"You're welcome. I figure I'll cook on Mondays and Wednesdays. You can have Tuesdays and Thursdays, if that's okay?"

"Works for me. That way we can both take the weekend off."

For a moment though his dad simply stood there taking him in. "I'm proud of what you did for me today, son. You're growing up."

"'Bout time."

His father shrugged. "I knew you'd get around to it. If you don't mind, I'd like to buy the bust you made of your mother when the committee sends it back."

"You don't have to buy it, Dad."

"Yeah, I do. It's an incredible piece and artists should be paid for their work."

Eli was humbled by that. "Okay. I'll figure out a price and let you know."

"Good."

Interacting with his dad made him think of Wyatt and all the things he was missing out on by not having one. "I'm going to teach Wyatt to skateboard."

His dad stopped in the midst of clearing the table. "That's nice of you."

"Most us kids have dads, but he doesn't and I just thought maybe I could be like a big brother or something. I talked to Ms. Gemma and she liked the idea."

His dad stared. "Who are you and what have you done with the boy formerly known as Eli?"

He laughed. "Stop it, Dad."

"I'm serious. Who are you?"

Eli eyed his dad with a growing fondness. They didn't usually talk smack to each other but he was enjoying it. "It may take me a while to save up the money for his gear, but it's something I want to do."

"I'll tell you what. I'll throw in thirty dollars to get you started. On your salary, Wyatt may be twenty-five before you save up enough."

"You got jokes tonight."

"I do, but only because I like who you're growing up to be."

The lump was back in his throat. "Thanks."

"I'll transfer the money into your account once I'm done in the kitchen. Proud of you, son."

Eli nodded.

Up in his room, Eli was on his back on his bed tossing a baseball from hand to hand while recapping the evening. His first attempt at dinner had been disastrous but everything turned out in the end. The praise he'd gotten for his efforts and for helping out Wyatt felt good and made him think he was redeeming himself in his dad's eyes. Eli didn't want the nasty smart-assed kid he'd once been to be his legacy. He preferred being thought of as mature and as his dad's best man. The offer made him smile again. Rocky would have Jack James jumping through hoops from Henry Adams to Saturn. Of course, she'd do it in a good and loving way. He wondered what his mom would think of his dad marrying again, and of her son finally getting his act together. He was sure she'd be okay with the upcoming marriage because she'd always wanted the people she loved to be happy, and as for Eli, he sensed that she was as proud of him as he was of himself.

Eli got up to start his homework. Although he was still disappointed with not winning the art competition it wouldn't stop him from sculpting. If anything, he was more determined than ever to make a name for himself through his art. He just hoped he'd get to do it in California. His phone sounded. It was a text from Amari: *Have you talked to Tamar yet?! Father's Day will be here in a hot minute!*

Chagrined, Eli put the phone down. He'd totally forgotten his mission. He put it on his to-do list and settled in to begin the assignment.

The following morning, Gen woke up excited. Her mobile home was coming today. Its imminent arrival and knowing Marie was back in her right mind made for a very happy Genevieve. Of course Riley and his hog were in town but nothing said she had to deal with them. All in all, her life was on track and the future looked bright.

Downstairs, she and Marie ate breakfast and for the first time in months actually shared a conversation. Gen asked, "So, what's on your agenda for today?"

"Going to go over to the Power Plant and talk to Trent. Need to make my peace with him and Lily, then get Rita Lynn's number."

"You're being very brave."

"Thanks," she said while mixing her eggs in with her grits the way she liked them. "And you? What's on your plate?"

"My mobile home of course."

Marie smiled. "Oh, that's right. Today's the day. Pretty exciting."

"Yes, it is."

"What time is it coming?"

Gen looked up at the clock on the wall. It was seven thirty. "They said they'd deliver it by eight, eight thirty. They have to hook up all the utilities but I should be able to move in hopefully by this afternoon." She felt like a little kid on Christmas Eve.

"Do you want me to drop you off on my way into town?"

"Would you, please?"

"No problem."

"That's another thing on my to-do list."

"What?"

"Buying a car. I need to learn to drive."

Marie looked impressed. "You're going all out."

"Tired of not being able to get around on my own. But first, my new home." Gen raised her coffee mug in salute. "To a new day for both of us."

Marie raised hers, too. "Amen."

To Gen's delight there were no problems with the installation or hooking up the utilities or the plumbing. As if the Fates were smiling down, all parties involved like the electric company workers showed up on time and by noon she, Lily, Bernadine, and Sheila entered the empty mobile home and looked around.

"It's almost as big as the ones on Tamar's land," Bernadine said, sounding impressed.

Sheila agreed. "Very spacious, Genevieve."

They were standing in the living room which was the space you entered when you first came through the door. There was a large window along the front wall and a matching one on the side wall. The living room flowed into the kitchen where the appliances she'd preordered stood ready to go. A hallway off the kitchen led to the back where the bathroom and two bedrooms were. She and her friends surveyed the larger one that she'd chosen as her own.

"This is nice, Gen," Lily said. "There's plenty of space for the queen-sized bed you ordered."

"When's your furniture coming?" Bernadine asked.

"Tomorrow. If I'd known the installation would go so smoothly I would've had everything delivered today." But she could wait another day. By tomorrow, she'd have a bed and a sofa and all the other pieces she'd ordered. Thanks to frugal Lily's help she'd been able to get what she needed to furnish the place and not be in the poorhouse afterward.

Lily said, "After the furniture comes, we can bring over all the stuff from the housewarming party that's at my place. Do you want help putting it all away?"

"That would be wonderful."

They moved back to the living room just as someone knocked on the door. Excited, Gen said, "My first visitor." But when she peeked through the window, her excitement died. "Dammit!"

"Who is it?"

"Riley."

Heads shook.

He knocked again. Louder.

Lily cracked, "You can't tell him to beat it, if you don't open the door."

Gen blew out a breath of frustration. "Lord, this man. I think he actually believes I'm going to let him live with me."

"You aren't going to, are you?" asked a wide-eyed Sheila.

"After what he put me through? Of course not." She heard him yell her name from his side of the door. Holding onto her temper, she pulled it open.

He smiled. "Hey, Genevieve."

"What do you want, Riley?"

"You were in such a hurry the other day we didn't get a chance to finish talking."

She asked again, "What do you want?"

"Can I at least come in?"

She studied him standing there in his dark glasses and worn black suit with the ever-present red carnation that was as fake as his smile. Everything in her wanted to slam the door in his face, but from somewhere inside came the reminder that she'd once loved this man. In tandem rose Reverend Paula's teachings: *kindness over rightness.* Gen knew she'd never take him back, and if talking to him would finally convince him of that then she would talk, otherwise she'd never be able to step fully into the new day she and Marie had saluted that morning. "Come in," she said tersely. She turned to her friends. "I need to speak with him. Can I call you later?"

They agreed and departed.

Alone with him she waited while he took a slow look around.

"This is nice," he said before bringing his attention back to her.

"I'm pleased with it."

"You know, the first time I saw you I thought you were the prettiest little thing I'd ever laid my eyes on."

She folded her arms and waited.

Her impatience seemed to throw him a bit and he cleared his throat. "You remember the first time we met?"

"I do. Clay brought you to Mal's eighteenth birthday party."

"Yep. Clay told me he was sweet on you, but the moment we were introduced I wanted to make you mine."

"Where's this going, Riley?"

"Just want to remind you how much we meant to each other once upon a time."

"You meant something to me but I never meant anything to you. Not really. Looking back, I think the only reason you courted me was to get next to my family's money and social status."

He startled, which let her know she'd hit the nail on the head, so she continued, "You married a naïve, small-town girl who'd never seen anything or been anywhere. You filled my head with all your big talk about our future and for forty years I was dumb enough to eat it up and believe you cared about me."

"I did."

"No. You didn't. If you had you would have gone to the doctor like I asked when I couldn't get pregnant."

He froze and stuttered, "I—I—."

When he looked away, she spoke with as kind a voice as she could muster. "I won't be letting you back in my life, Riley. I value myself too highly to be a victim again and I'm not apologizing for that."

"But I don't have anyplace else to go. What am I supposed to do?"

She threw up her hands. "Finally, the truth."

His jaw tightened.

"Did you think I wasn't smart enough to figure out why you're here?"

"If you hadn't walked out on me, I wouldn't be homeless."

"You're homeless because of you, Riley. Not me. You chose that damn hog over me. You chose to use Trent's name to steal that vehicle. Lord knows what else you have hanging over your head, but it's no longer my concern."

"You're mean, Genevieve."

"So be it, but read my lips. You will not be living with me. Not now. Not in the future."

They eyed each other like combatants in the ring. She didn't care about his anger. He needed to know where she stood and that she wasn't playing. "Anything else you want to talk about?"

"No," he snapped, and stormed out.

As the slam of the door faded away, Gen drew in a deep calming breath. She hoped he got it this time. If not, she'd explain it again and again until he did, or got tired of being told off. That twenty-year-old, naïve country girl he'd married was saddened by the failure of her marriage, but the grown-up Genevieve had already moved on.

Outside, Riley snatched open the door of Clay's truck and got in. He was so mad he could spit.

Clay asked, "Well?"

"She ain't taking me back."

"Told you that."

Clay drove toward town and Riley fumed. "Never cared about her anyway."

"Everybody knew that."

Riley stared.

Clay shrugged. "Marie tried to tell her. Her daddy tried to

tell her. Even I tried. But she was blinded by your BS and it took her forty years to learn who you really are."

"And who am I, Mr. Know-It-All?"

"A social climbing user with no conscience."

Riley's jaw dropped.

"You asked."

"Then why are you helping me?"

"For the ringside seat."

"What?"

"Let's just say I'm enjoying watching the man who stole my girl finally get his comeuppance."

Riley wanted to make him stop the truck and get out but he didn't have any way to get around or a place to stay, so he kept his mouth shut and tried not to think about Clay's description.

Arriving in town, Clay pulled up in front of what appeared to be a Quonset hut. Riley had never seen the place before. "What is this?"

"Kelly Douglas's beauty shop."

"Why are you stopping here?"

"So you can go in and ask for a barber job."

Riley's reply was dismissive. "I don't need you running my life, Clay Dobbs."

"Maybe not, but Bing will be back the day after tomorrow and you'll be needing money and someplace else to stay."

Riley's heart began pounding so hard he thought he might be having a heart attack.

Clay gave a smile that didn't meet his eyes. "I'll be at the Dog. Meet me there when you're done."

Riley decided he hated him. Hated him even more than he did Genevieve, but he had no choice but to get out. He walked to the door and silently cursed Clay when the truck pulled away.

Upon seeing Tamar July leafing through a magazine in one of the chairs, Riley wanted to run back out, but she glanced up and her sharp black eyes pinned his feet to the floor. "Afternoon, Riley."

"Uh, hello, Tamar."

"Used my grandson's name in vain lately?"

He hastily shook his head. "No."

"Good. I'd hate for him to have to give you another set of black eyes to match the one you already have. Nice shades."

Riley suddenly wished he'd stayed in LA. Since coming back he'd suffered nothing but blow after blow and now this day had gone from bad to worse.

A young woman holding a blow-dryer above the head of a Mexican woman he didn't know asked, "Can I help you?"

"Uh. I'm looking for the owner."

"That's me. Kelly Douglas. What can I do for you?"

"Name's Riley Curry. I'm told you might need a barber?"

"Really?" She glanced quizzically at Tamar.

Riley explained. "I—used to make my living as one."

Tamar said, "Town could use one, Kelly. Problem is, he's the only candidate."

"Is he trustworthy?" Kelly asked her while looking him up and down.

"No."

"Tamar!" Riley cried.

"You're not and everyone knows it, especially Genevieve."

Kelly froze. "Wait. Are you the ex-husband? The one with the pig?"

He nodded sorrowfully.

"I'm not hiring you. I heard the stories. She's godmother to my twins."

"Please. I really need a job. I'm homeless."

She threw back, "I heard you and that killer pig made her homeless once, too."

Riley turned to Tamar who responded, "Don't look at me. If the outlaw Julys were still alive you'd be stretched out on a flagpole with a flour sack over your head for what you did to my grandson."

Riley stiffened behind the shades. The humorous story of outlaw Neil July punishing storekeeper Armstead Malloy was an old Henry Adams legend. Malloy verbally defamed Neil's soon-to-be wife, Olivia, so to pay him back, Neil kidnapped him in the middle of the night. When sunrise came Malloy was, as Tamar described, tied fast to a flagpole and had a flour sack over his head. The only unamused person in town that day back in the 1880s had been Armstead Malloy.

Riley didn't want to beg, but, "Please. Just give me a chance. I promise to be the best employee you ever had."

The skepticism on the young woman's face was plain. "Come to think about it, I could use a barber, but I don't know about you. Let me talk to Ms. Brown. Technically this business belongs to her, so leave me your number."

"I—don't have a phone. You can reach me through Clay Dobbs, though."

"Okay. I'll be in touch."

He headed for the exit only to hear Tamar snap, "Riley!"

He went stock-still and turned.

"At least tell her thank you."

He took a quick look at the young woman's tight face. "Uh, thanks."

Kelly rolled her eyes. "Bye."

Feeling like a chastised child, Riley slunk out.

When Riley arrived at the Dog, Clay was in a booth eating. Mal was standing at the desk so Riley ignored his glare and quickly bypassed him and slid into the booth with Clay. He'd had enough of the Julys to last the rest of his life.

"How'd it go?" Clay asked, taking a bite of his sandwich.

"She wants to talk to Ms. Brown first. I told her to call you when she makes up her mind."

"Good. If she says no, Gary may have a job sweeping floors at the store."

Riley wondered how his life had gone to hell so swiftly. Granted, he'd done some things he now regretted, but he was the former mayor. He wasn't supposed to be sweeping floors or begging a little half-grown hairdresser for a job. And Clay? Riley had no idea that beneath that quiet laid-back demeanor lay the soul of a snake. That he would be enjoying Riley's misery was almost too much to bear, especially since Riley had always considered Clay one of his few friends.

"If you want to eat, go ahead and order. You can pay me back when you get hired."

Knowing the truth behind Clay's support, Riley didn't want to be beholden to him in any way ever again, but he was hungry and he couldn't think up a way out of this mess if he didn't fuel his brain, so he waved over a server and put in his order.

At the Clark home, TC greeted the girls after school, checked on the chili bubbling slowly to awesomeness in the Crock-Pot, and carried his cup of coffee and a few of the chocolate cookies he'd made earlier outside to the back porch. The spring weather seemed to be settling in for real, but it was still chilly enough in the mornings and evenings to need a jacket. Sitting in one of the chairs, he took in the unobstructed view of wide open fields still wearing winter's browns and golds, and savored the hush of the surroundings. Unlike back home, there were no sirens, horns, or bass blaring from cars, just the rustling breeze and the occasional birdsong. The calm allowed a man to think about many things. In his case two were most prominent and both were connected to Genevieve Gibbs. Being in her company opened a part of himself that had been on lockdown since Carla's death. He never imagined his heart stirring again, let alone contemplating courting a woman he'd known less than a month. It felt right though, and he wanted to explore what it might be like to be with someone he could laugh with, talk to and care about after so many years of going through life alone. The second was his reading problem. He'd decided to bite the bullet and ask her to be his tutor. If she distanced herself because of it, then she wasn't the lady for him. Taking out his phone, he called her.

Genevieve and Marie were in Marie's kitchen preparing to sit down to dinner. When her phone sounded and she saw TC's name on the caller ID, her brow furrowed.

"What's the matter?" Marie asked. "Please don't tell me it's Riley."

"It isn't."

"Then who?"

"Terence."

"Who?"

"Morgan Freeman."

Marie's eyes lit with amusement. "Then maybe you should answer it."

Gen picked up the phone. "Hey there," she said tentatively.

"Hate to bother you but I'd like to talk to you about something. Can I swing by after dinner and pick you up?"

"Where are we going?"

"How about the place where we had lunch the other day? I got Ms. July's number from Gary so we have permission."

Gen couldn't imagine what this might be about. "You aren't a serial killer, are you?"

He laughed. "No, ma'am."

"Okay. I guess so."

"Look, if you're uncomfortable . . ."

"No. I'm okay. How about six o clock?"

"Sounds good. See you then." And the call ended.

Marie, who'd watched the whole thing, peered at Genevieve's face. "A date?"

"I don't think so, but I'm not sure. He wants to talk, but he didn't say what about."

"Here?"

"No, at Tamar's picnic table by the creek."

"Sounds like a date to me."

"Hush," Gen replied, amused.

"Well, if he is a serial killer he'll never make it off the property because you know Tamar will be watching from the window with her shotgun by her side."

"I do." And she wasn't sure how she felt about that. On the one hand she liked the idea of Tamar acting as security but on the other hand, did she really want Tamar watching them? What if he kissed her? Immediately putting that out of her mind, she decided the Tamar factor didn't matter. What he wanted to discuss was more pertinent and she had to admit she was intrigued.

CHAPTER
11

On his way over to pick up Genevieve, TC grappled with what he wanted to say. He'd always been a straightforward kind of guy, but for some reason he wasn't sure simply blurting out his need for her help was the right approach. He was also nervous about how she'd react. He couldn't see her looking down on him because of his problem, so in theory he had no grounds for worry, yet it nagged him just the same.

When he reached her house, he drew in a deep breath, walked up to the porch, and pressed the bell. A tall, thin woman wearing cat-eye-shaped glasses opened the door.

"Hi. I'm here to see Ms. Gibbs."

"Come on in. She'll be down in a minute. I'm Marie Jefferson."

"I'm TC Barbour. Nice to meet you."

"Same here. Please, have a seat."

He sat on the couch.

"Gen says you're Gary's uncle."

"I am. His mother and my late wife were sisters."

"I see. We all thought real highly of Gary's mother."

He didn't know what to say to that so he simply nodded. When he heard footsteps on the stairs he stood. A second later Genevieve appeared wearing a soft gray turtleneck, jeans, and a smile that warmed him.

"Hello, Mr. Barbour."

"Hi. I hope this isn't too much of an inconvenience."

"No. Not at all."

Her roommate watched silently.

"Ready?" he asked.

"Let me grab my jacket."

She retrieved her leather from the closet and being a gentleman, he walked over to assist.

"Thanks," she said.

"You're welcome."

He saw approval in her roommate's eyes and said to her, "We shouldn't be gone too long."

She nodded and they departed.

Outside, he opened the door of his truck so she could get in. "This is nice," she said, checking it out.

"Thanks."

After taking his seat on the driver's side, he confessed, "Not sure why I wanted to go to the July place. I could've just as easily talked to you in your living room."

"Is that what you want to do?"

"No. I like the peace there."

"Then let's go to Tamar's, but I have to admit, I'm real curious about whatever this is."

"Sorry for the drama. It's not really a big deal, but it kind of is."

She had such a poker face he had no way of knowing what she was thinking, so he started the engine and drove off.

At the July place they parked and got out. The breeze blowing across the fields was crisp and bracing and the sun was making its way to the horizon. When they reached the picnic table, she sat but he stood with his back to her and gazed out at the slow-moving current in the creek.

"So, what did you want to talk to me about?" she asked quietly.

He grabbed his courage. "I want to learn to read." He let the words settle before turning to gauge her reaction. "Surprised?"

There was wonder in her eyes and then kindness. "I am. I'm pleased too, though. This couldn't have been easy."

He turned back to the creek. "No."

"Of course I'll help."

"Thank you."

Gen viewed the rigid set of his shoulders and back and wanted to smooth the tension somehow. His request could've knocked her over with a feather. Having worked with others with the same deficiency she sensed something else. "I don't think less of you, Terence."

He smiled. "Worried about that."

"No need to. I've been enjoying your company. This doesn't change that or who I perceive you to be."

He appeared more relaxed. "Good to know."

"When would you like to start?"

"Whenever you can fit me in."

"If you can give me a day or so to get my new place set up we can begin the lessons as soon as you'd like."

"That would be fine."

"And if you prefer to keep this just between the two of us, we can. I don't want you to be uncomfortable."

He nodded his thanks.

So for the next few minutes he talked about living with his lifelong problem, all the jobs he'd held and ultimately lost because of it, and the pledge he'd made to his wife.

"Do your children know?"

"Only Bethany. The boys don't."

Gen's heart went out to him in much the same way it had with Mrs. Rivard, but there was an added component—the connection being with him had created. She wanted him to succeed. That he would trust her with his secret and have the courage to ask for her help only increased his standing in her eyes.

"Brought you something." He reached into his coat and took out a small zip-locked bag and handed it to her.

"Cookies?" she asked, puzzled.

"Made them this morning. Thought you might like a couple."

She laughed softly, "Never had a man bring me cookies before." She opened the bag and took a bite of one. "Oh, these are good! Are you trying to butter up the tutor?"

"Figured a bribe might help me pass."

"You are something, Mr. Terence Barbour."

"You're pretty fabulous yourself, Ms. Genevieve Gibbs."

Genevieve went all sparkly inside. "How about you call me Genevieve."

"And you can call me TC or Terence."

"I think I prefer Terence."

"Then for you I'll be Terence."

A voice rang out. "Getting dark, Mr. Barbour. Time to take her home."

He froze and looked around.

Gen chuckled. "That's Tamar. She's probably been watching us since we got out of your truck."

"I didn't know we had a chaperone."

"She comes in handy now and again."

"I'll remember that for next time." He paused and said in a serious tone, "I want to thank you for making this easy."

"You're welcome. And thanks for the cookies."

"Anytime."

"We should probably get moving before she fires a warning shot over our heads."

"You're kidding, right?"

Genevieve got up from the table. "She loves that shotgun almost as much as she loves Olivia."

"Who's that?"

"Her truck."

His laughter rang out against the quiet. "Lord have mercy, this town."

"No place like Henry Adams."

They walked back. He handed her into the truck and drove her home.

When they got to Marie's he came around and helped her down. "Thanks."

"You're welcome."

"What's on your plate for tomorrow?"

"Taking Doc Reg to the airport in the morning. You?"

"Going to spend the day waiting on my furniture to arrive and putting away all the housewarming gifts my friends got for me."

"Sounds like fun. Okay. I'll walk you up."

"That's not necessary."

"Maybe if we were under twenty-five, but since we're not . . ."

Pleased by the show of chivalry, Gen surrendered and let him escort her to the door. When they reached it, she met his eyes. "Good night, Terence."

" 'Night, Teach."

Chuckling at that, she went inside. She was hanging up her jacket when Marie came out of the kitchen.

"Well? What did he want?"

"It was personal."

"Oh come on, Genevieve."

"Would you want me spreading your business?"

"There aren't any secrets in this town. Please."

Gen laughed. "True, but I'm not telling you."

"He didn't ask you to marry him, did he?"

Gen rolled her eyes. "No, Marie. Not walking down the aisle."

"He is kind of cute, though."

"And he makes fabulous cookies. Want one?" Gen tossed her one.

Marie caught it deftly and took a bite. "Oh, these are good. Cute and can cook? If you don't want him, I'll take him off your hands."

Genevieve laughed. "Going to my room now, Marie." She started up the steps.

Marie called after her, "I'm just saying."

Upstairs, Gen plopped down on the bed. She was still bowled over by both his request and courage. She'd do her best to honor the faith he'd placed in her. By the time they were done, he'd be able to conquer *War and Peace* if he wanted to. She helped herself to another of his cookies. And yes, he was very cute.

TC walked back into the Clark house feeling pretty good. Genevieve had been incredibly kind. He wanted to do something nice for her and he knew just the ticket. Gary was working late so he climbed the stairs and knocked lightly on Leah's door.

"Come on in." When she looked up from her computer screen and saw him, she said, "Hey Unc, did you talk to Ms. Gen?"

"I did." After dinner, he'd told her and Tiff where he was going but not why.

"You look pretty happy," Leah pointed out.

"I am. She's going to help me with something so I want to get her a housewarming gift."

"Like what?"

"Not sure, but she likes music."

"You could get her an iTunes gift card."

He thought about that but decided no. "I'd like it to be more personal—maybe a CD."

"Then you should try Amazon. Do you have an account?"

"No."

"I do. I can order it and you can pay Dad. My account is tied to his."

"Okay."

He watched her close out whatever she was working on and begin typing and clicking. He walked over to get a closer look. He couldn't read a word but was confident that in a few months he'd be able to type and click to his heart's content.

Tiff walked in. "What are you doing?"

"Unc wants to get Ms. Gen a housewarming gift. Maybe a CD."

Tiff came over and stood next to him.

"Did you get your laundry done, Lil Bit?" He'd introduced them to the washer and dryer a few days ago.

She nodded. "It's in the dryer. It's kind of nice not having to wait for Daddy to wash my stuff. Now I can wear my favorite jeans whenever I want. Thanks for teaching me."

"You're welcome."

Leah said, "Okay, we're at Amazon. Who are we looking for?"

"Wes Montgomery."

"Who?"

He rolled his eyes. "Greatest jazz guitarist to ever pick up an ax."

"If you say so."

He told her, "I still haven't had a chance to get my reading glasses replaced so help your old uncle out and read me some of those album titles." TC felt bad about lying to them again but decided once his lessons began he might tell them the truth. Knowing what great girls they were they might even want to help. But for now . . .

In the end, with the girls' help he found the CD he wanted and Leah closed out the purchase. "It'll be here maybe tomorrow. For sure the day after."

"Good."

Tiff said, "And you need gold paper to wrap it in."

TC was confused. "Why?"

"That's Ms. Gen's favorite color."

TC couldn't believe he was in a place where the people were so connected they knew each other's favorite colors. "Then gold it is. Thanks, ladies."

Later, TC was seated on the couch in the living room and watching the NBA when Gary came home from work. "Hey, Gary."

"Hey there, TC," he replied. He set down the soft-sided case that held his laptop and papers and tossed his coat over the chair. "Who's playing?"

"Golden State and Cleveland."

"Ah. Curry versus King James."

"Yeah, and Curry is lighting it up already. How'd your day go?" He pumped a fist as Curry sank another three.

"No complaints. Busted a couple of shoplifters. Argued with a supplier who tried to palm off a truckload of dead lettuce as fresh—the usual." He sat and eyed the game. "How was your day?"

"No complaints here, either. Took Trent to the airport. Asked Genevieve to teach me to read."

Gary sat up. "Wait. What did you say?"

TC smiled. "I asked Genevieve to teach me to read."

"What do you mean you asked her to teach you to read?"

"I can't read."

Gary seemed to finally get it. His voice dropped to a whisper. "You can't read? Since when?"

"Since forever."

"Are you serious?"

He nodded.

Gary fell back against the chair. "Wow."

"I'm what you call a functional illiterate. Have been all my life but being around Genevieve finally gave me the courage to do something about it."

Gary still looked stunned and appeared to have questions but didn't quite know what to ask, so TC helped him. "Hard to wrap your brain around it, isn't it?"

"Yeah. You're over sixty. How have you been able to get by?"

So TC took a few minutes to explain some of the techniques and strategies people like him used to make a way out of no way.

When he was done, Gary better understood and asked, "How can I help?"

"Not sure yet. I'll start lessons soon. Genevieve wants to wait until she gets settled into her new place."

"Are you going to tell the girls? I know they'd be supportive."

"Pretty sure I'll tell them at some point but not sure when. Wanted to let you know first."

"Okay. We're here for you."

"Thanks." It felt good having let Gary in on his plans and to have his support.

"And speaking of thanks, you've been a huge help to us. My stress level is way down. The girls are thriving. Tiff seems more sure of herself and I attribute that to you. Thanks," he said sincerely.

"You're welcome. I'm having fun."

"I'm glad you and Ms. Gen are hooking up. She's a great lady."

"Yes, she is."

Gary must have heard something in his tone because he

leaned forward and peered into TC's face. "Something else I need to know?"

"Nope."

Gary smiled. "Okay, Uncle Terence, be that way."

"Chili's in the Crock-Pot. Get yourself something to eat."

Gary shot him a grin. "Let me go up and see the girls first."

He climbed the stairs and a pleased TC went back to the game.

CHAPTER
12

Wednesday afternoon as her plane began its descent and the land below came into view, Paula thought back on the very first time she'd come to Oklahoma. It had been right after her mother's death and because her then fourteen-year-old self had no other family, her grandfather had agreed to take her in. Her mother Pat rarely mentioned the relatives she'd left behind in Blackbird, Oklahoma, so Paula knew next to nothing about them. Upon being met at the airport by her grandfather Tyree and her mother's younger sister, Della, Paula began to understand why her mother had been so close-mouthed. The distaste her grandfather displayed as his dark eyes raked her up and down was mirrored by Della. Instead of being met with the comforting open arms she'd imagined, there was a bristling hostility so chilling she wanted to run back to the plane. However, she had no choice but to follow them to his aging gray Buick in the parking lot. Too afraid to speak, she climbed into the backseat and rode the two hours to Blackbird without uttering a sound. Neither adult asked her about her flight, how she felt about her mother's passing or if she was hungry. Both adults stared ahead as if she weren't there. When the car left the interstate, the dirt roads they turned onto were foreign to a girl born and raised in Sacramento, as were the vast, undeveloped stretches of open land. The weathered houses they passed looked as tired and worn as the people she spied on the dilapidated porches, and the stillness and quiet made her feel as if she were entering a stagnant, lost-in-time world. Little did she know how correct that first impression would turn out to be.

The jolt of the plane's wheels making contact with the runway brought Paula back to the present. Knowing no one would be meeting her, she'd made arrangements for a rental car just as she'd done for last winter's visit. To his credit, her then dying grandfather tried to make amends for the painful years she'd spent under his care by asking for forgiveness and of course she'd granted him that, but she wondered if anything would ever totally eradicate the still open scars on her soul.

As she left the interstate and drove up the dirt road leading to her grandfather's place, nothing had changed. Houses were still in disrepair. Generations of men loitered outside the small concrete building that served as the general store. Teens who should have been in school walked down the edge of the road heading who knew where. Two of the girls had babies riding their hips and they all stared suspiciously as she drove by. As in many rural areas of the country the dropout rate and incidence of unwed teen pregnancy was high. Yet one more reason to be concerned about her young cousin, Robyn. Paula didn't want her searching for the love and validity she should be getting at home in a relationship that would leave her behind with a child of her own.

When Paula visited her grandfather in the hospital last winter he'd given her a key to his house so she'd have somewhere to stay when it came time for his funeral, or *home going* as it was sometimes called, because he knew he wouldn't see her again in this life. Inside, the shades were drawn and the space was filled with shadows and silence. The small front room still held the plastic-covered gold sofa and two matching chairs she'd never been allowed to sit on. Between the chairs stood a single end table that held his collection of decades-old issues of *Ebony* and *Jet* magazines. Both table and magazines lay beneath a thin layer of dust. Her attention moved to the wooden mantel above the old whitewashed brick fireplace often used for heating in the winter. On it stood Della's graduation picture. The sparkle in her aunt's young eyes and the smile on her face bore little resemblance to the bitter, tart-tongued woman she'd become. Beside it lay another picture turned facedown. With shaking hands and tears clogging her throat Paula picked it up and took in the portrait of her mother. The glass was dusty and dirty, but the smiling face resembled Della's so much they could've been twins even though Patricia was five years older. According to the story, the day her mother left Blackbird, Tyree placed the picture facedown. For all intents and purposes she became dead to him, and no one, not even Paula when she came to live with him, was allowed to look at it. The one time he caught her with the picture in her hands, he'd snatched his belt free of his pants and whipped her until she lay screaming and curled into herself at his feet. She never touched the picture again. Until now. Ignoring the dirty glass and the tears pouring from her eyes, she traced a loving finger down her mother's cheek. Going from her mother's abundant love to life with an old man who never offered a smile, let alone a kind word, had been so incredibly difficult she'd quietly cried herself to sleep each night for months. "I still miss you, Mama," Paula whispered.

"What the hell you doing in here!"

Paula didn't so much as flinch in response to her aunt's harshly voiced demand. While growing up, she'd learned to imagine being encased in battle armor to shield herself and her feelings from the verbal and sometimes physical attacks Della meted out with such twisted glee. That same armor enveloped her as she placed the picture upright on the mantel and replied evenly, "Papa gave me a key when he was in the hospital. He said I was to stay here when I came back for the funeral."

"He didn't say anything to me about you having a key." She was in her seventies now, average height and thin. The gray hair was severely pulled back and framed a dark face whose default expression had always been a mix of anger and disdain. Eyes gleaming with suspicion scanned the room as if to make sure everything was in its place. "Don't be bothering his stuff or thinking you're taking anything back when you leave."

"I'm not here for that. Just to pay my respects." She would be returning home with her mother's picture, whether Della pitched a fit or not. She also planned to clean up the place. Tyree Grant had been snake mean but he'd kept the house spotless and would be appalled by its present condition.

The sound of a car door closing caught Paula's attention. Della walked to the door and sneered through the screen at the unseen person. "Aren't you supposed to be at work?"

Seconds later, Calvin Tyree Spivey, her grandfather's out-of-wedlock son, entered. "Had the morning shift," he responded easily, his eyes shifting momentarily to Paula. "Saw the rental car, figured it must be Paula. Came by to see if she needed anything." He moved his attention her way. "Welcome back."

"Thanks."

"How was the flight?"

"Not bad."

He'd asked all the questions Della hadn't bothered with and it was a small balm. He was only a few years older than Paula. His mother, Anna Lee, had gotten involved with Tyree right out of high school. Much to Della's fury, her half brother had been shown all the affection she was denied. It also irritated her that he and Paula got along.

"Mama wants you to come to dinner tonight if you don't want to cook," Calvin said.

"I'd like that," Paula replied. While growing up, Della had forbidden her any contact with Anna Lee. "She still live in the same place?"

"Yes."

"She's having dinner with me and Robyn," Della declared.

That caught Paula off guard. She knew the only reason Della was laying claim to her time was to thwart Anna Lee and using Robyn as bait, but because Paula wanted to see her younger cousin, she ceded her aunt the round. "Tell your mother thank you for the invite. I'll take a rain check before I go home."

"No problem. I'll stop by tomorrow. Got some things I want to talk to you about."

"Like what?" Della demanded before Paula could reply.

In response, his eyes reflected a chill so reminiscent of

Tyree's, Paula was instantly transported back to her teen years when drawing her grandfather's ire could turn her to stone. Even Della took an unconscious step back. Then in a voice also reminiscent of his father's, Calvin stated, "It's none of your business."

Della's unbridled hate flared but he appeared unfazed. "I'll see you tomorrow, Paula."

"Thanks, Cal."

He left.

In the silence that followed, Paula knew retribution was coming. Della didn't like being challenged, especially by her father's bastard child and as always, Paula would have to pay, but just as Della's hand whipped out to slap her, Paula grabbed her aged wrist, held, and said through gritted teeth, "I've forgiven you for abusing me as a child but I will not let you abuse me as an adult."

Della showed surprise.

Reminding herself they were both children of God, Paula released her hold. "Now, let's go. I want to see Robyn."

Following Della in the rental car, Paula drew in a few deep calming breaths. The Bible said turn the other cheek, but she was pretty sure that didn't mean she was supposed to let her aunt assault her, and if it did, then she'd have to seek forgiveness in her nightly prayers. As a teen she'd endured whippings with belts, ironing cords, and doubled lengths of plastic-coated clotheslines. There'd been countless slaps to the face, punches to her chest and stomach and no one to make it stop. Her grandfather never intervened, nor did the neighbors. Della was the adult, Paula the child. No one in Blackbird saw fit to call the authorities. It just wasn't done. So she'd retreated into her books and got good grades and applied for scholarships, and eventually earned one to Spelman. On her eighteenth birthday, a letter arrived with a check for more money than she'd ever seen. It was her mother's life insurance money. It had been set aside for her and her alone. The check and scholarship were her ticket out of Blackbird and she never looked back.

Della's house was as run-down as its neighbors, and just the sight of it triggered painful memories. Paula parked and followed her up the warped wooden steps and inside. The dreariness of the interior was brightened by the smile that came over Robyn's face when she saw Paula, but the girl took one look at her grandmother and turned her attention back to stirring what smelled like a pot of beans on the stove. "Hi, Cousin Paula."

"How are you, Robyn?" Each time Paula saw her, Robyn's resemblance to her mother, Lisa, became more and more pronounced. Paula truly wished she knew why Lisa had left her behind.

"I'm good," she said, casting a wary glance at Della. "How was your flight?"

"It was fine. Come give me a hug."

She shot another quick look at her grandmother, placed the lid back on the large pot, and walked into Paula's embrace. Robyn's strong hug told all. Paula responded with all the love in her heart and silently prayed for the help the teen needed to be set free. After placing a kiss on the teen's forehead, Paula released her and asked, "How's school?"

"Good."

"Grades?"

Robyn offered a small smile. "Real good."

"Excellent."

Della asked, "You fry the chicken?"

"Yes, ma'am. It's in the oven keeping warm."

"Those beans done?"

"Yes, ma'am."

"Then let's eat."

The meal was a silent affair. Robyn seemed afraid to speak and Paula understood. What she didn't understand though was how Lisa could have abandoned her. Granted, Lisa and Della had never gotten along but to disappear for fifteen years with no word? "Chicken's good, Robyn," Paula said.

Robyn's eyes slid Della's way before she responded. "Thank you."

Della said sharply, "Finish eating and clean up. Need this kitchen mopped before you go to bed."

"Yes, ma'am."

Paula asked, "Do you have homework?"

Robyn nodded. "Yes. Geometry test tomorrow."

"Then how about I help you with the chores so you can get to your studying."

"She doesn't need help. Do you?" Della asked her granddaughter pointedly. Paula heard the veiled threat beneath the words and was certain Robyn did, too.

Her response was a softly spoken, "No, ma'am."

Paula wanted to insist but knew the price Robyn would pay if she forced the issue so she let it go. "Okay. Thanks for the great dinner. I'll be here until the funeral, so we'll talk soon."

"Okay," she whispered.

Ignoring the smugness in Della's eyes Paula rose from her chair. "I'm going back to Papa's. Aunt Della, if you need me, just call."

No reply was offered. Paula gave Robyn's shoulder a parting squeeze and left them alone. On the short drive back, she wiped at her angry tears and offered up a prayer on Robyn's behalf.

Inside her grandfather's house, she took her suitcase into her old bedroom and was again flooded by memories. The hard-as-a-rock twin bed was still there, as was the small, rickety nightstand that needed a magazine beneath one of its uneven legs to keep it upright. The walls appeared to have been painted at some point but they were still stark white. How many nights had she lain awake wishing to be elsewhere? In reality it had been four years' worth and each day crawled by like a century. Back then, her only escape had been school, where she'd been encouraged by teachers like Mrs. Cramer, who taught typing, and Mr. Ellis, who'd taught both English and Biology, and where she'd giggled with friends Fanny Jones and Kathy Stevens over the cute boys *du jour*. Over time, she'd lost touch with them, and wondered how their lives had turned out. Were Fanny and Kathy still around? She'd have to ask Calvin. It might be nice to reconnect. Putting the past aside, she unpacked and set about cleaning the house. She'd be staying at least until Sunday and the dust had to go. She found cleaning rags and detergent in the cabinet beneath the sink but when she turned on the tap the water came out in a thin stream and the pipes groaned in protest. Wondering what was up with that, she went into the bathroom and flushed the toilet. It worked but the bowl refilled at an incredibly slow pace. She hoped it wasn't something serious and made a mental note to ask Calvin about that too when he came by tomorrow. Issues with the water meant she couldn't mop the floors, but she didn't need water to dust or sweep so she threw herself into that. Once she was done the house looked better. She opened the back door and stepped out onto the small porch to get some fresh air. As she took in the large tree-lined yard the nightmare she'd had Sunday night came back. She saw her mother and the old woman digging, heard the butterflies moaning, felt their sharp wings beating like tiny razors against her face, but she remembered the skull in her mother's hand with the most clarity. It made her shudder and the sense of foreboding returned. Determined to ignore it, she walked back into the house and firmly closed the door behind her.

Because there was no Wi-Fi, Paula sat and read her Bible until nightfall, then prepared for bed. Passing her grandfather's bedroom, she gathered her courage and walked inside. The space was just as she remembered: same bed, dresser, and small closet. His presence was so strong she expected him to come up behind her and demand to know what she was doing. Shaking that off, she stepped in further. Growing up, she'd never been allowed in his room and she'd rarely violated the unspoken law even when she was home alone. She pulled open the closet door and the scent of Old Spice, his cologne of choice, wafted to her nose. Hanging inside were a few threadbare suits along with a small collection of blue and brown work shirts and pants that matched. She wondered if Della had plans for his things. For most of his life he'd worked for a wealthy white family in a town a few miles away as their handyman, doing everything from painting to lawn work to mopping their floors. The pay had been minimal but enough for him to stay on top of his bills, and it was steady. Paula had no idea what kind of financial shape he'd been in when he died or if he'd left a will.

She assumed Della knew the details. On the shelf above the clothes she spotted what appeared to be a thick book. Reaching up, she took it down. To her surprise it was an old photo album. Taking a seat on the bed, she blew off some of the dust and opened it. The photos were dull with age. There was one of him that looked to have been taken in his twenties. He was thin, dressed in a wide-legged pin-striped suit, and had a cocky smile on his handsome face. She could probably count on one hand the number of times she'd seen him smile. None had ever been directed her way. She turned more pages and found pictures of her mother and Della as youngsters and teens. The next picture stopped her heart. It was a wedding photo. The groom was her grandfather and the bride—a younger version of the old woman in her dream. Heart pounding, Paula read the name. Myrlie Parks. Her grandmother! Now she understood why the woman had looked familiar. Paula had seen her face in an album at Della's house years ago. Myrlie died when Paula's mother was in her teens. *What in the world!* She studied the picture again and in her face saw a resemblance to all the women in the family who'd come after her: Patricia, Della, Lisa, Robyn, and Paula herself. Unlike the families in Henry Adams no stories of Myrlie had been passed down. Paula knew her name, that she'd died, but nothing more. *Why were you in my dream?* There was no answer, of course. Closing the album, Paula placed it back on the closet shelf and left the room.

Later, lying in the dark on the hard uncomfortable twin bed, Paula's mind swirled with all she'd done, seen, and heard that day. There were so many unresolved issues, missing pieces, and pain. The priest in her said: Let go and let God. Paula hoped she could.

CHAPTER
13

The next morning back in Henry Adams, Clay and Riley were just finishing breakfast when Clay said, "Bernadine called a little while ago. Wants to see you."

Riley studied him over the cup of coffee in his hand. "She say what she wanted?"

"No."

Riley hoped it meant she'd be offering him the barber job. "Got some good news from the lawyer last night." Riley had spoken with him via Clay's phone.

"And?" Clay asked

"The dealership in LA dropped the charges."

Clay looked suspicious. "Why?"

"Because they got their vehicle back in one piece and didn't think it made sense to waste all that time and money trying to prosecute me. They took my age into consideration, too."

"So you got off scot-free."

Riley smiled smugly. "Yep. Just not allowed within fifty feet of their dealerships anywhere in the country and I can't set foot in LA County for the next three years. Which is fine and dandy because I'm never going back there anyway. Hate LA."

"What about the identity theft charges?"

"Dropped, too. Lawyer said he argued that I didn't do Trent any real harm. Didn't open a bank account, apply for a credit card, or sign his name to any documents. Apparently the prosecutor agreed." Riley guessed Trent wasn't going to be happy, but he didn't care.

"You were lucky," Clay said grudgingly, getting to his feet. "Let's hope you're lucky enough for Bernadine to hire you. I'll be ready to drive you over after you clean up the kitchen."

Riley froze. Wasn't he the guest? As Clay strolled out, Riley glared at his back but got up and got to work.

Once the kitchen was done, Clay drove him to the Power Plant and dropped him off. "Meet me at the Dog when you're done."

Riley entered Ms. Brown's office and tried to ignore the chill in her eyes as he took a seat.

"Riley," she said coolly.

"How are you, Ms. Brown? You wanted to see me?"

"Yes. Kelly said you stopped by her place yesterday wanting a job."

"Yes."

"And why should I hire you after all the commotion you've caused?"

He cleared his throat. "Well, I really need a job. I thought I'd run for mayor again in the next election but until then—"

The expression on her face stopped him cold.

"You plan to run for mayor again." It was a statement. Not a question.

"Sure. Why not? I have a lot of ideas that'll help this town grow." And he might find a way to prove his theory that she'd gotten her millions illegally.

She shook her head. "What's the latest on your court case?"

"The dealership dropped the charges." He didn't tell her the rest because it was really none of her business.

"I see." She didn't appear happy. "I made some calls last night to see if a barber was indeed needed and was told by men like Mal and others that there was, and that you were fairly decent at it."

"I was the best," he boasted. Inwardly though he was pleading for her to say he could have the job. Regardless of his good news, he was still flat broke and homeless.

"I'm going to give you the job temporarily."

Riley stiffened. *Temporarily?*

"If you prove yourself to be an exemplary employee over the next thirty days the job will be yours permanently."

Recalling being chastised by Tamar, he said, "Thank you, Ms. Brown."

She leaned forward. "But let me warn you, if you steal even a dime or do anything remotely illegal, Eustacia's lawyers won't be able to save you from *my* lawyers. Do you understand me?"

He nodded hastily.

"Good. Report for work tomorrow at nine and Kelly is in charge. Not you."

"Okay." He thanked her again and beat a hasty retreat.

Because the day was so nice the students at the Marie Jefferson Academy took their lunch outside and Amari asked Eli, "So are you going to talk to Tamar about the Father's Day party or not?"

"I am. Today. Promise."

Amari said, "Good, because I talked to my mom about helping us order the material for the flags and she suggested we come to the next Ladies Auxiliary meeting so they can assist with oversight."

Leah said, "That's a really good idea. Did you tell her not to tell your dad?"

He nodded. "She knows what's up. So who wants to go to the meeting with me?"

Devon asked, "Why do you get to go?"

"Because he has the gift of gab," Preston pointed out.

"Can I go?" Zoey asked.

"Sure."

"I want to go," Leah said.

Tiffany did too and so did Devon.

Amari threw up his hands. "How about we all go and be done with it?"

Everyone agreed. Except Wyatt, who sat eating silently. Eli glanced his way but said nothing. On the way back into the building, Eli stopped him. "Hey. You want to come by my house later and we go look at some skateboards?"

He shrugged. "Sure."

"Your enthusiasm is scintillating," Eli deadpanned.

Wyatt smiled.

That made Eli feel better. "I'll text you after I talk to Tamar."

Wyatt gave him a nod and walked away.

Eli was nearly at the door when Crystal stopped him and said, "Hey. What's up with you and Sam? You two haven't been joined at the hip lately."

He shrugged. "Split City. Her call."

Crystal searched his eyes. "You want her killed?"

He laughed. "No."

"Just checking. You're okay, though?"

"I am."

She nodded at him and went inside. Eli thought he couldn't have a better friend.

Heading to Tamar's after school, Eli didn't see her having an issue with them using her yard for the party, but he knew better than to assume when Tamar was involved. He'd sent her a text earlier, so she was expecting him. Walking to the porch, he thought back to the very first time they met. He and his dad had just arrived in town and Eli was an angry pain in the ass. She'd set him straight right quick, and he hadn't liked it, or her, at all. They ended up talking about his mom's death and when the conversation was over, he realized what a great lady she was. That she'd offered him pancakes that day hadn't hurt. He knocked. She opened the door.

"Come on in."

"Thanks."

She gestured for him to take a seat. She sat too and asked, "So what can I help with? Am I right in assuming this is another one of my great-grandson's grand ideas?"

"Yes, but it's a good one. We want to have a Father's Day celebration and your permission to have it here."

"Since this is Amari's plan I have to ask if the police will be involved."

"No, ma'am." Eli knew she was referencing an incident that took place the first year Amari, Preston and Crystal came to town. Amari's plan to help Crystal run away so she could find her bio mom went sideways and landed them all in the backseat of a squad car. It happened before he and his dad moved to Henry Adams. In a way he wished he'd been around to witness it, but in reality was glad he hadn't been.

"Good."

"Do you have a date for this?"

He gave her the date and watched her put it in her phone. She had to be the most tech savvy senior citizen he'd ever met.

"Okay," she said. "I have it marked. So tell me what this celebration will involve."

He told her about the food and the flags and the games they wanted to play and she listened attentively.

"Do the fathers know?" she asked when he finished.

"No. We want it to be a surprise."

"Pretty hard keeping secrets around here but it can be done."

"Leah's uncle, Mr. Barbour, has offered to help too, and Ms. Lily suggested we attend the next Ladies Auxiliary meeting so they could do the oversight thing."

"Good idea. This sounds pretty straightforward. You'll need tables, chairs—you can borrow those from the rec—plastic ware, plates, tablecloths, napkins, condiments—you might want to write all this down, Eli."

He startled. "Oh, sorry. You're right." He took out his own phone and made a list.

"I'll have Gary save potato sacks for the sack races. I'll tell them I need them so he won't suspect anything."

Eli liked having her on their side.

She asked, "If you think of anything else bring it to the meeting. I'll also let it be known that I need you children at that meeting so you won't have to lie about where you're going or why."

"Thanks, Tamar."

"You're welcome. So sorry neither you nor Crystal won the art competition."

"Yeah. Thanks. We were both pretty disappointed."

"Understandable, but you have a bright future. There'll be triumphs ahead."

"I guess."

"Gemma said you're taking Wyatt under your wing."

He wondered if there was anything in town that she didn't know about. "I'm going to try."

"That's a good thing, Eli."

"We'll see. He doesn't seem real happy about it."

"That's okay. You weren't real happy about me when we first met."

He grinned. "I was thinking about that on the way over. I was a mess back then."

"True, but look at you now. It's been a pleasure watching you grow into yourself."

Eli met her eyes and saw the kindness there. "That means a lot."

"Whether it does or not, it's the truth. No matter where you go you'll always take Henry Adams with you."

He made the split-second decision to seek her advice. "Is it wrong for me to want to go back to California?"

She didn't hesitate. "No. The spirit sets up its own call. Have you talked to your dad?"

"No."

"Why not?"

"He's just going to say no."

"And you know that how?"

"You sound like Crystal."

"Lord, I hope not. But then again, she's growing into herself, too." Her eyes showed her amusement. "Tell me what you've been feeling."

So for the next few minutes he poured out his heart and longings. She didn't interrupt. She simply listened. And when he was done, she said, "Either you ask your dad or don't. Both offer a path. If he says yes, you'll open the path that California offers. If he says no, your future will emanate from here. However, if you don't ask, you may never know what California brings. Does that make sense?"

He nodded.

"Step out on faith, son. You can't go through life cowering because someone might say no. If the Dusters had cowered none of us would be here today."

She was right, of course, and although he wasn't African American the lessons he'd learned about the Dusters and their quest were applicable to his own life.

"Does this help?" she asked.

"It does, Tamar. Very much."

"Good," she responded softly. "Keep me posted. I can't ask Jack for you but I'm here if you need to bounce things off me."

That meant a lot, too.

"Okay," she said, rising to her feet. "Go home so an old lady can go on with her day."

He stood, too. "Thanks, Tamar."

"You're welcome."

As he started to the door, she said, "Eli?"

He stopped.

"Your mother's real proud of you. Keep making her smile."

With a full heart, he stepped through the door and back out into the afternoon sunshine.

Buoyed by Tamar's praise and advice, Eli drove to Wyatt's.

"Why do you like skateboarding?" Wyatt asked when he got in the car.

"I'm an only child and when I started it was something I could do by myself."

"Never thought about it that way."

Eli said, "Look, if you don't want to do this and want to do something else, we can."

"No. It's okay. I've been looking at videos on YouTube. Can you do all those tricks?"

"Maybe not all but I'm pretty good. I'll show you my trophies sometime."

The wonder on Wyatt's face made him chuckle. "I ride like a boss, kid. Don't believe me—just watch."

Wyatt grinned.

And with that, Eli drove them toward Franklin for Wyatt's first visit to a skateboard store.

Inside, Eli nodded at the proprietor, a guy named Mike, and introduced him to Wyatt. He suggested one of his beginner's boards and they looked at a few. Eli rejected a couple of them because the balance was a bit off when Wyatt stood on them and another because the paint job was flat-out ugly.

Wyatt asked, "Are there any with maps on them?"

Mike stopped. "Maps."

"Yeah. I want to be a cartographer."

Mike seemed confused so Eli translated. "He wants to study maps."

"Oh." But he looked at Wyatt like he'd come from Mars.

Eli told Wyatt, "You can probably find some decals online for your board."

"Good."

In the end, they found a board to Eli's liking, along with

a helmet and pads for his knees and elbows. Mike threw in a cheap pair of gloves as well. Once the purchases were rung up they headed back to the car.

"Thanks, Eli. Never had anybody do something like this for me before."

Eli saw the sincerity in his eyes. "You're welcome. Just trying to be a friend."

And they drove back to Henry Adams.

When he walked in his dad said, "I just got a call from Sam's parents. She wants to finish out the year at Franklin High with her friends."

"Oh. Okay."

Upstairs in his room, all he could think was: so much for that.

Marie wasn't trying to be a friend to Rita Lynn, but she was sitting at her laptop waiting for their Skype connection to start so she could apologize and cross her high school nemesis off her 12 Step List. She'd already made her peace with Trent, who'd reacted in much the same way as his father in declaring he was just happy to have her back in his life. Marie wasn't sure how Rita Lynn would react so when her face came up on the screen Marie drew in a calming breath and said, "Hey, Rita Lynn."

"Hi, Marie. How are you? Good to see you."

"Same here. Look. I just wanted to apologize face-to-face for my actions during your trip."

"Not necessary."

"I think it is."

"I hurt you, Marie. You going off on me was a normal reaction."

"But I could've acted like an adult. As Genevieve said, my beef with you was forty years old."

"True, but I'll be visiting Henry Adams a lot and I just want us to go forward. We're too old to be rolling around on the floor."

Marie found herself smiling at that. "You're right. So, pax?"

"Pax. How are things there? What's Gen up to?"

"She just moved into her new mobile home."

"How exciting."

They talked for the next thirty minutes, which Marie found amazing, and when they were done and Rita Lynn signed off, Marie sat back and smiled. She'd made amends with everyone now and it felt good to be at peace with herself again.

She was picking up the phone to text Genevieve to let her know how things had gone with Rita Lynn when she heard a knock on the door. She went to the window and didn't recognize the dark blue minivan parked in the driveway but opened the door. A well-dressed woman in a business suit stood on the other side. She had light brown skin and appeared to be about Lily's age. "Ms. Jefferson?" she asked.

Marie heard traces of the South in her voice and replied warily, "Yes."

"We've never met but my name's Brandy French. I'm Brian's wife."

"Brian?" The name took a few seconds to register. When it did Marie's heart sped up. He was the son she'd put up for adoption. "Has something happened to him?"

The woman shook her head. "No, ma'am, but I wanted to talk to you. Is it okay if I come in? I promise not to take up a lot of your time."

Curious as to what this was about, Marie opened the screen and stepped back. "Come in."

The woman gave her a nervous smile. "Thanks."

They sat and Marie sensed the visitor choosing her words. "First of all," she said, "I didn't know Brian had come to see you, but when I found out I was pretty mad at the way the visit turned out."

"What do you mean?"

"Tell me if I'm wrong, but if I'd put a child up for adoption and that child suddenly turned up out of the blue, I'd assume the child wanted to get to know me, at least a little bit."

"You aren't wrong." The day had been painful. The visit left her so brittle she thought she might shatter into a thousand pieces.

"I want to apologize on behalf of me and the girls. Your granddaughters."

A startled Marie searched her face.

"When I found out how cruelly you'd been treated, I wanted to take a belt to him. He doesn't think sometimes. At all."

"Oh, Brandy," Marie whispered. "Thank you for this, but why are you here?"

"Brian felt real bad after I broke it down and explained to him how you probably felt, and we'd like to start over. We'd like to have a relationship with you. Him, me and the girls. Is that okay?"

Marie began to cry.

Brandy got up and took her hands. "Please don't cry," she said through her own tears. "I'm so sorry he's an idiot. And for what it's worth, his adopted mom, Janice, was pretty mad at him, too."

Marie looked up.

"She sends her regards and would like to meet you one day if you wouldn't mind. She raised him but you gave him life. She said a child can never have too much love."

Marie felt like she'd stepped into another dimension. "Are you in town on business?"

"No ma'am. I came all the way from Memphis just to see you. Took me a bit to find Henry Adams, but I'm here."

"Oh my lord. Is he with you?"

"No ma'am. Too ashamed to show his face. I'm here as the lead scout so to speak. He wasn't sure you'd agree to see him again."

"I would love to see him again, and I would love to have a relationship with you and the girls, and meet his adopted mom."

"Good. I feel so much better. Do you want to see their pictures?"

Marie realized she was shaking. "Yes. How old are they?"

"Dina is sixteen and Andrea is fourteen."

Brandy handed over her phone. "They favor their dad a lot, which means they favor you a lot."

Marie could barely see them through her tears. "They're lovely."

"They come from lovely stock."

Marie laughed. "May I keep you?"

"Yes, ma'am. I'll be here until the Good Lord turns out the lights."

Marie stood, opened her arms, and Brandy walked into the embrace. Marie whispered, "I'm so glad you're here."

"Me, too."

As Marie savored the fullness in her heart, Reverend Paula's advice rose in her mind: *Make peace with yourself so your blessings can flow . . .* Marie was glad she had.

For the next two hours Brandy and Marie forged a bond Marie had craved since giving up her son at birth. When time came for Brandy to return to the airport for the evening flight back to Memphis, they made arrangements to meet again, this time with the rest of her family. "Is it okay if we come back for Mother's Day?"

Tears stung Marie's eyes again. "Yes. That would be very okay."

They shared a final parting hug and Marie knew her life was now complete. Heart full, she watched Brandy back the van down the driveway. As she drove away, Marie waved, wiped her tears, and picked up the phone to call Genevieve to share her spectacular news.

After talking with Marie, Genevieve put down her phone and wiped away her own joyful tears. What exciting news. She was so elated for her best friend and couldn't wait to meet the son and his family. She was also happy for herself. Her furniture had arrived. Gazing proudly at it and all the beautiful touches supplied by her friends, she decided that she and Marie were the two most blessed women on the planet.

She was on her way to the kitchen to cook her first meal when the doorbell sounded. She opened the door and there stood Terence.

"I know I probably shouldn't have just dropped by without calling first, but I brought you a housewarming gift."

She was so glad to see him and he was so good-looking it took her a moment to remember her manners. "Come on in, please."

He entered and looked around. "This is nice."

"It is, isn't it? Have a seat."

"No, I'll only be a minute." He reached into his coat and withdrew a small square object wrapped in gold foil paper. He handed it to her. "Brought you something to thank you for your kindness. The girls said gold is your favorite color."

Gen was having difficulty breathing. "It is. May I open it?"

"Of course."

She pulled off the paper. It was a CD of Wes Montgomery's greatest hits. "Oh my."

"I hope you don't already have it."

"I don't," she said, flipping it over to read the names of the selections it held.

"I had Leah order it for me. She said Amazon would get it to me faster than trying to find it in a store."

"Amazon is amazing. This has all of his classics, including 'Bumping on Sunset.'" It reminded her of their first meeting. Going forward, she'd always associate the tune with him.

"Yes, it does."

"Thank you so much. This was very sweet of you."

"Glad you like it."

"I do."

They stood in the silence, pretending they weren't staring at each other and failing miserably. Gen wanted to ask him to stay for dinner but she wasn't that bold yet. He solved the issue by saying, "I'll let you get back to your evening."

An invitation to stay and have dinner almost slipped out. "Thanks for dinner. I mean for the CD." Embarrassment burned her cheeks.

He smiled. "Can I take you to the movies tomorrow night?"

When she finally regained her ability to speak, she said, "Yes. I'd like that."

"Good. I'll pick you up at seven."

She walked him to the door. "We can start your lessons whenever you have the time."

"Okay, let's talk about it tomorrow."

"Sounds good. Thanks again for the CD."

"You're welcome. See you tomorrow." He gave her a wink and walked back out into the evening's fading light.

Genevieve closed the door and with her back pressed against it slowly melted to the carpeted floor. Kicking her feet with joy, she crowed, "I have a date, ladies and gentlemen. A real live date!"

CHAPTER
14

Having received a text from Calvin that he'd be by around three, Paula drove over to the nearest fast food place to grab breakfast and stopped by a small grocery for provisions to get her through the weekend. As she placed her items on the belt, the cashier, a short Black woman with a kind smile, asked, "You visiting, ma'am?"

Paula wasn't offended. This was a small town and unfamiliar faces stood out. "Yes. I'm here for my grandfather's funeral."

"What's his name?"

"Tyree Grant."

The cashier paused in the midst of ringing up her order. "Della's daddy?"

"Yes. I'm his granddaughter, Paula."

The woman studied Paula's face. "You're not Della's child."

"No, she's my aunt. My mother was Patricia. Della's older sister."

The woman seemed to be thinking, then said, "I remember now. You're Anna Lee's niece."

Paula froze.

But the woman was checking the display on the register and didn't notice Paula's shocked face. "That'll be fifty-five seventy-two."

Moving like a zombie Paula swiped her debit card and was handed the receipt. The woman finished by saying, "Condolences on your loss, honey. If you see Anna Lee, tell her Gaylene said hi."

"Thank you. I will," Paula managed to whisper.

Outside in the car, Paula sat and drew in a couple of deep breaths, hoping to calm her racing heart. *Anna Lee's niece?* All her life, Paula wondered who her father had been. Her mother always waved the question away by saying it didn't matter and after a while Paula stopped asking, but she'd assumed her mother had gotten pregnant after leaving Blackbird by a man in California. She cast her mind back to her teen years with her grandfather and vaguely remembered Anna Lee having an older brother, but couldn't recall if she'd ever met him. For sure she didn't know his name. She drew trembling hands down her face. Were she and Anna Lee really related? After driving to Tyree's to put the food away, she got back in the car and headed to Anna Lee's.

"Paula!" Anna Lee exclaimed happily when she answered the door. "Come in. How are you, honey?"

"I'm well."

"Have a seat. It's so good to see you."

The gold couch and chairs were encased in plastic. "Good to see you, too."

For a woman who'd gone to school with Della, Anna Lee Spivey with her red bob wig, long fake nails, and carefully applied makeup was still a beautiful woman. The skinny jeans and low-cut blouse showed off a trim but buxom figure. There was gold in her ears, hanging from her neck and circling her wrists.

"Can I fix you a drink?" she asked, walking over to the cut-glass decanters sitting on a glass tray on top of a large black piano.

"No, thank you."

"Oh, that's right. You're a preacher now. Sorry. Mind if I have one?"

"No."

"I know it's not noon yet, but what else is there to do in this godforsaken place? We drink, steal each other's husbands and wives and call it living." She raised her glass to Paula in salute and downed a shot. Pouring herself another one, she took a seat on one of the chairs. "My condolences on your loss."

"Thanks. My condolences to you, too."

"Thanks. For all his faults, Tyree was good to me and my son. Not sure how we would've survived without him. Have you seen Della?"

"Yes. Yesterday."

Anna Lee sipped and shook her head. "The devil's hand-maiden. If she could've figured out a way to kill me and not get caught I'd've been dead for thirty years now. We've hated each other since high school. Stole Louis from me junior year and I never forgave her."

Louis was Della's first husband. He left her for another woman, or so the story went.

"Paid her back, though. After graduation, I stole her daddy." She winked and raised her glass again. "Wasn't hard. Every woman in town knew Tyree couldn't keep his pants zipped after his wife died."

Paula didn't want to hear any more. "Can I ask you a question?"

"Sure."

"Are we related?"

She paused. "Yes. You're my niece."

Paula now had the truth but wasn't sure what to do with it.

"Pat never told you who your father was?"

"No."

"Your daddy was my brother, Darren."

"Is he still alive?"

"No, honey. He died in prison about fifteen years ago now."

"What was he in prison for?"

"He and some three guys robbed a bank over in Tulsa. One of his buddies shot and killed a guard. He got the chair. Darren got life."

Paula thought she was going to be sick.

"I can't believe she didn't tell you. He wasn't all that bad growing up. Yeah, he was in and out of trouble, but it was petty stuff. Shoplifting. Stealing cars. That kind of thing."

A thousand questions ran riot in Paula's head. "So, did he know she was carrying me when she left town?"

"Everybody knew, and she didn't leave town on her own. Tyree took her to Oklahoma City, gave her fifty bucks, put her on a train, and walked away."

Her eyes widened.

"That's what some families did with unmarried pregnant young women back then. Kicked them out. Now me, I come from a long line of bastards so when Tyree knocked me up my parents didn't trip. He didn't either once he found out the baby was a boy. Can you spell hypocrite?"

Paula was filled with so many conflicting emotions. Her

poor mother. "So was my father already in jail when I came to live here?"

Anna Lee nodded. "Yes. He went in a few years after Tyree put Pat on the train."

Paula wondered if her mother knew that and was the reason she kept saying it didn't matter. Paula was going to have a lot of prayers to offer up later. A lot. "Does Della know the truth about what happened? She told me my mother left here willingly."

"We were five years younger than Pat, so I don't know for sure. Only reason I know what happened was because my uncle was the one who drove them to Oklahoma City."

Paula had heard enough. Overwhelmed, she stood.

Anna Lee said, "I'm glad you got away from here and made something of yourself, Paula. You're one of the lucky few."

"It's never too late to change your life."

She scoffed. "Yeah, right. I barely finished high school. I have no skills to speak of and I'm of a certain age. Go where? Do what? I was born here. I'll die here. Maybe in my next life." She drained her glass, got to her feet, and walked over to the piano.

Paula prayed that she'd somehow find peace in her life. "Thank you, Anna Lee. I'm going to take off. I'll see you later."

Anna Lee waved dismissively and was pouring another drink when Paula walked out the door.

She sat in the car a moment and replayed the startling revelations. All she could think about was how terrified her mother must have been the day Tyree took her to the train station and walked away. Had she cried and begged him to change his mind? What went through her mind when the train pulled out and she knew she was alone and on her own?

Heartbroken, Paula started the engine. Driving back, she could barely see the road for her tears.

Calvin showed up that afternoon as promised. "Mama told me you dropped by earlier," he said when Paula opened the door to let him in.

"I did."

They both took seats and Paula continued, "And I found out that I'm your niece and your cousin."

He nodded. "I know. Crazy, right?"

"That's a pretty apt way to put it. Did you know?"

"I did. Figured you did, too."

"No. I thought my father was someone she met in California. Della always said my mother left here willingly because she was uppity and thought she was better than everybody else."

"I've learned that if Della says it's raining you'd better get up and go look. Sorry for your pain."

"Thanks." She remembered describing Blackbird as a snake pit. Little did she know the snakes in her own family would deliver the most venomous bite.

"You okay?"

"Trying to decide. It's not every day you learn your father was serving life in prison. I'm usually the counselor, not the one in need of counseling. I'll be fine. Just need time to process it all." *Why had Della lied?*

"How about we ride up to Boley for some dinner. Nice little place there that serves pretty good food. We can talk while we eat."

"I'd like that." She suddenly remembered what she was supposed to ask him. "Did Papa ever mention anything about problems with the plumbing?"

"What's it doing?"

She took him into the kitchen and showed him the weak stream of water.

"Might be the sump pump needs looking at," he said. "No telling how old the thing is. I'll get somebody to check on it."

"Any idea how much it might cost?"

He shrugged. "We'll cross that road when we get to it."

"Okay."

On the drive to Boley, she surveyed the passing landscape. "What's it like in the townships these days?" At one time the state had been home to over fifty all-Black townships. Now only a handful remained.

"Folks are hanging on. Doing the best they can with what they have. It's tough, though."

"Why did you stay?"

He shrugged. "This is my home. Mama wouldn't know how to live anywhere else and probably neither would I."

"And your kids. How are they?" He and his wife, Shannon, had been divorced for decades.

"Families of their own now. My daughter Michelle's in Oklahoma City. David's down in San Antonio. Both are doing well. I don't see them a lot, though."

Paula heard the sadness in his voice.

He asked, "What about you? How's life?"

"It's good. Too scared to complain." They laughed. She told him about Bernadine and Henry Adams. "She and the town have been a blessing to me."

"No sweetheart? Your religion lets you marry, right?"

"Yes, but there's no special person in my life. Still waiting on God to send me someone." She'd never admitted that out loud before. *Ask and ye shall receive*, the voice in her head said. She smiled inwardly and turned her attention back to the landscape.

Calvin was right. The food at the little joint in Boley was great. As she ate her collards, sweet potatoes, and catfish, she asked him, "So what did you want to talk to me about?"

"Tyree's will."

"I wondered if he had one."

"Oh yes, and Della's going to stroke out."

"Why?"

"He didn't leave her a dime."

For some reason Paula didn't find that surprising. "So is this like a life insurance policy?"

"No. It's a stock portfolio worth about two hundred and fifty thousand dollars."

Paula's eyes went wide as plates. "What?"

He smiled and nodded. "And he left half of it to me and the other half to you."

Paula's fork slipped from her hand and clattered to the floor.

CHAPTER
15

Riley had Clay drop him off bright and early for his first day at work. In fact, he beat Kelly there.

"Morning," she said as she unlocked the door. "Thanks for showing up on time."

Feeling self-important, he followed her inside. She hit the lights and put down her bag. "You'll use that station over there," she said, pointing to a chair and a table.

"No barber chair?"

"Did you bring one?" Her frosty eyes held his and when he couldn't stare her down, he shook his head.

"Then you'll use that one. If you work out, Ms. Brown will get us a real one."

"What about clippers?"

"They're in the drawer."

At one time he'd owned a collection of expensive barber tools but sold them to a pawnshop when he and Cletus went on the lam after Morton Prell's death. He was pretty sure she'd gotten substandard ones but when he opened the drawer and saw the quality of the scissors and clippers neatly laid out on a barber towel, she must've seen his surprise.

"I do know what I'm doing, Mr. Curry."

He didn't want to admit it but apparently she did.

She continued, "Aprons are there. Put the dirty ones in the hamper beneath that table."

He looked to where she pointed.

"Your broom and wastebasket are behind you."

He swiveled.

"Questions?" she asked.

"Lunch?"

"Half an hour. And for now you'll work part-time. Tuesday nine to three. Thursdays nine to three. Saturdays same time. If your clientele picks up we'll add more hours."

Riley wasn't pleased. He'd been counting on a forty-hour week but kept that to himself. "Tips?"

"What you get you keep. Everything else you bring to me and I'll put it in the safe."

"Which is where?"

"You don't need to know."

He growled silently. He didn't like her. At all.

"Here comes your first customer. Have a good shift."

Clay walked in and she called out in a cheery voice Riley didn't know she possessed, "Morning, Mr. Dobbs."

"Morning, Kelly. How are the twins?"

"Giving the day care people over at the school fits, but they're well."

He took a seat in the chair and Riley thanked him for coming in.

Clay's response, "You can't pay me what you owe me if you don't make any money."

Riley growled silently for the second time.

"Oh, and Mal said to tell you he'll be by later," Clay added. He sighed. It was going to be a long first day on the job.

But it turned into a fruitful one as word of his services spread. He cut Mal's hair and then the doctor married to the singer—he didn't remember their names. Sheriff Donovan stopped in along with a couple of his deputies. Two construction workers came in on their lunch hour followed by a Mexican guy who introduced himself as Luis Acosta, the town's fire chief—which was news to Riley because he didn't even know Henry Adams had a fire department. He decided maybe working for Kelly and Ms. Brown wasn't going to be so bad after all. Not only did he make a wallet full of tips, he saw his customers as potential supporters if and when he decided to make a run for mayor.

By quitting time at three he felt pretty good, and then Clay showed up.

"Bing's back," he told Riley. "You and Cletus can stay tonight but you need to be out by noon tomorrow. Meet me at the rec when you're through here."

Wearing the mocking smile Riley had grown to hate, Clay strolled out.

Riley was stunned. He knew Bing was due back and that he'd have to move out eventually, but by noon tomorrow? Where was he going to stay? More importantly, if he couldn't rely on Clay's help anymore, how would he get to work?

"What's the matter?" Kelly asked from across the room.

Riley didn't want to tell her but he knew he had to. "Clay's kicking me out and I need a place to stay."

"Starting when?"

"Tomorrow at noon."

"You're going to need a way to work, too, now?"

Angry and grim he gave her a terse nod. "Probably."

"You made the shop a decent piece of change today and I want you to stay on. You can't live with me but I can swing by and pick you up as long as it's not too far from town."

Riley stared.

She shrugged. "I'm a businesswoman, Mr. Curry. No more, no less." That said, she resumed sweeping up the hair near her station.

When his shift ended, instead of meeting Clay at the rec, Riley walked down to the Power Plant to see Bernadine Brown instead.

Inside, he knocked on her partially opened door.

She looked up. "What can I do for you, Riley?"

"I need a key to the door of Eustacia's place."

"Why?"

"Me and Cletus are going to move in."

She studied him for a long moment. "You know there are no appliances or utilities."

"I do, but Clay wants me out tomorrow and I need a place to stay so I can keep my job. Kelly said I can ride in with her on the days I work."

"That's nice of her. Your first day must have gone well."

He nodded and waited.

She finally opened a drawer and pulled out a key ring. There was one key on it. She handed it to him.

"Thank you."

"You're welcome."

He exited and a very thoughtful-looking Bernadine watched him go.

* * *

Eli and his dad were watching for his grandparents to enter baggage claim at the Hays airport. Eli had been allowed to leave school early to make the ride and the other students were left in the hands of Ms. Marie. He wasn't sure how this visit was going to go but his dad looked kind of tense, so Eli hoped the weekend wouldn't be a disaster. When they finally appeared, his grandfather Jack Sr. waved and his grandmother Stella smiled and blew a kiss. Hugs were shared and after the luggage was retrieved they made the walk to the parking lot to the car.

Stella said, "Goodness, Eli, you get taller every time I see you."

Jack Sr. cracked, "Goodness, Stella. You say that every time you see him."

She playfully hit him on the arm. "Quiet, you." She turned to her son. "So, Jack. How are things in my favorite small town?"

"Hopping as usual. Now that weather's better, Trent and his crew are going to be building up a storm. We should have a new swimming pool by the Fourth of July."

"That sounds exciting."

Eli agreed. He couldn't wait to dive off the high board. He wondered if Wyatt knew how to swim.

The luggage was put in the bed of the truck and everyone piled in.

Jack Sr., riding shotgun, said, "I still can't get used to you driving a truck, son."

Jack smiled. "It's the ride of choice out here because of the winter weather."

Stella asked, "And how's Rocky?"

Jack steered them off the airport property. "She's doing well. She's looking forward to seeing you two again." They'd last visited at Thanksgiving.

"Looking forward to seeing her again, too."

Eli met his dad's eyes in the mirror.

She must have seen their look because she said, "I know you think I don't approve of her but I do. Especially now that I've rebooted myself."

Eli wondered what that meant.

Jack Sr. chuckled softly. "Oh, here we go."

Eli's dad grinned and asked, "And that means what, Mom?"

"You know how much I love Oprah."

"Yes, I do," he replied, sounding amused.

"Well, she talks a lot about embracing the inner you, so I've been doing that. I'm meditating and given up being judgmental and temperamental. I've even taken up yoga. I'm learning to embrace my inner Stella."

"And how is that working for you, Dad?" Eli's dad asked.

"Pretty damn well. I no longer want to bury her in the backyard five days a week."

She cut him a look. He leaned over and kissed her cheek. "You are better, lovey."

"Thank you. I've been trying to get him to go to yoga class too, but so far nothing."

"I don't look good in a leotard."

As the truck filled with laughter Eli thought the weekend might not be so disastrous after all.

Eli's dad said, "Well, since you're brand-new, Mom, you should know that Rocky and I are getting married."

Silence.

Jack Sr. cracked, "Embrace your inner Stella. Take a deep cleansing breath."

She leaned forward and playfully popped him on the back of his head. "Stop. That's great news, Jack. It really is."

Eli's dad asked him, "Is your grandmother's nose grow-ing?"

Eli laughed. "Doesn't look like it."

Stella countered, "I was just taken by surprise."

"Whatever you say, Mom."

Eli wanted to ask her how could she not want his dad to be with someone as awesome as Rocky, but being the kid he knew his job was to sit and keep his mouth shut, and besides, his grandmother was speaking again.

"Your dad and I have good news, too. We're in the process of selling the house so we can move to Henry Adams."

Eli blinked as his dad asked, "Really?"

"Did you think I was kidding at Thanksgiving when I told you how much I loved the town?" she asked.

Eli changed his mind. Yep, the weekend was going to be a disaster after all. Big time.

While Wes Montgomery's greatest hits played through the Bluetooth speaker she'd been surprised with at Christmas by the kids, Genevieve prepared for her date. Because Terence was taking her to the rec and not the opera there was no need to get dressed to the nines but she did want to look nice. She considered the white cashmere turtleneck she'd been dying to wear but the thought of accidentally dropping taco sauce or mustard from a hot dog on it made her nix the idea and put it back into the closet. She settled instead on a black merino wool sweater with a bateau neck and a pair of black velveteen straight-leg jeans. A girl could never go wrong with black, and it would go well with the silver jewelry she planned to wear. Her wardrobe decisions made, she got dressed.

By six thirty she was ready for his arrival. She was also a

nervous wreck. It had been so long since she'd been out with a man she felt like a long-tailed cat in a room filled with rockers, as her mother had been fond of saying. Thinking of her mother made her wonder what she'd think of her daughter's new life. The women of the twenty-first century had more freedom and options than her mother's generation and Gen was glad. Home and children were no longer the whole world and they could be more than teachers, nurses, and secretaries. A part of herself regretted having stayed married to Riley for so long, but because she couldn't change the past her choice was to step boldly into her future. The sound of the doorbell broke into her musing. *Terence.* Would he be part of that future? Truthfully, she hoped so. Tonight would be another new beginning.

She walked to the door and let him in.

"You look nice," he said.

"Thanks. You do, too."

"Thanks."

He was wearing a navy blue knit collared shirt, a black leather jacket, and gray slacks. A thin silver chain peeked through the undone buttons at his neck and the signature silver hoop hung discreetly from his ear. Fighting to corral her nerves, she said, "Let me get my jacket and we can go." At the closet, she took down her red leather.

"Here. Let me help you with that," he said.

She loved his old-school manners but having him near enough to notice the heat of his body touching hers shot her already soaring nervousness into the stratosphere. "Thanks," she told him once the jacket was on. Hoping he didn't see her shaking hands, she picked up her purse and they stepped out into the fading evening light.

In the truck he put the key in the ignition. Before starting the engine, he glanced her way and confessed, "I haven't done this dating thing in a while so I'm a bit nervous."

His honesty was endearing. "Truthfully, so am I."

"Oh, good." He sounded relieved.

She could already see the looks they'd get in the auditorium. "We're going to be the talk of the town when people see us together, so be prepared."

"I'm okay with that. How about you?"

"I'll be fine." And the envy of every unmarried woman of a certain age in the place. He was handsome, fit, and with her. A girl couldn't ask for more.

When they entered the auditorium the surprise and raised eyebrows on the faces of Marie and her friends at the concession stations made her smile inwardly, but she set their interest aside to consult with him about where they should sit.

"You pick," he said to her.

They decided on seats in the middle and she noticed him discreetly eyeing the crowd.

"You were right. We're getting a lot of looks," he said.

She saw Clay checking them out, and thought she saw regret in his eyes before he turned away. "I know. As I said, talk of the town. Are you still okay?"

"I'm with the prettiest lady in town, so I'm definitely okay."

The heat in her cheeks made her drop her eyes shyly. When she raised them he was smiling.

"How about I get us something to eat?" he asked. "What would you like?"

"The grilled chicken tacos and a cola."

"Got it. Be right back."

So thankful to have such a wonderful guy in her life, she

was taking off her coat and settling into her seat when Lily walked up. A smiling Gen knew she'd come to grill her. "Yes?"

"So, you were ogling him at the town meeting that night."

"Go away," she told her. "Aren't you supposed to be serving hot dogs?"

"Is he nice, Gen?"

The idea of him made her melt inside. "Nicer than any man I've ever met."

"Good. Enjoy yourself. But no necking when the lights go out. There are children here."

Gen laughed at her outrageousness. "I'm going to hit you with my purse, Lily July."

A chuckling Lily took off and left her alone.

Still smiling, Genevieve found herself wondering what being kissed by Terence might be like. Hastily putting that out of her mind, she turned her attention back to the crowd. The teens were down front in their usual spot, huddled together discussing lord knew what. She supposed if it was something serious the town would find out soon enough. Continuing to scan the room, she saw Mal and Bernadine looking for seats. When they waved, Gen waved back. She stole a glance over at Clay again. He was talking with his buddy, Bing Shepard. She hoped ending her relationship with him wouldn't negatively affect her friendship with Bing because she liked him a lot. Turning from them she checked to see if Terence was in line yet. He was. Standing a bit away from him was Luis Acosta holding a tray filled with snacks and drinks. He was talking with Jack, Eli, and Jack's parents. Surprised to see Stella and Jack Sr., she wondered how long they'd been in town.

Standing in line to put in his order, TC knew he was being scrutinized but he didn't make a big deal out of it and nodded politely in response to those who nodded his way.

"Mr. Barbour?"

The voice froze him and everybody else. He glanced over into the assessing eyes of Tamar July. "Yes, ma'am?"

"Your intentions?"

He didn't play dumb. He knew better. "Strictly honorable."

"Good. She's had enough heartache." As if his answer was all she was after, Tamar walked off and a pleased TC took his order and went to rejoin Genevieve.

When he reached their seats, she took the cardboard tray from his hand. "You survived, I see."

"Got grilled by Lady Shotgun."

"What did our matriarch want?"

He liked the way her eyes brightened when she smiled. "Asked me my intentions."

She went so still, he knew to reassure her. "I told her they were strictly honorable. And they are."

She searched his face as if trying to gauge the truthfulness of his declaration. "That's good to know."

"I'm looking forward to whatever the future's got in store for us, Genevieve."

"As am I."

That pleased him because the idea that such a sweet classy lady would enjoy being with him in spite of his faults was humbling. "Then let's have some fun."

"Let's," she echoed softly.

The movies on the docket that evening were *Transformers*

3 and *Coming to America*. While they waited for the entertainment to begin, they ate and talked quietly about starting his lessons on Monday.

"How long do you think it will take?" he asked.

"Depends on how much help you'll need at the outset, but you're motivated and that means a lot."

He was motivated and planned to do whatever it took to be successful. He had a gorgeous teacher, not to mention a box filled with decades of greeting cards waiting to be read.

Their talking was interrupted when Gary and the girls stopped by on their way to their seats.

"Well, look at you two," Gary said with surprise and approval in his voice. "How are you?"

TC grinned. "We're good." He hadn't said anything to Gary about his date.

Tiff asked Genevieve, "Did you like the CD we helped Uncle TC pick out, Ms. Gen?"

"I did."

Leah glanced between TC and Ms. Gen and grinned. "I see you, Unc. You go."

He chuckled. "Thanks, Leah."

"We're going to go find some seats," Gary said. "Enjoy the movies." The Clarks moved on.

Mal walked up next. He nodded tersely at TC before saying, "Hey, Gen."

"Hey, Mal." TC noted that the diner owner still acted as if he wasn't sure he wanted TC hanging around his friend.

"Treat her right," Mal warned.

"That's the plan," TC said. "Square business."

Mal drew back and looked impressed. "Okay, then."

Beside him Genevieve did an eye roll.

When Mal moved on she blew out a breath. "Lord."

"He's just concerned about you."

"I understand that and I'm real appreciative, but my goodness."

A moment later, Amari stood before them. After silently glancing between the two of them, he asked, "You two dating?"

TC heard Genevieve's sigh and he replied, "Yes."

For a moment the teen didn't respond. He finally asked Genevieve, "He okay?"

"Yes, Amari. Very okay."

"Good. Be nice to her."

"I will. Promise."

Amari disappeared into the crowd.

"You have lots of knights, my lady. Guess I'd best be on my best behavior."

She chuckled. "Guess you'd best be."

Down front, Tamar walked onto the stage and the auditorium quieted. "Welcome everyone," she said into the mic on the podium. "I have some housekeeping to take care of first. Jack and Rocky? Where are you?" She shaded her eyes and peered out into the crowd.

They stood and waved.

"Come on up."

Up onstage, the two moved to the podium. The mic picked up Jack asking Rocky, "You want to tell them?"

"I thought you were going to do it." She was decked out in her black motorcycle leathers.

Jack sighed and the crowd laughed. "Okay. I've asked Rocky to marry me, and lo and behold, she said yes."

Applause rang out. People jumped to their feet. The place went nuts.

Taking in the pandemonium, TC leaned over and asked the wildly applauding Gen, "Is this a big deal?"

"Yes, it is!"

On the stage, Jack said, "We don't have a date yet but we'll be throwing a She Said Yes Party at the Dog next Saturday and I hope you'll join us." He asked Rocky, "You have anything you want to add?"

"Nope."

More laughter and the newly engaged couple left the stage. Tamar moved back to the mic. "That's it. Lights, please!"

The lights went down and the opening action began. Gen's hand was on the armrest. When his hand covered hers, she linked their fingers and settled in to enjoy the movie.

It was nearly midnight when he drove back to her home. As they sat in his truck with the soft jazz playing through the speakers, Gen said sincerely, "I had a really nice time."

"Me, too. How about we do it again next Friday?"

"I'd like that."

For a moment all they could see was each other. He finally broke the spell. "Come on. I'll walk you to the door."

Once there, they stood under the porch light while she searched her purse for her keys. With them in hand, she said, "Good night, Terence."

He placed a kiss on her forehead and whispered, "Good night."

Senses racing, she held his eyes and didn't know what to say or if she was supposed to say anything.

"Was that okay?" he asked with a half smile.

"Yes."

"Don't want to rush things."

"I appreciate that." Her heart was rushing enough for the entire town.

Neither seemed able to move, though. A few more seconds ticked off and he said, "Baby, I'm content to stand out here and look at you all night, but we'll probably freeze, so go on inside."

It was the closest Gen had ever come to swooning. *He called me baby!* "All right. Good night." She went in and closed the door softly behind her. As soon as she let out a sigh her phone sounded. The caller ID showed Marie's name. Gen laughed. "Hello."

"Okay, Miss I've Got a Secret—spill it. Chapter and verse and don't leave a thing out."

"What a nice time," Stella James said on the drive back to the house after the movies. She and Eli were in the backseat of the truck. His dad was behind the wheel and Jack Sr. was riding shotgun. "This is why I want to live here," she added. "What other communities do this kind of thing?"

Jack Sr. said, "It was fun. I'd never seen *Coming to America*. What a hoot."

Eli was glad they'd had a nice time.

Stella asked, "And this is every Friday night?"

"Yep," Eli said.

"Wonderful." She then asked, "Jack, don't you worry about Rocky riding that big motorcycle?" After the movie, Rocky had offered up her goodbyes and roared off.

His dad responded, "No. She built that bike herself. She's been riding since she was a little girl."

Even though she'd claimed to have rebooted herself, Eli saw his grandmother shake her head with what appeared to be disapproval. He was disappointed.

"Then I hope you aren't going to let her ride when she gets pregnant."

Eli found that unbelievable but up front his dad laughed it off.

"What's so funny?" she asked.

Eli couldn't see Jack Sr.'s face but sensed his grandfather's eye roll.

"Rock and I aren't having kids, Mom."

"Why on earth not? You aren't too old."

"Yes we are, and besides, she doesn't want kids."

Jack Sr. warned, "And before you ask why, Stella, it's not any of your business."

She gave a small huff. "Then I suppose after we move here, I'll have to content myself with spoiling my *only* grandson."

And then his dad said something Eli would remember for the rest of his life.

"Eli won't be here. He's going back to California for school."

Eli stared. His heart began pounding and he thought he might faint—except guys don't faint. Somewhere off in the distance he heard his dad asking, "Isn't that right, Eli?"

Eli blinked. It took his tripped-out brain a few seconds to reconnect his ability to form speech. "Yeah." His dad was grinning at him in the rearview mirror. *OMG! OMG!*

Later, after the grandparents climbed the stairs to the guest bedroom, the still-thunderstruck Eli stared in awe at his chuckling dad, who boasted, "Got you, didn't I?"

"Yeah. Does that mean you were just punking me?" He prayed that wasn't the case.

"No. It was the truth. Or have you changed your mind?"

"No!" he replied hastily. He scanned his dad. "But how did you know I wanted to go? We never even talked about it."

"Geoff's mom called me the day you asked Geoff to talk to her about staying with them."

It never occurred to Eli that Geoff's mom would call his dad, but he supposed being a parent she would. Parents, like kids, tended to stick together.

His dad continued, "Truthfully, when she called I told her no. I didn't think you were responsible or mature enough to be so far way. And I have to take some of the blame for that. I've been coddling you since your mom died. I thought you had enough on your plate without me demanding you pull your weight."

He thought back to the conversation he'd had with Crystal when she called him out for basically being spoiled. Once again, she was right. "So what changed your mind?"

"You."

Eli wasn't sure he understood.

His dad must've seen that confusion because he explained, "You've grown up this spring, Eli. I never thought you'd try and make my life easier by making me dinner, but you impressed me that day even if you did try and burn the house down."

Eli smiled at the memory of all the smoke pouring out of the oven.

"And then there's Wyatt. Taking him under your wing was just as impressive. You're not the boy you used to be, and it's been a pleasure watching you taking steps to turn yourself into the man you may one day become."

Eli dropped his head and swore he'd punch himself out if he started to cry. "Thanks, Dad," he whispered.

His dad gave him a crooked smile. "I've also been in touch with Amari's grandmother. She's an artist, you know."

He did. He met her last winter and she seemed like a pretty okay lady, but he had no idea what she had to do with this.

"She told me about a community college near where she lives that offers great academics and a fantastic art program."

Eli waited.

"She lives near Malibu and has what's called a mother-in-law apartment above her garage. She's offered it to you for as long as you want if you decide to attend that school."

His eyes widened.

"After I convince your grandmother that she doesn't want to live here, how about we fly to Malibu and check out the school and the apartment?"

"Hell yeah! I mean—"

His dad laughed and opened his arms.

Eli didn't hesitate. He entered the embrace and hugged his dad like he was eight years old again and in that hug was pride, joy, and love. When they stepped back both had wet eyes. Eli dashed his tears away with the back of his hand. "Too old to be crying."

"If you say so."

They spent a few silent moments taking each other in before Eli said softly, "You parent like a boss."

"High praise. You're welcome."

Upstairs in his bedroom, Eli jumped up and down and did some happy-dance moves. He wanted to throw open his window and scream out his joy into the night. He looked through his blinds to see if Crystal's light was on. It wasn't but he sent her a text anyway. He was so excited he texted in all caps. *DAD LETTING ME GO TO CALI!!!!!*

She replied: *Stop yelling! Trying to sleep. Happy for you.* ☺

Grinning, he sat on his bed then fell back on the mattress. *Wow!*

Over at Eustacia's place, Riley tried to get comfortable on the sleeping bag he'd borrowed from Clay but the kitchen floor was hard. Cletus was snoring on the other side of the room, blissfully ignorant of the challenges his owner faced. For the one hundredth time Riley wondered how he'd sunk so low. To hear Genevieve tell it, his plight was his own fault and for the first time Riley had to agree. He was almost seventy years old and had nothing to show for it but a six-hundred-pound hog he could barely feed. He didn't like examining his life because to do so would be to acknowledge Clay's correct assessment of who he was. *A social climbing user with no conscience.* He could argue that the hand he'd been dealt by life had given him no other choice, but that would be too easy, and it wasn't the truth. He was the only child of a single mother who'd taken in laundry to pay the bills. More often than not it hadn't been enough, so she'd shoplifted at the grocer's and helped herself to whatever she could find of value in the homes of the folks who hired her in to cook or clean. They spent his formative years moving from place to place, often one step ahead of the law, while his mother fed herself on delusions of one day being as rich as the people she worked for or saw in the magazine and the movies. In her mind, she was going to invent something that would make them a ton of money, or catch the eye of a rich man who'd buy her a big house and a fine new car. Never mind the reality of her fourth-grade education or the holes in the soles of their shoes or the shacks they were forced to live in. It was going to happen. Someday. Soon. She'd died while he was in high school and went to her grave still convinced her life was destined to be paved with gold. Before she passed away she urged him to marry up. Find himself a rich girl so he'd never have to be hungry or go without again. And he had. Genevieve Gibbs. The only daughter of the wealthiest colored undertaker in Graham

County, Kansas. He'd helped himself to her status and her bank accounts and, like his mother, fed himself on deluded dreams. Genevieve was right when she accused him of never having cared for her. In truth he hadn't. He saw her only as his stepping-stone to greatness and it hadn't mattered if the ladder to success was a bit crooked because he was on his way to the top. So, he'd tried to sell the town out from under the Julys and Jeffersons—the Dusters be damned—he was going to be rich. When the arrival of Bernadine Brown put an end to that scheme, he threw in with the cadaverous Morton Prell only to have those ambitions squashed by Cletus. Literally. And now, he was lying in the dark on the litter-strewn floor of the trashed and abandoned house of yet another woman he hadn't cared about but used. He turned over, trying for a more comfortable spot, but like his life there wasn't one. Sighing, he knew what he had to do. Forget the schemes, scams, and delusions of grandeur and step into the real world like the rest of humanity. If he didn't, he'd be on the floor of life until he went to the grave and there'd be no one to blame but himself.

CHAPTER
16

Della made it clear she didn't want Paula involved with the service, but that didn't prevent Paula from honoring her grandfather according to her own traditions. So, on the morning of the funeral, in the pre-dawn quiet of his house, she read aloud from the Book of Common Prayer. *"I am the resurrection and the life saith the Lord; he that believeth in me, though he were dead, yet shall he live, and whosoever liveth and believeth in me shall never die . . . Blessed are the dead who die in the Lord; even so saith the Spirit, for they rest in their labors."*

Next, came Psalms 46, 90, and 121, followed by two readings from Isaiah—25: 6-9, *He will swallow up death in victory*, and 61:1-3, *To comfort those who mourn*. She ended with Psalm 27 and the King James version of the 23rd Psalm. Closing the Bible, she whispered, "Rest in peace, Papa," and rose to begin her day.

The wake had been held last night at Della's house. Paula drove over to pay her respects and to see if her aunt needed any help, but upon arriving she'd received such a hateful glare she hadn't stayed long, telling herself she didn't want to add to Della's grief. The funeral slated for eleven would be held at the local Pentecostal church where she assumed Della was a member. Calvin offered to drive her over but she'd declined. She wanted to drive herself. That way if she needed to leave right after the service she could and he'd be free to concentrate on comforting his mother, Anna Lee.

Paula arrived at the small cinder-block church a half an hour before the service was due to begin. She found a parking space on the gravel lot and got out. Two women and a man dressed in their Sunday best made their way to the door and she followed them. One of the faces was vaguely familiar but the others were not. After all, she'd left Blackbird almost forty years ago and her face was probably unfamiliar to them as well, but at the door, she was approached by a woman wearing all white.

"Good to see you, Paula. Nan Willis. We were in typing class together freshman year."

The prompt was helpful. "Good to see you, too, Nan. Been a long time."

"It has. I heard you were here and that you're a reverend now?"

"Yes." Paula had chosen not to wear her collar out of respect for Della's wishes.

"Are you helping with the service?"

"No. Just here to pay my respects."

"Della said no, I take it."

Paula didn't respond.

"You'd think she'd appreciate having a woman of God in her family, but she is who she is."

Paula remained silent.

"Well, let me get inside. I'm working with the Nurses Guild today. Need to let Pastor Gordon know I'm here. My condolences on your loss."

"Thank you." The Nurses Guild, a staple at Black churches, were at funerals to help those overcome by grief. She wasn't sure if they'd be needed.

Inside, Paula nodded at the six people in the pews and wondered how large the gathering might be. A red-eyed Anna Lee and a stoic-looking Calvin were seated up front so she went to greet them. She didn't see Della or Robyn and assumed they'd arrive with the casket. Della hadn't shared any details about the funeral home and Paula hadn't pressed.

"Why aren't you with Della?" Anna Lee asked after they'd shared hugs.

"Wasn't asked."

Anna Lee shook her head and dabbed at her tears with the tissue in her hand. "And she calls herself a Christian."

Not wanting to feed dissension, Paula said, "It's okay."

"No, it's not. You're family just like she is."

"You can sit with us," Calvin offered.

Paula thanked him and sat silently in the quiet of the small sanctuary. The things she'd learned from Anna Lee about her past continued to ache inside and would undoubtedly do so long after she returned home. She didn't doubt her ability to handle it. After all, she had God on her side. She just hoped her mother was at peace.

The numbers of people who'd come to pay their respects didn't increase. According to Anna Lee, Tyree hadn't set foot in a church in fifty years.

Della and Robyn arrived a short while later and were escorted to the front pew by two solemn well-dressed men Paula assumed were from the funeral home. The casket was rolled in and the top opened. Della had on a black suit and a large black hat with a nose-length veil. Robyn was in a simple but dingy white blouse and blue skirt.

Anna Lee leaned Paula's way and whispered, "Why does Della look like she just stepped out of Nordstrom's and Robyn from the thrift store?"

The contrast was noticeable but Paula didn't respond. She did however get up and walk over to where they were sitting. She wanted to give Robyn a hug. They hadn't had any time together since the dinner at Della's and she was saddened by that. While speaking with Robyn in hushed tones to ask how she was doing, Paula ignored Della's icy demeanor. When Paula finished speaking with Robyn, she said to Della, "My condolences on your loss, Aunt Della."

She didn't reply.

Releasing a quiet sigh, Paula walked over to the casket and looked down into the face of the man who'd asked for her forgiveness on his deathbed. "Rest in peace," she said to him and returned to her seat.

The service was short—only a few prayers. There was no choir, sermon, or eulogy. Only later would she learn that Tyree insisted that he be buried without ceremony and would probably haunt Della for eternity for putting him on display in a church.

The burial took place at the old cemetery outside of town. There was no marker. By the time the pastor released them, Paula was numb inside. All she wanted was to go home to Kansas and lick her wounds, but there was more to do.

Calvin stopped her and Della to say, "Tyree's lawyer wants us to meet at Mama's place at two o'clock to go over the will."

"What will?" Della demanded.

Calvin didn't address that. "I'll see you both at two."

As Della and the silent Robyn walked to their car, Paula checked her watch. It was nearly one. There would be no repast so she had time to drive back, grab a bite to eat, and gird herself for Della's reaction to Tyree's startling last will and testament. It wasn't going to go well.

The lawyer, a tall, powerful-looking man with ice-blue eyes, arrived promptly at 1:55. Della didn't or couldn't hide her shock when Calvin ushered him in. His name was Martin Jeddings, and he was the lawyer for the Crane family, who'd employed Tyree.

"My condolences," he said to start things off. "The Cranes send their condolences as well. Mr. Tyree will be missed. I know it's been a trying day. I won't keep you long but I need to go over a few things. The Cranes, with Mr. Tyree's consent, began investing a small portion of his salary in stocks about forty years ago, so you can imagine how much those investments have grown."

Paula saw surprise fill Della's face before her aunt asked, "How much?"

"His portfolio is worth a bit over two hundred and fifty thousand dollars."

Her eyes widened and Paula braced herself for Della's reaction to the revelation the lawyer was about to share.

Jeddings continued, "There are two beneficiaries, and his instructions are that the portfolio be divided equally between his son, Calvin Spivey, and his granddaughter, Reverend Paula Grant."

Della cried angrily, "What! There must be some kind of mistake. My name should be on there, too. I'm his daughter, Ardella!"

Jeddings looked uncomfortable. "He left you the property at 662 Lawson."

"I don't want that damn house!" she screeched.

"I'm sorry, ma'am, but—"

Calvin got up and went to her. "Della—"

She shook him off. "Get away from me, you bastard! Look at those papers again, Mr. White Man, and find my damn name! Look again!"

"I'm sorry, ma'am."

"Sorry?" she raged. "After all I did for him. After cooking and cleaning and putting up with his whoring ways! I even killed—"

The hair rose on the back of Paula's neck.

Jeddings's attention snapped to Della.

"You killed—what?" Calvin asked urgently.

"I killed my *life* because of him! I hope he roasts in hell!" She grabbed her purse and stormed out.

In the silence following her exit, a thoughtful-looking Jeddings remained focused on the door.

When Calvin's startled eyes met Paula's she didn't know how to respond.

Anna Lee, seated on the piano bench on the other side of the room, said matter-of-factly, "I told Tyree fifteen years ago that hateful bitch killed Lisa."

Paula spun.

Wearing a grim smile, Anna Lee raised her drink in toast.

Back at her grandfather's, Paula hoped Anna Lee was wrong and that Della hadn't killed her daughter. Such an act was too horrific to contemplate but the images from the dream with her mother and the skull continued to haunt her. Stepping out onto the back porch, she scanned the trees and the open field behind the house. Was her cousin Lisa buried out there somewhere? Gooseflesh traveled up her arms and she hugged herself. She'd come back for a funeral not knowing she'd be stepping into a nightmare. Her thoughts moved to Robyn. If Della was indeed responsible for Lisa's death what would happen to her? Who would claim her and raise her? Paula knew very little about the teen's father and had no idea if he still lived in Blackbird or was an active participant in his daughter's life. Being a woman of faith she knew it was best to turn this over to a higher power, but letting go and letting God was difficult because she wanted to do *something* even if she didn't have a clue as to what that something might be, so she prayed and girded herself with the knowing that He had this in hand.

She wanted to see Robyn before flying home and even though she knew Della would probably say no to a visit, Paula called her anyway.

"What did you do to my father to get him to leave you his money?" Della demanded when she answered the phone.

"I didn't know anything about the will until Calvin shared the information the day after I got here."

"Liar!"

Paula held onto her patience. "I'd like to see Robyn before I leave in the morning."

"And I'd like the money you and that bastard cheated me out of. You can't see her. Take yourself back to Kansas. I don't ever want to see you again."

"Della—"

But she'd ended the call.

With a heavy sigh, Paula went into the bedroom to pack.

The next morning, she called Calvin to say goodbye.

"It was good seeing you, Paula."

"Same here. You'll keep an eye on Robyn?"

"Sure will. I'll send somebody to look at that sump pump, too. If Della doesn't want the house maybe Jeddings can work it so Robyn can have it. She might want to live there once she turns eighteen and can get away from Della."

That gave her hope. "When I get home, I'm going to call him and make arrangements for her to have most of my share of the portfolio."

"That's real generous of you."

"She needs options and having money will give her some. My mother's insurance money changed my life. I want to do the same thing for Robyn."

"Sounds good. Make sure you text me when you get back so I'll know you got home safely."

"Will do, and I'll be in touch."

"You'd better," he said with affection in his voice. "Take care, Rev."

"You, too."

Before leaving for the airport, Paula took one last look at Tyree's house. Ghostly memories of all the heartache, bitterness, and pain made her never want to return. With that in mind, she placed the key he'd given her on the mantel in the spot where her mother's graduation picture, now cushioned inside her suitcase, had lain facedown for over fifty years, and with nothing else to hold her, she closed the door and walked to the car.

Since he didn't have to work Sundays, Riley used the time to begin clearing out the debris littering Eustacia's place. The looters had left a broom so he started upstairs in one of the bedrooms he planned to use as his own. He didn't have a bed so he'd still be sleeping on the floor but it wouldn't be in the kitchen and it would be clean. Cletus was outside eating the last of the rice cereal purchased for him by Clay. Riley had made enough in tips to be able to buy more but he also had to feed himself so economically the situation would be tight until he got his first paycheck. Deciding not to worry about that or the rest of his problems for the moment, he looked around for something to put the pile of rubbish into so he could haul it downstairs when he heard knocking on the front door. Puzzled by who it might be, he went downstairs to see.

It was Ben Scarsdale, the California animal trainer. Seeing him filled Riley with panic.

"Hey there, Riley," the older man said, showing an easy smile. "How are things?"

"Uh, good, Ben. How'd you find me?"

"Got a nephew who's a cop with the LAPD."

Riley swallowed and blinked. "What can I do for you, Ben?"

"Came to collect the four thousand dollars you owe me."

The panic increased. "I'm a little short on cash at the moment."

"Figured that. Not a problem, though. Have a court order here," he said, showing Riley the papers he held. "Going to take Cletus back with me."

Riley gasped. "No!"

"You look surprised. Did you think you'd never have to pay me?"

Sweating under Scarsdale's now icy-blue glare, Riley tried to think. He'd been able to bamboozle the man before. "How about we try and work something out?" he asked congenially.

"No thanks. You're a liar and a cheat—two qualities honest men abhor. Where's my hog?"

"You can't have him," Riley declared firmly.

"Court order says I can. Got a nice county sheriff named Will Dalton standing out by his car just in case I need assistance."

Riley peered past him and sure enough Dalton was down by the road. Parked in front of the patrol car was Scarsdale's familiar blue truck. A large metal trailer was hitched to the back.

"I'm calling my lawyer!"

Scarsdale shrugged. "Go right ahead. In the meantime, Cletus and I are heading home." He pulled a silver whistle out of his shirt pocket and blew into it twice. A minute or so later, Cletus came trotting around the side of the house.

Riley snarled, "Clete, go back and finish your breakfast." He leaned toward Scarsdale to let him know he meant business. "He's not leaving."

"Sure he is. Watch."

Scarsdale waved his arms toward the road and a man Riley knew to be the trainer's assistant stepped out of the blue truck. He moved around to the trailer, opened the back, and unfolded the heavy ramp. Down the ramp came the white sow, Cleo. Riley's eyes went wide. She was the sow Cletus had been sweet on in California. Upon seeing her, Cletus raised his snout and squealed. She squealed in reply. Cletus set off toward the road.

"Cletus, get back here!" Riley demanded.

Cletus turned, eyed his *former* owner for a second, and kept going.

"Cletus!" Riley ran to stop him, but he was no match for a

six-hundred-pound hog. When Riley tried to grab him, Cletus grunted angrily and bit him on the hand. Riley yelped with pain and jumped aside.

Upon reaching the truck, Cletus followed Cleo up the ramp. Once the hogs were inside the assistant closed them in.

Scarsdale walked over and cracked, "True love is a beautiful thing, isn't it?"

"Please don't take my hog, Ben," Riley pleaded. "He's all I got. Please, I'm begging you. Let me pay the bill over time. Please."

"See you around, Riley."

A minute or so later, Ben's truck pulled off, followed by the sheriff in his patrol car. With tears in his eyes, a devastated Riley watched them drive away.

Eli and Wyatt were going to spend the afternoon at the skate park, so Eli came downstairs to let his dad know he was leaving, but the only person there was his grandfather, who was watching the Sunday news programs and reading the Franklin Sunday paper. "Hey. Where's Dad and Gram?"

"Out driving around. He's showing her the sights."

"Not much to see."

"I know, and maybe once they're done she can drop this whole moving to Henry Adams idea."

Eli was surprised. "You don't want to move?"

"Of course not. I like the town and the people here, but my life and hers is back east."

"So why does she want to move?"

He shrugged. "We're getting up in age and our friends are dying pretty regularly now. I think she's just feeling a little lost. Not handling being an old lady very well. And she misses your father."

Eli sort of understood. "So is your house really on the market?"

"It is, but I'll be calling the Realtor when we get back. This charade has gone on long enough. I love my wife, always have, but you get to the point where somebody has to be the adult and pull the plug on silliness. And that's what this is." His grandfather set the paper down. "So, back to California, huh?"

He nodded and sat down.

"Excited?"

"I am." Eli spent a few minutes telling him about his plans and Rita Lynn's offer.

"That's pretty nice of her."

"Yeah, it is. Nice of Dad to let me go, too. He was worried at first that I might not be mature enough." Eli then told him about the circumstances that made his dad change his mind.

Jack Sr. nodded approvingly. "My son is a better dad to you than I was to him."

"Why do you say that?"

"I never had time for him—too busy being college president, which meant he had to spend his life being the son of the college president. Instead of letting him play ball and do the stuff normal kids got to do, his mother and I pushed him to excel academically because of who we were."

Eli nodded. "It was pretty embarrassing having the only dad who didn't know a shortstop from a wide receiver. He's better now. Rocky's a big sports fan, so he's had to learn in order to keep up with her." Eli then asked something he'd been wondering about. "Do you not like her, too?"

His grandfather chuckled. "Are you kidding me. She's as gorgeous as a sunrise and rides a hog. I'm just surprised she's choosing to be with a nerd like my son."

"So is he. I like her a lot."

"That's the only thing that matters. Your grandmother always wanted your father to marry someone who could trace their bloodlines back to the *Mayflower*, but her blood's not that blue and neither is mine. More silliness."

"Are you two still flying home today?"

Jack Sr. nodded. "Flight's at five. Your dad's taking us to the airport when they get back. Are you going?"

"I'm supposed to be spending the day with one of the younger kids at the skate park, so I may not be back in time. Do you mind if I don't?"

"No. Go have your fun. It's been good being with you this weekend."

"Same here." The past few minutes had been one of the best moments. They'd never talked alone like this before.

"In case you don't make it back, give me a hug," Jack Sr. said.

Eli didn't hesitate.

When they parted, he said, "See you next time, kiddo."

Eli nodded. "Have a safe flight. Give Gram my love."

"I will."

Eli went to the garage and started his car. He sent his dad a text to let him know where he was going, then backed out of the driveway and drove over to pick up Wyatt. When he got to the house he hit the horn a couple of times. Wyatt came out right away but Eli noticed he didn't have anything in his hands but his board.

"Where's your helmet and pads?" Eli asked when he got in.

"Don't need them."

Eli looked to heaven for strength. "Go get your gear."

"I don't need it!"

"Yeah, you do."

"You don't wear any."

"That's because I'm a boss. You've been riding less than a month. Go get your damn gear or we don't go." He wondered if this was what it was like to be a parent and have a kid.

Wyatt huffed, stormed out of the car and went back in the house. A couple of minutes later he returned carrying his helmet and pads.

"Happy?" Wyatt asked.

Eli rolled his eyes and drove them away.

In spite of the tense start they had a good time. Wyatt fell and busted his butt a couple of times but Eli refrained from referencing the necessity of safety gear or saying, "Told you so!"

Eli also knew that as a responsible person he should be home to see his grandparents off, so after ninety minutes in the bowl he and Wyatt headed back to Henry Adams. As they rode, Eli said, "Just so you'll know, I'm going back to California for school in the fall."

Wyatt looked stricken and the reaction pulled at Eli's heart. "Brain's getting his driver's permit in a few weeks so you'll still have a way to get to Franklin and ride your board."

Wyatt didn't reply.

Eli glanced over and the mutinous set of the kid's jaw made him decide to never ever have a kid. "Maybe you can fly out and see me while I'm there. I'll teach you to surf. Can you swim?"

"Yeah. Learned at the Boys and Girls Club. Why are you leaving?"

It was hard not to see the hurt in his eyes. "I miss it. Bad."

"I miss Chicago."

"Then you understand."

"Yeah."

For a moment there was silence. Wyatt's attention was focused on the passing landscape. Eli wondered if he was thinking about his old hometown.

"Can I really fly out to California and see you?" Wyatt asked.

"Yes. We'll figure out how to pay for it when the time comes. Maybe we'll get Miss Big Bucks Zoey to loan us some paper."

Wyatt smiled. "She probably would. I'm going to marry her one day."

Eli almost drove off the road. After recovering he asked, "Really? Does she know?"

"Nah. She will though, eventually."

"Okay, then." Eli realized there was a lot more going on in Wyatt's cartography-centered brain than he let on. *Marry Zoey?* Eli vowed to move back to Henry Adams just to be able to watch that play out.

By then they were back on the street where they lived. Eli pulled up in Wyatt's driveway.

"Sorry for being a pain in the ass before," Wyatt said.

"No problem. Thanks for hanging with me."

"You won't tell Zoey what I said."

"And have her punch me out? Not a chance. The conversation was just between us."

"Okay. Thanks, Eli."

"You're welcome."

He went inside.

Eli drove home and arrived just in time for the ride to the airport. His dad was pleased.

CHAPTER
17

Early Monday morning, TC drove Roni Garland to the airport. When he mentioned to her again how much she resembled the singer Roni Moore, she finally confessed that she and the singer were one and the same. TC felt like an idiot but she just laughed and said, "Gotcha!"

He was still smiling about that when he arrived at Genevieve's place for his first reading lesson. The memory momentarily chased away his jitters but as soon as he pressed her doorbell they returned.

"Morning, Terence," she said when she opened up.

"Morning, Genevieve. How are you?"

She stepped back to let him enter. "Doing good. Do you want some coffee before we start?"

"That would be good."

"Have a seat." She crossed the room to the kitchen. "Your book is there on the coffee table. The title is: *Yes We Can Read*."

He picked it up and checked out the sunset-colored cover. On it was a circle encasing the silhouettes of three people who had their arms raised and legs tucked up as if jumping for joy. He guessed they were celebrating being able to read. He hoped to be jumping with them soon.

Genevieve returned with their coffees, spoons, and a small, gold-colored sugar bowl. "Not sure how you take it. I have some artificial sweetener if you prefer."

"The real stuff is good." He doctored his brew, took a sip, and sat back against the sofa to savor the pretty lady seated by his side. "How come nobody told me that Roni Garland was superstar Roni Moore?"

She smiled over her cup. "Finally figured that out, did you?"

"Yeah."

"There aren't many secrets here but she's one. She even built a recording studio in town so she wouldn't have to leave her family. We love her a lot."

"She seems pretty regular."

"She is. Are you ready?"

He nodded. "Nervous, though."

"It's okay." She reached over and rubbed his forearm supportively. "It'll be fine." She picked up the book. "As I said earlier the title is—*Yes We Can Read*." And she put her finger on each word as she spoke them. She moved her finger down to the white words below the title. "This says: *The one to one reading scheme for learners 8 to 80.*"

"That's me."

She smiled. "The book comes from England and I find it to be super helpful for getting people started. I have a video from them that I want you to see." She opened her laptop. When she was done typing and clicking he watched and listened to an Englishwoman explain how much the book and her tutor helped her overcome her deficiency. Her testimonial was followed by a few more. Each person gave various reasons why they were coming to reading as adults and the challenges they faced beforehand. TC found their stories moving and as they went on to talk about how they felt once they were able to overcome their deficiency he was inspired by the pride and happiness they displayed.

When it was over Gen said, "This will be you very soon. Promise."

He had no doubts.

She scooted closer so they could both see the book. Her nearness was pleasantly distracting so he forced himself to concentrate on the task at hand and not on the faint heady scent of her perfume.

The first page was filled with pictures of objects representing each letter of the alphabet. It started with an apple and ended with a zipper. She had him name each picture. Some, like the orange, rainbow, and snake, were no-brainers. Others took a bit more thought. The picture of the dragonfly actually stood for the word *insect* and the letter *i* and she had to turn the book a bit so he could identify the picture of a pan which represented the letter *p*.

"The neat thing about these pictures is that they also have the shape of the letter they represent. This apple for instance—notice the shape?"

He did.

"It's shaped like a lower case *a*. The little leaf on the bottom of the apple represents the tail the *a* has when you see it in print."

He studied the pictures. He knew his letters and thanks to her explanation understood the concept almost immediately. The recognition made him smile. "That's pretty clever." The duck was positioned to look like a *d*. The egg had a crack across its front that made it resemble a lower case letter *e*.

She continued, "And each picture also gives the sound of its letter. Reading is as much about how a letter sounds as it is about knowing the letter's name."

So they spent quite a while going through the sounds. She had him repeat each one a number of times until they covered them all.

"And that, my Terence, is your first lesson."

Surprised, he checked his watch. Sure enough, the hour was over. Time had flown by.

"You have homework, however."

He grinned. He was half in love with her already.

She handed him three color copies of the picture page. "I want you to spend some time tracing the shapes of the pictures with your finger. Do it four, maybe five times. Then use a pencil directly on the sheets. It will help you visually connect the shape of the letter with the sounds once we start actually reading."

He studied the sheets. "Okay."

"Bring them with you for next time."

"Yes, ma'am."

"How do you feel?"

"Like I can do this."

She gave him a nod.

Their gazes held and when his attraction to her rose and reasserted itself he leaned over and slowly kissed her. A few lazy seconds later he pulled back. She opened her eyes and whispered, "The school frowns on students kissing the teachers."

"I'll remember that for next time," he said, adding, "I figured we'd get this first one out of the way. Yes? No?"

She nodded. "Yes."

In a voice as sincere as his intentions he said, "Thank you for the lesson."

"Thank you for the kiss."

"Anytime."

"What's on your agenda for the rest of the day?"

"Picking up the colonel at the airport. He went to some kind of security trade show in Phoenix and then Gary wants me to go with him to the Dads Incorporated meeting tonight. He said it's like a support group for the dads here?" TC was still thrilled by the sweetness of the kiss and he wanted another.

"Yes, they meet, drink beer, and try and come up with ways to keep the kids and the Ladies Auxiliary from taking over the world."

He laughed. "Sounds like it might be fun."

"They have a good time, or so I'm told."

He gathered up his sheets. "I should get going. Thanks again."

"Here to help."

She walked him to the door. He placed a kiss on her forehead. "I'll text you later."

"Bye."

Feeling like a million bucks, TC stepped out into the late-April sunshine.

Later that afternoon, TC was so engrossed in his homework at the dining room table, he didn't realize the girls were home until Tiff asked, "Hey Unc. What are you doing?"

His first instinct was to hide the sheet of pictures but he

decided to tell the truth because there was no shame in what he was doing. "Homework."

She looked confused. "Are you taking a class?"

"Yes. Learning to read."

He watched Leah stop on her way to the coat closet and turn his way. "Read what? Are you taking a Spanish class?"

"No. English."

Now both girls looked confused. "Are you talking like English Literature?" Leah asked.

"Nope. I'm just learning to read, period." Because Tiffany was closer to him, he handed her the sheet.

"This is the alphabet."

"Have to start at the beginning."

Her eyes went wide as dinner plates and she whispered, "You really can't read?"

Leah made her way to his side. "Quit playing," she warned, sounding like Crystal. But when Tiff showed her the sheet, she studied it and went still as a post on the side of the road.

She too whispered, "Oh my goodness. You weren't playing."

He shook his head. "Ms. Gen is tutoring me."

"Wow," Leah said, viewing him intently. "That takes a lot of guts, Unc. I'm really proud of you."

"Me, too," Tiffany added. "Do you need our help?"

"Maybe later. Right now I'm still learning shapes and sounds."

"We can drill you if you want."

Their caring spirits touched his heart. "I'd like that. My next lesson is Wednesday, so how about we do the drilling tomorrow. I want to get my bearings with the sheet first."

Leah handed it back. "Sure. Just let us know."

Tiff asked, "Does Daddy know?"

TC nodded. "I told him a few days ago,"

"Okay. Let us know when you're ready for help."

"Will do."

They headed to the kitchen for their after-school snacks.

"Ladies?" he called.

They looked back.

"Thank you."

They grinned.

Glad to have them in his life, he went back to his sheet.

TC found the Dads Inc. meeting pretty interesting. Gary invited him because of the semi-dad role he was playing with Leah and Tiffany. The men met at the Dog, and over munchies, beer, and soft drinks for Mal and Bobby, they talked about a bit of everything. The news that Genevieve's ex had had his hog repossessed made for quite a few chuckles followed by a semi-serious debate as to whether to offer him help in rehabbing his trashed house.

Trent said, "After being handcuffed and taken to jail in front of everybody in the area because of him, I say let him rot."

Mal said, "Understood, but you got your pound of flesh with his two black eyes. I say we give him a hand. He's pretty low right now and he is a good barber."

Reg said, "Kindness over rightness, right?"

Luis Acosta said, "I'm still trying to understand how you re-po a hog?"

Laughter followed that.

In the end, nothing was decided about helping Curry.

The next topic made TC's ears perk up.

Trent asked, "Does anybody know what our kids are up to? There's been a lot of sneaking around lately. Meetings with the Ladies Auxiliary. Meetings in my basement that supposedly have to do with something Tamar has assigned. Lily insists I'm imagining it, but I can smell it when Amari has something cooking."

Barrett agreed. "Preston asked me if I was going to make a family crest, what would be on it. When I asked him why, he played dumb and said—school project."

Jack smiled. "Liar, liar, pants on fire. I haven't assigned anything of that nature."

Mal said, "As long as whatever they're up to doesn't involve the police I'm good."

TC knew the mystery had to do with the kids' Father's Day extravaganza but he kept his mouth shut. He didn't want to be known as Uncle Snitch and besides, the men would find out soon enough.

They talked next about the newly formed fire department, the ground breaking for the pool, and a host of other items. For a small town there was a lot going on and TC was glad to be in the mix.

When he and Gary got home he went up to his room and called his daughter.

She answered on the second ring. "Hey, Daddy."

"Hey there, baby girl. How are you?"

They spent a few minutes talking about her job and the weather before he told her about his lessons.

"Oh, Daddy, that's wonderful. I'm so proud of you. I think I'm going to cry."

He smiled.

"I'm serious. I'm searching my desk for tissue as we speak. So tell me about the lessons, the tutor, all the stuff."

So he did.

"She sounds great."

"She is. I like her a lot. In fact, we're dating."

"Get out! You? Dating?"

He laughed.

"Have you told the boys?"

"Not yet."

"Oh my goodness, I may faint now."

"You are such a drama queen."

"Please. It's not every day I hear you use the word *date* in a sentence. In fact, you've never used that word. Ever."

"Things have changed." Genevieve's face floated across his mind and he sighed inwardly. "You're going to love her, Beth."

"Hold up. Listen to your voice. Daddy, are you in love with this lady?"

He laughed again. "And if I am?"

Her end of the line went silent.

"Beth?"

He heard her blow her nose, then say, "If these people fire me because I scared off the clients with all this mascara running down my face it'll be your fault."

"Stop playing. You are not crying."

"Want to bet? I'll send you a picture after I hang up. I'm so happy for you. When do I get to meet her?"

"I'd like to bring her to Hawaii with me this summer if she'll agree, and you don't mind sharing me."

"You know I won't. Wow. My daddy's in love. You know Mom's in heaven smiling."

"I know. She made me promise to go on with my life and find someone. Took me a while but I have."

"Awesome."

They spoke for a few more minutes and after sharing *I love you*s, ended the call.

A few seconds later, her picture arrived on his phone—red eyes, runny mascara and all.

Paula, having all but made her peace with her Blackbird, was preparing for bed, when she got a text from her uncle Calvin. *Need you here asap. Lisa's skull found. Della in jail.* Stunned, she read it again and when she could breathe, she called Bernadine.

Bernadine's pilot Katie Sky landed Paula at the Tulsa airport the next day. Calvin met her outside the terminal. "Who do you know that owns a private plane?" he asked. "This is the first time I've ever been to this terminal."

"The lady I work for."

"Wow."

"I wanted to get here quickly."

He stashed her suitcase in the backseat of his truck, and a few minutes later they were on their way to the interstate.

"So the skull is Lisa's."

"Yes. They found it yesterday morning and used dental records last night for confirmation."

Paula shivered. "I dreamt about my mother and a skull a few days before I flew in for Tyree's funeral."

He glanced her way. "You know we country Black folks set a lot of stock in dreams."

"I know, but I didn't want to talk about it." And didn't now. It was all too eerie. "So was it found in Tyree's backyard?"

"Yeah. Sump pump company found it when they dug up

the ground to check on the plumbing. Wasn't buried very deep. The police think all the lye and chemicals may have dissolved the rest of her body, but they're still digging."

"Why'd they take Della in? Did she confess?"

"No, but Jeddings apparently talked to the county prosecutor after her performance the day he told us about the will. When the skull was found the police were called of course, and based on what the prosecutor was told by Jeddings he had Della brought in for questioning."

Paula was confused. "Did Jeddings know Lisa?"

"I don't believe so, but the prosecutor did."

Paula's eyes shot to his. "How?"

"His name is Jeff Case. He's a member of the Case family that Tyree worked for. Lisa was his babysitter when he was growing up."

"Oh my lord."

"And because Della is relying on a lazy court-appointed lawyer, she agreed to take a lie detector test, which she failed."

"Can that be used against her?"

"I don't know, but they have charged her. Second-degree manslaughter for now."

"She needs a good lawyer."

"Tried to tell her that, but she just cussed me and told me to get out of her face."

Paula sighed. "Has she made bail?"

"No. She wouldn't let me help with that either, so she's still locked up."

"Where's Robyn?"

"With my mama."

"Is her dad around?"

"Yeah, but his wife won't let Robyn stay there. I talked to

him earlier. He's perfectly willing to sign papers to let her stay with you until she's eighteen if you're willing to have her."

"Of course, she's welcome to stay with me if she wants. Poor baby. Probably feels like no one wants her." Paula remembered feeling that way while staying with Tyree.

"Good. I'll let him know, and you can talk to her when we get back."

"What an awful mess."

"You got that right."

The moment Paula entered Anna Lee's house, Robyn ran to her and Paula held her tight while the teen cried as if her heart was breaking. "It's okay, baby," Paula whispered. "It's okay. You're going home with me."

In a voice raw with anger and pain, Robyn said, "She killed my mother. I hate her."

"We don't know that for sure. It might have been an accident. Please don't add more hate to this, Robyn, please," Paula pleaded.

Paula and Anna Lee eventually calmed Robyn down enough to convince her to go and lie down. Once she was asleep, Paula closed the bedroom door softly and rejoined the concerned-looking Calvin and his mother. "I'd like to go and see Della."

Anna Lee said what Paula already knew. "She's not going to want to see you. You may as well get Robyn's things and go on back to Kansas for now. We'll keep you posted on the court dates and all that. Trial probably won't be for months."

"I still want to see her and pray with her. Maybe she'll surprise me."

Anna Lee said, "I doubt that, but Cal can run you over to the jail. I'll stay here with Robyn."

On the drive with Calvin, Paula asked the question she most wanted answered. "If she did kill Lisa—why? The day of the funeral she made it sound as if it might have had something to do with Tyree."

Cal shrugged. "Who knows? Like you said, maybe it was an accident and she or they panicked."

Paula wondered if the truth would ever be learned.

To Paula's surprise, Della agreed to see her. Escorted out of the back by a deputy and wearing gray prison garb, she took a seat behind the glass and picked up the phone so they could communicate.

"Came to gloat, did you?" Della asked acidly.

"No, Aunt Della. I came to ask if there's anything I can do to help, and to pray with you."

She responded with a bitter chuckle. "I don't need your damn prayers. All I need is for you to take your pious ass back to wherever and hope I never have to see you again." She replaced the phone and without sparing Paula another glance had the guard take her back.

Hurt and disappointed, Paula walked with Calvin out of the building and back to the car.

On the flight home to Kansas, while Robyn stared out the window at the darkening sky, Paula replayed the visit in her mind. She'd done everything she could to offer Della an olive branch, only to have it slapped aside. She could've helped her aunt find a good lawyer and maybe make bail so she wouldn't have to be locked up until her case came to trial, but Della was in charge of her own life and she'd have to accept that. Getting Robyn back and settled in would be her priority going forward. Della's future was now in the hands of God.

Warm weather ushered in the month of May and all the flowers Sheila Payne planted around town a few years back were in bloom once again.

Kelly continued to pick up Riley on the days he worked and although he was still blue over Cletus and sleeping on the floor at Eustacia's place he kept his nose to the grindstone.

TC worked diligently on his lessons. Gary and the girls helped by ordering books like *Hop On Pop* by Dr. Seuss and others geared toward new readers, and listening to him read aloud. He had a ways to go to be as proficient as he needed to be but his reward was the time spent with Genevieve. They went to the Friday night movies, had dinner at her place and the Dog, went for drives in his truck, and yes, there was kissing.

The Ladies Auxiliary meeting was held at Gen's place one evening during the first week of May and once the old and new business items on the agenda were dealt with, President Lily said, "Okay, time for a life check. What's going on with everyone?"

Roni spoke up first to tell them about a two-week summer tour of South America that was in the works and that she'd be taking Zoey with her. "She's never been there. Now that the new CD is done, I think we're due for some mama and daughter time."

Gen and the others thought that a great idea.

Lily then asked, "Marie. How're things going with your son, Brian, and the family?"

Genevieve loved the way Marie beamed every time the subject came up. "I speak with my granddaughters at least twice a week via Skype and a few days ago his adoptive mother Janice and I spoke on the phone for almost an hour. We're both educators."

Sheila asked, "Are they still coming for Mother's Day?"

Marie began to cry. "Yes. And I can't wait."

She was sitting on the couch next to Gen. Gen put an arm around her and hugged her like the BFF that she was.

Marie said through her tears and the tissue in her hand, "I'm so happy."

"We're happy for you," Tamar said.

"Thanks for putting up with me this past winter. You have no idea how much it means to have you all as friends."

Gen said, "Through sickness, health, and craziness."

Everyone laughed and a few of the ladies wiped away their own tears.

Luis Acosta's mother-in-law, Anna Ruiz, asked, "Paula, how's Robyn settling in?"

"She's settling. Painfully shy, though. Leah and Tiff had her over for a sleepover this past weekend. She did okay, Leah said, but my aunt kept her away from stuff like the boy bands and the Internet, so the Clark girls are helping to bring her up to speed on pop culture stuff, too."

"And how's school going for her?" Bernadine asked.

"Jack says she's incredibly smart and there's no reason for her not to graduate with Eli and Crystal. We've been looking at colleges but I'm not sure if she's confident enough to go away yet. We'll see, but I'm giving her all the love and support I can. Counseling her, too."

Gen asked, "And your aunt?"

"Still incarcerated. Trial will be sometime in the fall."

Tamar said, "I know you're a very strong woman, Reverend, but don't try and carry this burden alone. If you need help I expect you to throw up a hand."

Paula smiled. "Yes, ma'am."

Gen thought Paula needed to hear that. Women tended to suffer in silence under the weight of their lives, often to their detriment, and sometimes until it was too late.

Lily asked, "Anything else?"

Gen took in a deep breath and said, "Yes. How do you know when you're in love?"

Later, once her friends were gone, Gen sat in her now quiet living room and smiled, thinking back on the looks on their faces when she first popped her question. She knew it would throw them for a loop. After they recovered from the shock, their answers ran the gamut from silly to profound but each one served to verify what she herself already knew. She was in love with Terence. She loved his smile, his strength of character—the vulnerability he showed by seeking help with his reading. She also loved that he made her smile and most of all she loved that he wanted her to be Genevieve. He'd never tried to force her to be anyone else. He'd taken who'd she'd presented herself to be and been as okay with her as she was with herself, and that meant the world. And no, they hadn't known each other long, but she could spend her remaining days learning as much about him as he was willing to share and offer him the same. What to do with her revelation was yet to be seen. She'd sworn her friends to secrecy; however, this was Henry Adams, and for all she knew everyone in the tri-county area now knew how she felt about Terence Christopher Barbour.

As if cued, he called, "You ladies done plotting to take over the world?"

"Yes, so I hope you have your bunker dug?"

"On my to-do list," he replied, sounding amused. "In the meantime, do you have plans for Mother's Day weekend?"

"No. Why?"

"Stevie Wonder's coming to Kansas City. Figured I'd ask my best girl if she wanted to go?"

"Yes! Oh my goodness!"

He laughed. "Then I'll get the tickets. You find us a hotel since you probably know the city better than I do. Separate rooms of course, and because this is my gift to you for being such a great teacher, I'm footing the bill."

Gen didn't know anything about his finances. She almost asked if he was sure about paying for the entire weekend, but she swallowed that and instead asked, "What kind of hotel?"

"Fancy. Room service. The works. I want this to be special."

For her it already was. "Okay. Fancy it is. I haven't seen anything about him coming to town. How'd you find out?"

While they discussed that, Eli and Crystal were seated outside on the Dog's back dock savoring the end of their shift and enjoying the warm clear night. The moon was out and the stars sparkled like bits of bling on black velvet.

"So, how was the trip to Cali?" she asked.

"Good. Amari's grandparents are super nice. My dad and I toured the school and checked out the apartment I'll be staying in. They have an old Honda in the garage they never use, so they're going to let me buy it for a dollar."

"Sweet."

"Yeah. Their place is near the ocean so I'll get to surf again, too."

"Since when do you surf?"

"Since I was about ten."

"Never knew that. What else don't I know about Eli James?"

"That I'll miss you a lot when I go."

"Nah. You'll meet some tall, tanned, lanky blonde and be like, Crystal who?"

"Never."

She turned to him, held his gaze for a long few moments before focusing back on the night.

Feeling his emotions starting to twist, he changed the subject. "So what have you decided? You staying here in town?"

"Yeah. Going to work on bringing my grades up and then see about going east. Maybe to Pratt."

"You could always come west to Cali with me in the fall."

"I know, but I figure I'd stick around—keep Amari and Preston in line, make sure Devon doesn't get any more insufferable than he already is, and watch over Miss Miami. Being big sister is a lot of work, but somebody has to do it."

He nodded.

There was a long silence.

He looked at her and she at him and she said, "Even after

you find that blonde, I'll still have your back anytime, any-where. If you ever need me just send up the bat signal."

"Will do," he said softly. "Same goes for you."

She leaned over and kissed him gently. "I'll miss you too, Eli."

As he sat there stupefied and reeling, she went inside.

As Mother's Day weekend approached, the kids went to the mall with their dads to pick out gifts and with the help of those same moms and the Ladies Auxiliary, continued work-ing on their super-secret Father's Day event. Trent kept pres-suring Lily to tell him what they were up to and she kept insisting he was imagining things. Marie was going crazy get-ting her house cleaned and ready for her special guests, and Gen was given a fancy homemade apple pie by Mrs. Rivard on the day of her last lesson. Gen had a surprise for her, too—a tote full of brand-new books to read to her granddaughter and Mrs. Rivard thanked her through her happy tears.

In anticipation of her weekend in Kansas City with Ter-ence and Stevie, Gen made an appointment with Kelly to get her hair done. When she walked into the shop, Riley was seated in his barber chair waiting for his next customer. Gen nodded. He nodded in reply and she took a seat on the couch to wait her turn. Taking out her e-reader she went back to the story she'd started a few days before, but couldn't help but take a peek at Riley while she read. He'd lost weight. The black suit he used to wear so proudly looked as run-down as he did. Karma had obviously taken its toll. Because her life was so spectacular she wanted everyone she knew to be just as happy, so she felt bad that he wasn't, even though he'd stolen from her and been nothing but a pain in the rear during the last few years of their marriage. "Riley?"

He looked up.

"I heard about you losing Cletus. My condolences. I know how much you cared about him."

He nodded tightly. "Thanks, Genevieve."

To her surprise he walked over and said, "And I want to apologize for doing you so wrong. If there was a way I could make it up to you, I would. You didn't deserve what I put you through."

Genevieve wondered who this man was and what he'd done with the Riley Curry she once knew. "I appreciate that, I really do."

"Just wanted you to know." He then asked her, "Are you happy, Genevieve?"

She thought about her life and about Terence. "I am. Very much."

"Good. Good." He gave her a nod and went back to his chair.

After Kelly finished her beautician's magic, Gen paid her, gave Riley a parting nod, and headed up the street to the Dog to meet Terence for lunch. She was struck by how badly she felt for her ex-husband. That he had actually apologized and in a sincere manner no less had to count for something, so while she walked, she took out her phone and made a call.

When Kelly drove Riley home, he took a look at all the trucks out front and froze. His first thought was that the place was being repossessed and he wanted to wail, but then he saw Trent and Mal and Clay and some of the boys. They were carrying wood and what appeared to be windowpanes and a bunch of other construction type objects. There were men on the roof and others going in and out the front door.

"What's going on?" Kelly asked, peering through the windshield at the activity.

"I don't know."

"Looks like they're working on your house."

"Yeah. It does." So stunned by what he was seeing, he had trouble opening the car's door so he could get out. When he finally succeeded, he said, "Thanks for the ride, Kelly."

"You're welcome."

She drove off and he made the walk to the house.

Mal met him halfway.

"What's all this?" Riley asked.

"It's called kindness over rightness."

Riley was confused.

"Translation—you seemed to have learned your lesson and a couple of guardian angels think you've suffered enough."

"Huh?"

"Translation number two: Genevieve's got a big heart. Too bad you treated her like crap. Now come on. We have work to do." And he walked off.

Not wanting his tears seen, Riley dashed them away with the back of his hand and hurried to catch up.

That night, Riley looked around the clean house and felt more grateful than he'd ever been in his life. He had lights, a working furnace, and hot water from the new water heater. According to Mal, in a few days appliances would be delivered. A knock on the door broke into his thoughts.

He opened it to find Bernadine Brown standing on the other side, and he froze.

"Evening, Riley."

"Ms. Brown."

"May I come in?"

He nodded hastily.

Once inside she glanced around. "I see the electricity is on."

"Yes. Did Genevieve really make this happen?"

"She did."

His lips tightened with how humbled he felt.

"Very special lady, that Genevieve," she said.

He nodded.

"Here's the deal, Riley. When she called and asked if I would help you, I naturally hesitated but like her I think you've been through enough. I called Eustacia and made her an offer for this house. I am now your landlord."

His eyes went wide.

"And as your landlord I needed this house brought back up to code. All repairs should be finished in a few days. Mal said he told you about the appliances. He also said you're sleeping on a sleeping bag on the floor?"

Riley nodded and the embarrassment kept him from looking her in the eye.

"A bed will be delivered in the morning."

"Thank you."

"You're welcome. I'll forgo your rent for the next three months so you can buy clothes, groceries, etc., and get back on your feet. In exchange you will treat this house as if you are paying the mortgage. I don't mind you having a pet but no hogs. Understand?"

He nodded.

"Any questions?"

"Yes. Why are you helping me?"

She assessed him for a moment. "Because mine is the hand that turns this little portion of the world, and no one in that world, not even you, should have to sleep on the floor in a trashed house, especially since you seem to have acknowledged the errors of your ways. So don't screw this up."

"Okay."

"Have a good evening."

And she left.

In the silence following her departure, Riley thought back on all the horrible ways in which he'd disrespected Genevieve and yet she still found it in her heart to help him when he needed it the most. He'd never be able to repay her for what she'd done for him, but he'd try his best to do so. This morning he'd been living in his own personally made hell and now, because of her he was smiling in a place that was as close to heaven as a sinner like himself would probably ever get.

CHAPTER
19

Gen was in heaven on the way to the airport with Terence. They talked, listened to lots of Stevie Wonder on her iPod, and generally had a good time. When they reached the airport property and he drove past the regular parking garage, she asked, "Where are we going? You just passed the parking garage."

He looked over and smiled. "Just sit back. Got a surprise for you."

"What are you up to, Terence Barbour?"

He waggled his eyebrows and she laughed.

The surprise turned out to be one that rendered her speechless when he took their luggage out of the truck, escorted her into the terminal, and they were taken by a member of security to a small, white private jet.

"Oh my lord. Is this Bernadine's plane?"

"Yes. When I told her I needed the weekend off to take you to the concert, she decided to make our weekend even more special by offering her plane and pilot both there and back."

As the pilot approached, Gen could only stare. She'd never flown on the jet before but she'd heard all the stories and knew that the female pilot was appropriately named Katie Sky.

"Welcome," Katie said in her island accent. "Are you ready?"

They were, and a short while later were winging their way to Kansas City where thanks to Lily a nice town car was waiting. They were then whisked to their hotel. Their rooms were directly across the hall from each other. With the car and the lady driver at their disposal for their stay they dressed and had a nice dinner, then had her take them on a tour of the city.

Riding in the backseat with his arm around her holding her close, Gen gazed out at the lights of the city at night. "I always find the lights of big cities so beautiful."

"Do you?"

"I do. Being from Henry Adams where the nights are black as pitch, I'm always struck by the contrast."

"Those dark nights have their own beauty, too. Never seen the stars the way I can see them in Henry Adams. I noticed that my first night there."

She smiled softly. "Big-city guy. Little country girl."

"Beautiful little country girl."

She snuggled closer. "Flatterer."

"It's the truth." He leaned down and placed a kiss on her forehead. "Thanks for coming with me."

"Thanks for asking."

They parted at the doors of their rooms. "I'll see you in the morning, Terence." Rising on her toes, she kissed him.

"'Night, baby."

They both enjoyed the concert that next night. Even though Stevie was no longer Fingertips young, he still put on a fabulous show. She and TC sang and danced along with the crowd on the many, many favorites he performed from his groundbreaking album *Songs in the Key of Life*, and when it was over, they rode back to the hotel physically but jubilantly exhausted.

When they reached their rooms, she said, "I'm too wound up to sleep. Why don't you come in and we can talk for a little while."

And as they talked, laughed, and rehashed some of their favorite moments from the concert, TC realized he wanted her in his life for the rest of his life. Everything about her drew him in. From her smile to her intelligence to her charm and big heart. He'd heard about her hooking up her ex even though the man was an ass and should've been tarred and feathered for treating her the way he had.

"Been thinking," he told her. She was standing at the window looking out at the lights of the city.

"About what?"

"Me and you."

She came over and sat down next to him. "And what have you concluded?"

"That maybe next weekend or the weekend after we should fly to Vegas and get married."

She stared and smiled. "Really?"

"Yep. I'm love in with you, little country girl."

"That's good because I'm in love with you, big-city guy."

He laughed. "So is that a yes or a no?"

"That's a yes."

"Cool, then I can give you this." He reached into his sport coat jacket and withdrew a small navy blue velvet box. He liked how wide her eyes stretched.

"You already bought a ring?"

He nodded.

"Nothing wrong with your confidence, is there?"

He chuckled. "Hold out your hand, please."

When he slipped the sparkler on her finger she started to cry and threw her arms around his neck and cried harder. He held her tight. "I love you."

"You've just made me the happiest little country girl in the world."

"And you've made me happy as well." He drew back so he could see her face. "Let's have some fun."

"Let's, but I want to elope."

"What?" He laughed. "Why?"

"Because I don't want to fight Bernadine. She gave Lily fits when she and Trent decided to get married. I know her. She's going to want a big fat affair and I just want to be your wife."

He found that so endearing he loved her even more, if that were possible. "We can probably find a cheap flight to Vegas from here."

"You're right. But what about your job? She's expecting us back on Sunday."

TC had no answer for that. He enjoyed his job and preferred not to get fired.

"Tell you what," she said. "I'll just call her, tell her what's going on, and she'll be too happy for us to fuss much."

"Do your thing."

So she did and in the end, she was right. So right, in fact, Bernadine offered Katie and the plane for the flight to Vegas and back home on Tuesday.

Gen came back and sat down and snuggled close to her husband-to-be. "I was worried about needing clothes but we'll be on our honeymoon, so I don't think that will be a problem, will it?"

He stared and then howled with laughter. "No. Clothes will not be an issue."

She looked up and smiled. "Good."

The day of the Father's Day event was sunny and warm. The dads were awakened with calls from Tamar and told to report to her house no later than ten. Since it was Tamar, they all did as told and were surprised to see her field decked out with tables, chairs, and the grills manned by Clay and Bing already fired up. The parade of flags started promptly at 10:30. Wyatt, bearing the newly created purple-and-black Henry Adams flag, led the procession. He was followed by the other kids carrying purple-and-black flags that represented their fathers and in some cases themselves. Amari and Devon's July flag had a raptor in full flight holding a flute in one of its talons. Preston's had the Marine globe and a telescope. Leah and Tiff's flag had a large cornucopia with a comet blazing above it. Zoey's was a caduceus surrounded by musical notes. Eli, wearing his cap and gown, held a flag that featured an open book and a surfboard standing on end. Alfonso and Maria Acosta had a map of Mexico—drawn by Wyatt—with a fire truck on it. The fire chief wiped away tears.

Having helped with the preparations, Bernadine had seen the flags before but the dads hadn't and the smiles of pride on their faces was a for-real Kodak moment. There were games, food, and music. The flags standing upright in their stands were a sight to behold and fluttered in the breeze like a gathering of kingdoms from *Game of Thrones*. She always enjoyed her town's celebrations just as much as she enjoyed the people she now considered family. The newlywed Genevieve and TC were sitting with Marie, who was eagerly anticipating an extended visit from her granddaughters come summer. Paula and the shy Robyn were sitting with the Clarks. As far as Bernadine knew there'd been no further word on the fate of Paula's still-jailed aunt—only that her trial was slated for November. Bernadine watched Eli and Wyatt compete as a team in the sack race. Eli would be their first chick to leave the nest. She was glad that he'd be watched over by Rita Lynn so his dad wouldn't have to worry too much about him. His future was bright. Her own chick, Crystal, was going to stick around, and Bernadine was okay with that. Crys wanted to stay in one of the apartments that would be opening up in the newly renovated Henry Adams Hotel and Bernadine was okay with that as well. In truth, she wasn't ready for her daughter to fly away—at least not just yet. Bernadine spotted Riley sitting with Clay and Bing. So far he hadn't screwed up, but she still wasn't ready to completely trust him. With that in mind, she'd be keeping a sharp eye on him going forward. All in all, things were going well in the little town where she lived. This was Henry Adams, however, so anything could happen. For the moment though, as the man she loved walked up and gave her a kiss on the cheek, she had no real complaints. Life was a blessing.

EPILOGUE

Kauai—a few months later

While Gen and TC's daughter, Bethany, went off to spend the day at the botanical gardens, TC took his box of greeting cards out to the suite's balcony overlooking the ocean and removed the lid. Picking up the top card, he slipped it out of its green envelope and read the Father's Day greeting sent to him last year by his son Keith. That he could actually read the words gave him chills and put tears in his eyes. For the next hour, he made his way through the stack and each and every one he read filled his heart to bursting. The last one was handmade. It came from Bethany and by the date written on the bottom she'd been seven years old. She'd drawn a picture of a little brown-skinned man standing on top of a big, blue-colored world. Printed below it were the words—*You are the best daddy in the whole wide world! Love Bethany.* By then he was crying openly and had to get up and stare out at the ocean until he regained his composure. Genevieve had given him such a precious precious gift and it was one he'd treasure for the rest of his life. He thought about his first wife, Carla. He didn't think Gen would mind that he felt good about finally keeping his promise. He glanced down at Bethany's card in his hand and felt the emotion rise once more. *I can read!*

AUTHOR NOTES

Stepping to a New Day is our seventh trip to the little town of Henry Adams, Kansas, and I hope you enjoyed it. According to a recent 2015 study there are 32 million (1-7) functionally illiterate adults like TC Barbour in America. UNESCO defines the term functionally illiterate *as a person who may be able to perform basic reading and writing, but cannot do so at the level required for many societal activities and jobs.* As our world becomes more and more technically complicated, many of our neighbors are being left behind due to their lack of reading proficiency. If you know someone who might benefit from the book Genevieve used in her tutoring sessions, or are in need of a good resource for a literacy program in your community, please go to the website: http://www.gatehousebooks.co.uk/yes-we-can-read/. Or look for: *Yes We Can Read* on Amazon.

Stepping to a New Day offered new futures for many of our beloved Henry Adams residents. I thought Genevieve needed love after all she'd been through, and Uncle TC turned out to be a perfect match. This book tied up some loose ends while leaving us with unanswered questions. Has Riley really changed his ways? Is Cletus gone for good? If Reverend Paula's mean old aunt Della did indeed murder her daughter, why? And my favorite—is Wyatt really going to grow up and marry Zoey? I'd stay tuned if I were you. As we say on my Facebook page: *Stay calm and move to Henry Adams.* (Oh, if only we could.)

Until next time—happy reading,

B

THE BLESSINGS NOVELS BY
BEVERLY JENKINS

**STEPPING TO
A NEW DAY**

**FOR
YOUR LOVE**

**HEART
OF GOLD**

**A WISH AND
A PRAYER**

**SOMETHING
OLD
SOMETHING
NEW**

**A SECOND
HELPING**

**BRING
ON THE
BLESSINGS**